BLOOD CURSE

Book 2 in the Branded Trilogy

Tammy —
 Your support, encouragement and honesty mean the world to me. Thank you for taking on the tough job as my editor.
 Love you long time ♡
 Kat Flannery

KAT FLANNERY

BLOOD CURSE
Book 2 in the Branded Trilogy

Copyright © 2014 by Kat Flannery. All Rights Reserved.

No part of this publication may be reproduced, stored in a retrieval system, or transmitted, in any form or by any means, electronic, mechanical, photocopying, recording, or otherwise, without prior written permission from the authors.

This is a work of fiction. Names, characters, places and incidents either are the product of the author's imagination or are used fictitiously. And any resemblance to actual persons, living, dead (or in any other form), business establishments, events, or locales is entirely coincidental.

http:// www.katflannery-author.com

FIRST EDITION TRADE PAPERBACK

Imajin Books — www.imajinbooks.com

October 1, 2014

ISBN: 978-1-77223-003-1

Cover designed by Ryan Doan — www.ryandoan.com

Praise for BLOOD CURSE

"*BLOOD CURSE* by Kat Flannery sucks you in and keeps you on the edge of your seat from the first page to the last. I fell in love with Pril, Kade and the relationship that blooms between them. While there are sparks between them, Ms. Flannery weaves her tale without having a sex scene. In a market where sex scenes are a dime a dozen it is refreshing to read a perfect blend of romance and intrigue without having sex forced on you. Without giving any spoilers you will see the lengths Pril will go through to keep her daughter safe from the men of the Monroe family. They believe the way to break the curse sworn on them by Pril's sister, Vadoma, is to kill her child, Tsura. The very thought of this would turn anyone's heart ice cold, unless of course you were the head of the Monroe family yourself. If you are a lover of Gypsies and all things magical, this book will engage you heart and soul. I highly recommend reading *BLOOD CURSE*. For if you do, you will be enthralled, entertained but never disappointed." —Sandra Bischoff, author of *BEYOND TIME*

"Engrossing, enchanting and suspenseful. *BLOOD CURSE* (Book 2 in the Branded Trilogy) is the perfect blend of paranormal, history and romance. The prequel is as impossible to put down as its predecessor, *LAKOTA HONOR*. Flannery deftly weaves a tight plot filled with mystery, emotional detail and heart-thumping action." —Kim Cresswell, award-winning author of *REFLECTION*

"Ms. Flannery has crafted a taut story deeply embedded with gypsy lore, along with the fanatical fear of witches that permeated the time period. Pril and Kade's love grows slowly, and surprising betrayals and revelations will keep the pages turning. Tragedy and unwavering perseverance fill this wonderful tale to a surprise ending. A richly-woven tale of early America and gypsy lore." —Kristy McCaffrey, author of *INTO THE LAND OF SHADOWS*

For my Grandma, I hold the memories within my soul.

"There is no charm equal to tenderness of heart." —Jane Austen

Acknowledgements

BLOOD CURSE wouldn't be possible without some very important people. Tammy Ivanchanko, for her guidance, advice and keen sense of grammar. Cheryl Kaye Tardif, my publisher and good friend for pushing me to write stories I never thought possible. Todd Barselow, senior editor at Imajin Books for his exceptional skills and easygoing attitude. You make edits a breeze. Krysta Ivers, my cousin, for adding to *BLOOD CURSE* with your beautiful poem.

My readers, without you I would not be doing this. I am grateful for each and every one of you, and I thank you with all of my heart.

Thank you to my husband, Edwin, for always supporting me even when I'm neck-deep into a story and not asking why dinner is not made. My sons, Skylar, Seth and Samuel for giving me a reason to smile every day and offering feedback on my fight scenes.

I love you all.
Kat

A twisted knife into the back.
Betrayal beyond belief.
Magic that is stained so black,
No good can bring relief.

Guilt and shame torment the soul,
For grief with heartbreak in its wake.
A pain so immense it's dug a hole,
And left nothing else but hate.

Selfishness devours the mind.
Decisions are made in vain.
One cannot turn back the time,
And erase what's on the slate.

But love can unfreeze the coldest heart,
And right the worst of wrongs.
Even in souls turned so dark,
Filled with hatred that holds on.

The grasp that once held tight,
Telling one to loathe,
Forgiveness will soon fight,
And force it to let go.

With emotions in excess,
Some will rise and others fall.
Souls are put to the test,
But will love conquer all?

—Krysta Ivers

"Upon mine death for the blood ye have shed, every daughter born to ye shall die before it draws breath, to which ye will know pain and worse, I cast unto ye mine blood curse."
~ *Vadoma*

PROLOGUE

The moon hurled shades of green and grey across the starless black sky. Waves rolled up onto the docks, rocking the boats tied there. The water pooled around his booted feet as he walked briskly along the wooden boards. The air reeked of fish and sea, and he tucked his chin into the raggedy coat, inhaling the stale garment. One hand in the pocket fingered a piece of rope while the other pulled open the door to The Cat House, a brothel on the docks.

Men of all kinds sat at the tables. Smoke, laughter and mugs clinked together. He ignored them all to take a seat at the table in the corner.

"Can you guarantee this to be done?"

"Of course."

"You must kill him, and bring the child to me."

"Consider it done."

He shook his head. "You must make sure he no longer breathes."

"Indeed."

"Do not be fooled. He is tough and knows his way around a sword."

"I am not concerned."

He nodded and slid a brown package, tied with twine, across the table to the broad-shouldered man on the other side.

Long slender fingers reached out and picked up the package.

"A name?"

"Kade Walker."

CHAPTER ONE

1723, Appalachian Mountains, Virginia

Pril Peddler lifted the green shawl from her trunk and wrapped it around her bare arms. The change in seasons brought a damp chill to the morning air, and the heavy woolen wrap kept her warm. She peeked at the small face, huddled under the blankets at the back of the wagon. The charm above the child swayed on the string Pril had hung it from. A dull ache hummed in her chest when she thought of the horrific loss her clan had been dealt.

The evil was near, and she'd need to work another spell to keep them safe. Late for counsel with her brother, Galius, she kissed the soft cheek of her daughter before heading to the door.

Hand up, she shaded her eyes from the bright sun as she stepped from the back of the vardo. She pulled the heavy burlap curtain down to close the opening and walked toward Galius.

"Your steps are light this morning, Sister. One would think you did not want to be heard," Galius said as he stirred the coffee beans inside the metal pot.

Tension twisted her gut. He was right. She did not want this counsel. She did not know what to say. She let the flicker of merriment in her brother's eyes wash over her, relaxing the muscles in her shoulders.

"My step is the same." She poked him with her finger, trying to ease her own nerves and his as well.

His lips lifted as if to smile, and she held her breath. It'd been weeks since he smiled. Pril's heart ached, and her lips trembled.

He held up the bubbling pot. "Would you like a cup?"

She inhaled the aroma of strong coffee beans and nodded, taking a seat on a wooden stump by the fire.

He handed her a cup and sat down across from her.

The wood crackled, and sparks jumped from the heat onto the ground in front of her. She tipped her chin, concentrating on what to say next. Ever since the murder of her niece, she'd not been able to hold a conversation with either of her brothers without offering apologies. This morning was no different. She could not look Galius in the eyes and see the anguish and sorrow within them.

The Monroes had come again.

They'd never be safe.

She blinked away the tears hovering against her thick lashes. Tsura was asleep in her wagon, while another was lost to them forever. The door of her brother's wagon creaked open, and Milosh's wife, Magda, stepped out. Black circles settled around her sunken eyes, and Pril felt the stab in her chest once more. Long brown hair fell untied down the woman's back. The black clothes, she'd put on weeks ago, hung on her body unchanged and wrinkled from sleep. Milosh came from behind their wagon, a jar of honey in his hand. Pril stood when Galius' large hand grabbed her wrist.

"They are not wanting to see you today, Sister."

She heard the regret in his voice, swallowed past the guilt in her own throat and nodded. Milosh hadn't spoken a single word to her since the death of his child. He blamed her, and it was clear so did Magda.

"I...I'm so sorry, Galius."

He didn't reply right away, and without seeing it, she knew he had wiped the tears from his eyes. "Alexandra's death is not your fault."

The words were spoken because they needed to be. Gypsies stayed together no matter what. They were family. There was no truth to his words, and Pril knew it.

"Are you going after them?" she asked.

"I hold no power. No spells flow from my lips. I am strong, yes, but they are stronger." He stared at her, his eyes pleading. "We need the pendant."

Guilt thickened her tongue. The gritty residue clung to her lips and tasted bitter.

The talisman had been in their family for generations, blessed by each new Chuvani. Vadoma had promised her the pendant before she died, but Pril never saw it, and there had been no time to search for the jewel when they fled.

"Without the pendant we cannot break the curse. We cannot protect our people."

She knew this. They all knew this, but no one had a clue as to where the talisman was. She'd tried to call an image forward, to make a finding spell, but nothing worked.

"We have lost one of our own. Our clan is frightened. They have lost faith. We cannot fight the Monroes. We have neither the numbers nor the skill." He took a long drink of his coffee. "And neither do you."

She glanced at him.

"I know you, Sister. You're planning to take Tsura."

Pril sighed. She did not know what else to do. The Monroes were coming for her child. Alexandra had died because of that. Milosh and Magda hated her.

"Running is not going to change anything."

"It will save lives. It will…help Milosh and Magda to heal."

"No, it will not. Running will get you and Tsura killed, and that is all."

"How can you look at me when you know what I've brought to our family, when you know that this is all because of me?"

Galius blew out a long breath that moved his thick beard from his lips. She watched, through tear filled eyes, as his bottom lip quivered.

"Vadoma put this burden on you. For that, we do not judge."

Their sister had died a vile death. She'd betrayed their clan and had been hung while being burned. Pril ached for her sister's guidance and counsel. She yearned to know that what she was doing was right.

"We had a plan, and up until Alexandra's death it worked. We will rethink and come up with something better—stronger."

The plan was simple. Dress the girls as boys, and the Monroes wouldn't find them. But someone had figured out Alexandra was a girl. Someone had told the Monroes. They came for her, stealing the precious child in the middle of the night. The morning two weeks before, as the clan frantically searched for her, a harrowing scream Pril would never forget echoed across the land. Milosh found his daughter's body by the river, her neck broken.

She raised a shaky hand to her mouth so she wouldn't let out the sob she held against her lips.

"I have enough for one more protection spell." She had lied. Her forehead ached because of it.

He glanced at her, his eyes showing no emotion. "You will concoct another."

"I cannot."

He frowned.

"The spell has the oil Vadoma blessed. Without it, Tsura is at the mercy of the Monroes, and so are we."

Galius pumped his large hands into tight fists. "Surly you can think of another?"

"I cannot. Vadoma placed the blood curse. It is only with the blessed oil that I am able to create the spell to keep danger away. The oil is almost gone."

He worked his jaw. "That gypsy whore—

She held up her hand to stop him from blaspheming their sister. It wasn't right. It brought evil to curse your own, and Pril would have none of it.

"Our sister had her reasons. Leave it be."

"Reasons? She betrayed us. Left us with a curse we cannot break and wealthy plantation owners hunting our very hides—killing our children!"

She hung her head unable to look at him. What could she say? He was right. Her very niece had died but thirteen days ago.

"Where is the book?"

Throat tight and dry, she refused to meet his gaze. The book held her mother's spells. Only she knew where it was, and unlike the pendant, she'd not lose it.

"I have it safely tucked away."

"Is there no spell for what we need?"

"The child is not of my blood. I cannot protect her, or the others, like she can."

Tsura was Vadoma's child, but Pril raised the girl as her own.

"And she is gone."

"Has been nigh on four years."

Galius' face softened. He placed his hand on her shoulder. "I need to speak with Milosh. We may have to move again, once he's healed." He gave her a light squeeze and walked away.

Pril watched through hooded lids as Galius moved toward Milosh. The two shook hands and embraced. She longed to be enfolded in Milosh's arms, forgiven of all her transgressions.

She wiped at the tear on her cheek. He'd not consider it, for he despised her. Magda placed her head on her husband's shoulder. Their love was strong, and she prayed it would get them through their grief.

She brought the cup to her lips and sipped the now cold coffee. Memories of a time, when life was simpler, brushed her mind. There were no worries. No threat of the Monroes hanging over them. They were free. Now, they never stayed in one town longer than a month. The Peddlers wandered the land, searching for a safe haven where they could raise their children.

The rustle from the other wagons brought her head up, and she watched as the rest of the clan rose for the day. Sisters Sabella and Sorina exited their vardo and smiled at her from across the yard. The two girls had joined them a few years ago, when the Monroes had attacked their family, burnt the wagons and killed most of them. Both unwed and beautiful, they were very good at creating new balms and potions to sell at the markets. Sorina enjoyed living with the clan, and she loved to visit with the others, while Sabella never spoke and preferred to remain alone.

She lifted her hand and waved. She liked the sisters and had shared dinner with them many times.

Her brothers knew the truth about Pril's child and had made a pact to never speak a word of it to anyone. She, on the other hand, was finding it difficult not to tell the others. Each time they hid the children, packed in the middle of the night, or took turns guarding the camp, she felt the stab of guilt twist in her heart.

"Mama?"

Pril turned, mug still in hand, and gazed at her daughter. Black corkscrew curls fell around her plump cheeks and clung to her pink lips. She wondered what her hair would look like grown out and knew, if the Monroes did not stop their relentless hunt, she'd never see the day.

There were days when Pril herself forgot, only ever seeing her child in long pants, cotton shirt and a cap. But in the evenings, when the moon was bright, she cherished the mother-and-daughter moments they had in their wagon. Pril told her daughter made up fairytales of Kings and Queens. She'd allow Tsura to play with her dolls and try on the lovely dresses Pril had secretly made for her.

She held out her hand and watched as Tsura ran to her. At four she didn't understand how to use her gifts, which sometimes resulted in accidents. But it wasn't the mishaps that had her worried. It was the mixture of good and evil, within the girl, that she feared.

"Oh, my sweet. What has you up and out of the vardo already?"

Tsura's green eyes locked with hers. "I had a bad dream."

Pril straightened. Dreams were the way her people saw the future, or the past. Tsura had them often. She took the girl's hand and led her back to their wagon. She smiled at those they passed on the way. Her shoulders straight, she remained the same not to draw anyone near. Once inside the wagon she closed the flap, and waited a few minutes before she sat on the bed beside her daughter.

"What did you see?" she asked.

"Blood, Mama. Lots of blood."

She squeezed the blanket on the bed to stop her hands from shaking. "Whose blood?"

The child shook her head, black curls bounced up and down. "I do not know."

Pril pulled her daughter close and kissed the top of her head. Tsura went very still, and her tiny body grew hot. She sat back and gently placed Tsura away from her. Past lessons had taught her well.

"Sweetheart, are you okay?"

Beads of sweat formed at Tsura's hairline, to drip down her forehead and cheeks.

She was careful not to touch her and placed a hand beside her daughter's instead. The heat from the girl's flesh warmed her hand, and the wagon grew hot.

"Tsura, look at mama."

Green eyes that showed a red rim around the color stared up at her. Pril wished she could do more to help her child. When Tsura got like this, Pril knew she couldn't control what her body was doing. She wanted nothing more than to help her daughter learn how to use her gifts. With Vadoma gone she would have to learn alongside Tsura.

"Mama?"

She smiled, watching as the redness left Tsura's cheeks. She reached out to sweep back the wet curls hanging in the girl's eyes.

"I'm sorry." Tsura hung her head.

She pulled the girl into a tight hug, her body still hot, but Pril didn't care. "You are learning," she said.

She felt the nod against her chest and squeezed her tighter. Thankful once more that she was safe. "What were your thoughts?"

"I was angry."

"How come?"

Green eyes peered through black lashes. "Because Alexandra's gone."

She ran her finger along her daughter's round cheek. She pushed aside the guilt pressing against her soul. "We are all very sad."

"I've seen the man who stole her."

Pril waited until her heart resumed its normal pace and asked, "You saw him?"

She nodded.

"What did he look like?"

"He was a negro."

That was odd. The Monroes always sent a well-dressed aristocrat to do their dirty work. Were they enlisting the help of their plantation workers now? That would explain why none of the Peddlers spotted the well-dressed killer. The Monroes had sent a slave.

"But, mama?"

"Yes, dearest?"

"The man did not kill her. He tried, but he could not do it."

"How did Alexandra die?"

"I do not know."

Pril pulled her close. If Alexandra hadn't been killed by the slave, then who had taken her life?

"And mama?" Tsura whispered. "They killed him."

Pril ran her palms down the front of her skirt as uneasiness settled deep within her, and the soup she'd eaten for dinner churned in her stomach.

The Monroes were near once more. She'd not done the protection spell over them all, the one she'd said countless times before, to protect Tsura and the others from harm. She used the oil on Tsura, thinking she'd concoct a different spell for the others—but she'd forgotten, and now Alexandra was gone.

She hung her head. *How could I have been so foolish? I am the reason my niece lies within the cold ground.* There was nothing she could do to stop the desolation as it crawled up her spine and curved her back. Life was precious—even more so when it was a young one. It was any wonder Milosh blamed her so. The shame covered her and blurred her sight as tears washed her cheeks. She'd been selfish when she should have rationed the oil and cast the spell—strengthened the charms.

She pulled the jars from the shelf. Rosemary, bark and the remnants of the oil her sister had blessed. The jar was empty, except for the thin layer that clung to the glass walls.

Pril did not receive the gifts her sister had. Vadoma had been the firstborn daughter to Imelda, the enchantress. Their mother had been very strong in her magick, aiding those in need with potions and spells. Pril held no such power. Her only gift was the counting of the spells. She could not move things, throw a beam or have seeing dreams. She was useless.

She blew out a breath and stared at the last of the oil. There was enough to strengthen the charm, but not cast a full protection spell. She'd known this when she used the oil for Tsura a month ago. But now that her niece was gone, the act of what she'd done came down upon her, weighing on her heavily. She leaned into the counter and pressed her fingers to her temple, massaging the strained blood vessels.

She took the jar and stepped outside into the darkness. The clan asleep for the night, she went to Mortimer, her Ox, tied behind the vardo.

"Hello, my friend." She stroked his rough fur. "I need but one drop this time."

The ox turned his head toward her and bowed.

She smiled.

"Good boy."

Quickly, she slid the needle along his neck enough to produce one drop of blood. She held the jar next to Mortimer's neck, watching as the blood ran into the glass mug and mixed with the oil. She dipped her finger into the mixture and ran it along the scratch.

"For the gift thou hast given, receive mine with love." She watched as the wound healed.

Inside the vardo, she stoked the fire in the small cook stove and placed an empty pot on the burner. She pinched the rosemary, a symbol of Vadoma, and dropped it into the jar of oil to swirl with the spice. She watched as it mixed together with the oil and blood. Next she took the bark from the forest and dropped it into the pot. The bark sparked. She poured the mixture of oil, blood and rosemary into the pot, listening as it bubbled and hissed.

"Protect mine child from the evil that hunts. Keep her spirit hidden to their wants."

The liquid evaporated into a cloud of smoke, and she watched as it drifted over the child to settle on top of her sleeping form.

CHAPTER TWO

Kade Walker eyed the wagon in front of him. He'd never seen such artistry before. Hand-painted green and yellow vines curved along the outside walls to cover the black boards. He set his jaw. There was no damn way he was going in there. He pulled his collar up and pushed his hands into his long coat. What the hell was the matter with him? He was crazy to think he could get answers from a fortune-teller, a damn gypsy no less.

He shook his head. He'd tried everything else. Followed every damn lead that came his way—investigated every gypsy camp he'd come across, and he'd still come to a dead end. This was the last place he wanted to be, but time was running out. He'd been told the woman inside could see the future, that she had some sort of magic. He clenched his fist. There was no such thing.

What he needed was a sign—an epiphany that he was on the right trail.

Voices inside the wagon grew louder, and he watched as a young woman and her son exited. His chest constricted. The woman held a handkerchief to her cheek and the boy tightly to her side.

"Awe, hell." He spun on his heel determined to find another way to get information.

"Sir, would you like to know the days ahead of you?"

Kade stopped. *Shit.* He turned to face the gypsy and was not prepared for the sight before him. Balancing herself on the top step, the gypsy woman stared down at him. Long red hair, the color of crimson, fell to the middle of her back. The heavy tresses, pinned up on the left side with a large bejeweled broach, swayed behind her. Her hand on hip, a bright blue scarf tied around her waist hung at an angle. He followed the line of her flowing black skirt to the hem where a black slipper peeked out. A beige blouse fell loose around her breasts and could slip from her shoulders at any moment. Had it been another time, another place, he'd have wondered what gypsy jewels lay beneath the thin fabric. She jingled when she moved, and he pulled his gaze from her attire to the metal bracelets around her wrists and the tiny bells hanging from her neck.

Kade narrowed his eyes. He knew a liar when he saw one, and this colorful gypsy fit the bill.

She smiled, but the emotion never reflected in her vague eyes.

The gypsy camp was a twenty-minute ride from town, and he was surprised at how many people came to buy the potions, healing balms and homemade honey. *Fools.* Couldn't they see these lowlifes were scam artists? He was never one to believe in this kind of bull. Yet, when he scanned the area, men, women and children stood in long lines waiting for the gypsy wares.

"No. I need not know of the days before me," Kade said, placing his palm over the dagger hanging from his hip.

Her dark eyes narrowed. "Hmmmm, you are not a believer?"

"Humph. Precisely." He turned to leave.

"Are you afraid, Mr. Walker?"

Kade stopped. "Do I know you?"

She shook her head.

He did not like this one damn bit.

"Allow me to help you. Please, come inside." She disappeared behind the brown sack hanging in place of a door.

He shook his head and climbed the three steps leading into the wagon.

Two windows on either side of the carriage lit the small room, and he scanned the space in the moderate light they provided. A navy carpet, with gold flowers stitched into it, lay on the floor. Wooden cupboards lined the walls to the end where it seemed the room stopped abruptly. A square table with two chairs stood to his left, and across from that was the stove. The room smelled of spice, and when he inhaled, the scent of cinnamon stuck on his tongue.

She pulled out a chair and motioned for him to sit across from her.

He lifted the handmade seat and eased into it. Afraid he'd bust the delicate chair, he refrained from putting his full weight on it. He never took his eyes off the mystical woman across from him.

"You've come to hear your future?"

Kade cleared his throat. "If you say so."

Her red eyebrow lifted. She grabbed his hand and turned the palm upward.

He yanked his hand from hers.

She snickered, the sound rustic and musical at the same time.

"I need to see your palm in order to tell you of the days that are ahead of you," she said.

"Do you not have a glass ball, or some other contraption you see into, and pretend to tell me of my life?"

She observed him, her lids half closed, and he shifted in his seat.

"You are aware of the glass ball?" she asked.

"I've heard tell of it."

"Well, I do not own one, never have. The answers are within your palm." She motioned for him to place his hand in hers.

He open and closed his fist before inching it toward her. He didn't feel right. Something was wrong, and he couldn't put his finger on it.

The gypsy examined his hand before she closed her eyes and hummed a haunting tune. A bell rang somewhere in the room, and Kade had to stifle a laugh.

"Mr. Walker, I need you to close your eyes while I summon my ancestors."

"What ancestors?"

"The ones who will tell me of your future."

He snorted.

She glared at him from across the table.

"Please, close your eyes."

"No."

"If you do not believe in what I do, Mr. Walker, you may leave," she spoke through tight lips.

"Lady, I don't believe a damn thing you say."

She threw his hand from her, and the bracelets on her wrists jingled. "Then why have you come?"

That was a good question. A last chance effort at finding answers in the wagon of a gypsy? Hell, he didn't know. He thought he did, but as he sat across from the mystical woman, who bore her evil eyes into him, he had no damn clue why he'd come here other than desperation. But he wasn't going to tell her that, and he wasn't going to take any ridicule from a woman who professed she could tell the future.

"That is none of your concern, Gypsy,"

"Pril. My name is Pril of the Peddlers."

He shrugged. Her name did not matter to him. "Do you think me a simpleton? Anyone with eyes in their head can see what you are doing is a fraud. You, Gypsy, are a liar. In fact, I'd bet good coin the bell rang from the back room you've cleverly hidden."

Her gasp told him he was right.

"The potions and balms, your cohorts claim to cure damn near anything with, are nonsense as well."

"I've never been—"

"You and your people should be ashamed of yourselves. You have deceived the poor citizens of Riverbend so that you may steal their hard earned cash."

"That is absurd."

"I will say you're very clever, Gypsy, and thus far it has worked for you. How you figured out my name is beyond me, and I don't much care. The truth is that you're a con." He stood. "Ancestors talking to you? What a load of shit."

"Mr. Walker, you obviously came for a reason and are too frightened to hear the truth." She pointed her long finger, and the silver bracelets clinked. "Go from my vardo at once."

"I'll go when you return the money you've made today to those poor people."

"I will not."

"You have deceived them."

"I have deceived no one. I tell them what they want to hear."

Kade spun on her. "Precisely! You give them false hope."

"I do no such thing," she hissed.

He stood a foot taller than her and stepped closer to scare the little twit, but instead of retreating, she gave him a shove.

"You have overstayed your welcome, Sir. Now get from my vardo."

He burst out laughing. "I see I've hit a nerve, *Miss Pril of the Peddlers*. Is there not some sense of dignity left inside your gypsy heart?"

Pril's whole body shook with anger. The nerve this man had. He was bigger than Galius, and yet she was not afraid. Her brothers would say her temper was one of her worst traits, often landing her in a heap of trouble. Mr. Walker was lucky she did not own a gun. A bullet in the kneecap would surely put him on his knees, and at her height no less, so she could clock him square in the jaw.

"I am happy to do what I do," she said, chin tipped. "I offer a means for those wishing to know the days ahead. As for our goods, they are made from what you see in the forest and within the ground you walk upon. The healing elements they hold are from the earth, not our chanting over them."

"It is witchcraft, and you could hang for that."

She fisted her hands and took a giant step into him so her breasts touched his chest. "We practice no such thing," she ground out.

"Talking to spirits, telling the future, and claiming your wares have healing powers is not witchcraft?"

"You bastard." She raised her hand to strike him when he caught her wrist and stopped her.

The door to the private room opened, and Pril turned to see her daughter, green eyes full of anger.

"Tsura, no." She moved to go to her, but he held her wrist. A violent wind blew Tsura's hair up and knocked the dishes from the shelves. Tsura threw out her hand; with it she sent a force so strong it slammed into Pril and Mr. Walker, throwing them through the doorway.

Pril squeezed her eyes shut until they landed with a hard thud on the ground. She took slow short breaths that were followed by a stinging in her side as she tried to regain her composure. Her head hurt, and when she opened her eyes the sky spun around her. She waited a few more moments before deciding she'd better remove herself from Mr. Walker's chest. She rolled to the right, and a sharp pain sliced through her back. Her ribs ached, and she inhaled raggedly against the discomfort. She was sure she'd broken more than one. The bone throbbed against the skin.

She leaned to the right, pressed her elbow into the ground and slowly elevated herself. She brought her left arm around her midsection and cradled her broken ribs when she saw the blood. Her heart skipped, and she searched among the crowd for a familiar face. She spotted Sorina's bright orange shawl coming toward her. There was a small puddle of blood at the base of Mr. Walker's neck, and she gagged. The sight of blood had her vomiting into a pail before, but today she'd need to keep her composure. She didn't think her broken ribs would fare too well from the heaving she'd do.

"Are you all right, Pril?" Sorina knelt beside her. The woman had a light flowery voice, and Pril often thought it resembled that of an orchid—subtle yet refreshing.

"My ribs are broken," she said. "Please, tend to Mr. Walker. He is in far worse shape than I."

Sorina's blue eyes searched her face for any signs of doubt, and when Pril nodded, the women turned toward the man lying unconscious on the ground.

A crowd had gathered, and she didn't know what to tell them. She decided to ignore their questions, the looks of concern and concentrate on Mr. Walker's ashen face. *Please, let him live.*

Sorina carefully turned his head and gasped when she saw the large gash. "He will need to be stitched."

"He breathes?" she asked.

Sorina nodded.

She had to get up. She needed to help her friend, and see to Tsura—make sure she was okay.

Stefan and Galius pushed through the people.

"What happened?" Galius asked.

Pril gave him a look.

He nodded. No further explanation was needed. Her brother came to know when Tsura was involved.

"Are you okay?" he asked his thick eyebrows pulled together with concern.

"It seems I've broken a few ribs." She inhaled, not prepared for the powerful ache in her side which caused her to involuntarily groan.

He nodded, and without further conversation he bent, picked up Pril and gently set her on her feet.

"We need to move him," Stefan said.

"You will be all right?" Galius asked her.

"Sorina will aide me."

The men hoisted Mr. Walker and carried him to the supply wagon behind Pril's.

"What happened?" Sorina whispered.

"We...he slipped leaving the vardo. I tried to help him." She prayed her friend would believe the lie.

"All is well, good people of Riverbend," Sorina said, smiling at the crowd around them. "Mr. Walker slipped while exiting Pril's vardo. She tried to aide him and in turn fell, too. They will be fine in no time." She waited until they disbursed before she placed her arm around Pril's waist. "Come now, friend. I need to wrap you tight."

"I need to see Tsura."

"After I've examined you."

Pril stopped. Each breath was paired with a pain so intense it penetrated across her middle, and she gasped. "No, right now."

Sorina sighed. "Very well."

It'd taken Pril the better part of an hour to calm her daughter down, and in the end she placed a sleeping spell over her. The ox charm hung from the bed where they slept, and she grazed it with her fingertip. If something ever happened to Tsura, Pril would die. She'd need to examine her mother's book again for a new spell, one she could create to protect Tsura and the other children. There had to be something she'd missed.

She frowned. The powers Tsura held were difficult for even Pril to understand, but she needed to find a way to show her how to control them. She'd watched her sister as they'd grown and was often bewildered by all the possibilities her magick held. But Tsura was different—Tsura was stronger.

At four years old, she was a Chuvani but no Peddler saw her as such. They were a band of misfit gypsies from all different clans. When Vadoma died, Pril and her brothers decided to go off on their own. The Renoldi clan they'd grown up with didn't need to suffer for Vadoma's sins, and because Pril refused to give up the child, it put them in danger.

She bent and brushed her lips over Tsura's forehead before leaving to go stand by the table.

"She sleeps?" Sorina asked as she brushed her long black hair from her shoulder to lay across her back.

"She does."

"Come, let me bind your ribs and give you some tea that will relieve the pain."

Pril removed her blouse.

"Had you been wearing a full corset your ribs would still be intact," Sorina said and snickered.

"That may be so, but surely I would've punctured my heart from the corset bone itself." Pril hated the corset; instead she wore a short stay that only went a bit below the breasts allowing her midsection to be free of anything tight and encompassing.

"I am afraid you will need to wear one for the next week."

She groaned.

"We won't do it up too tight, but you'll need to sleep with it on as well."

"Very well." She pulled the unpleasant contraption from the trunk and handed it to her friend.

The woman wrapped it around Pril's midsection and wove the silk through the holes lacing it. "Hold on," she said while pulling the silk together to bind her stomach, ribs and lungs tight.

She whimpered as Sorina tied the back. Her ribs seemed to hurt more with the corset than without. Unsure if she should sit, she remained standing and watched as Sorina mixed the Horsetail tea.

She hated the herb. It tasted awful and smelled worse, too. For all the good it did she knew, even before Sorina handed her the cup, she'd not be able to drink it.

When the other woman wasn't watching, Pril opened the jar of mint leaves, took one sprig along with one stem of lavender and dropped them into the mug.

"Mint and lavender do thy duty, remove thy stench upon the touch of mine lips," she whispered so Sorina did not hear and lifted the glass, drinking the entire contents in one gulp.

"I cannot believe you drank it so fast. It usually takes me an hour to get it down my throat."

"I like to get the bad stuff over with as quickly as possible." She licked the mint from her lips to hide her smile.

Pril met Stefan and Galius outside of the supply wagon. Galius, the larger of the two men, stood with his muscled arms folded over his chest. Black hair fell in unruly waves around his face, clinging to his full beard. She slowed her steps and inhaled. Galius was angry. *Damn it.*

"How is he?" she asked and wrapped her arm around her waist. It still hurt to breathe, and Sorina said it would until the ribs became one again.

"He is still unconscious," Stefan said in low tones as his blue eyes roamed her body.

It'd been two years since she'd called off their engagement. She never loved him and only allowed the courtship because her brothers had pushed her into it. Galius wanted to see her safe and content while Milosh wanted to be rid of the burden she and Tsura caused.

Stefan had come to them like the others in the Peddler clan, a loner cast from his own people and from the terror of being a gypsy. But even after all this time he still pursued her.

The air puffed from Galius' nose onto her forehead. She stepped to the side away from his irritation.

Stefan placed his hand on her arm and grabbed her palm, lacing his fingers with hers. "Sorina may have something to wake him," he said.

She pulled her hand from his and crossed her arms.

"Sorina sits with Tsura," she replied.

"The clan needs wood. Go and fetch some," Galius finally spoke and gave the other man a glare fit to melt ice.

Stefan's gaze swept over her.

"Now," Galius said.

He rushed off to do Galius' bidding.

She shivered. "He needs a wife."

"He needs to be reminded that you are not his pet," Galius growled, staring after Stefan.

"Yes, well that is unlikely to happen until he meets someone else."

Galius' gaze went over her head, and his strong jaw flexed.

She placed her hand on his arm careful of her ribs. "What is wrong, Brother?"

His eyes, the same almond-color as her own, stared down at her. "We need to discuss Tsura."

Pril straightened her shoulders and stood a few inches taller. There was going to be no discussion. "No."

Galius' lips thinned. "No?"

"She is my daughter. I will decide what is best for her."

"That may be true, but she has become a constant issue." He looked around them before lowering his voice. "One that has Milosh chomping at the bit to rid the clan of."

"No. I will not allow him to touch her."

"Nor will I, but he is grieving, and while that will allow him some margin of grace, I cannot see past the anger and hate I witness in his eyes when he looks at Tsura."

She stepped back. "He hates her?"

"I am afraid so, and his wife is not far behind in her feelings."

Pril had known Milosh blamed her for their troubles, blamed her for the death of his child, but to hate Tsura—to hate a little girl. Her heart sunk. The weight of what she was up against almost buckled her knees.

"I will offer guidance, Sister." Galius placed his arm around her shoulders.

"He cannot be trusted," she whispered.

"Neither can our clan."

"What do you mean?"

"Milosh has taken it upon himself to speak with a few of the others."

"About Tsura? About the hunt?" Her heart raced, and her chest seized.

He nodded.

"The child is not safe. We are a small clan, one who cannot fight the Monroes, and we are tired of running. If Milosh can cast doubt into their minds we are doomed."

"There must be something we can do—some way to stop him."

Galius took her hand.

"I have asked for counsel with him, and...you are to be there."

She hung her head.

"I cannot."

"Sister, you must. Tsura needs you."

She couldn't see his face past the tears gathering in her eyes. "He hates me. I am the reason Alexandra is gone."

"Look past your nose, and see that he is your brother. He is mourning his daughter. He will come around. I have faith in that."

She nodded, but deep in her soul she knew that hate had consumed Milosh, that he'd stop at nothing to see her in the same anguish as he.

CHAPTER THREE

Jamestown, Virginia

Silas Monroe stood outside the bedroom door, listening to the frantic cries of his wife while in labor. Soon he'd know if the blood curse had been broken.

"It is a girl." The midwife's words floated toward him, and hope sprung in his chest, kicking his heart into spasms. He went for the knob and was stopped by Beth's harrowing scream. He pressed his fingers into the handle until his knuckles went white. Anger seeped into the crevices of his soul, taking up residence, and his sorrowful eyes slanted. He placed his forehead against the wall.

The girl was still alive. The damn gypsy child still existed. He gnashed his back teeth together, clenching his jaw until the muscle ached. Beth's low wail slammed into him, and he swayed. He could not go in there. He could not see the anguish upon his wife's frail face. He could not explain that they'd try again to find the girl, that maybe next time she'd have a boy. He'd promised her over and over that it'd be done, the blood curse would be broken and three times he'd failed. Three times he'd buried his daughters. THREE. And now he'd bury the fourth.

Silas pulled back his arm and punched the wall as hard as he could. The horse-hair wig he wore fell into his eyes, and he reset it, just as the pain shot up his hand. It wasn't enough. He needed to hurt, to expel the anger within him. He hit the wall again, and again and again. Blood smeared the flowered wallpaper and ran down his forearm. His fingers and knuckles throbbed, but he didn't care. Nothing compared to the agony he felt right now.

He pushed from the wall and went in search of his brothers. The dark hallways of the Monroe mansion were quiet at the late hour. The servants were all asleep, except the ones tending to his wife. His chest tightened. Beth would not want to see him. She'd shut him out like all the other times. He feared for her sanity, saw the circles under her eyes, heard the quiver in her voice and knew she'd changed.

He didn't light a candle, for he could walk the halls with his eyes closed and not get lost. The darkness allowed him the privacy to release two teardrops. He let them remain on his cheeks, feeling the cool air as it dried them.

What would he do now? Who could he send to kill a child? He thought of the slave, Elijah. The man hadn't returned after they'd received the letter telling them it was done. He'd sent Jude to kill him. His wife and child asked for him on a regular basis. He couldn't even pretend to care about their loss when his was so much more intense.

He found his brothers in the library, both with a glass of scotch accompanying solemn looks. Hate boiled within him, and he swallowed past the fire in his throat. Hiram turned. Every time Silas looked at him he saw weakness, and he wanted to slap it from his face.

The brothers didn't need to ask him, the slant of his eyes told them that soon they'd bury another niece.

"We killed the wrong one," Jude growled and kicked the ottoman out from under his feet.

Hiram glanced away, silent.

"The damn slave killed the wrong girl." Silas picked up the bottle of scotch and threw it across the room. Glass shattered onto the floor, and no one moved. "The wrong bloody child!"

"He said she had the mark—she was branded."

Silas remembered the mark behind Vadoma's left ear. The child had the same one.

Hiram ran his hand through his shoulder length hair. "There has to be another way. We cannot keep killing children." He turned toward Silas, and his brown eyes begged. "I cannot sleep at night for my transgressions."

Silas curled his lip, and he spat onto the floor. "You coward. You're a part of this blasted curse like the rest of us." He stepped closer. "Do you not remember the rope I placed around the gypsy's neck? You were there. You watched her convulse until she died."

Hiram averted his eyes.

"Search your memories, Brother. We burned her until there was nothing left but ash!"

"Stop," Hiram yelled.

"You were always weak." Silas yanked Hiram's drink from his hand, and lifting it to his lips he drank it all in one swig. "What will you tell your wife when she has to bury a daughter?"

"I do not know," he whispered.

"You've been lucky thus far, Brother. God has granted you twin boys. But evil walks among us and always will until we kill that damn gypsy child."

"But we have killed so many," Hiram whispered.

Silas slapped him across the face. "And we have lost many."

Hiram grabbed Silas' collar and tugged him close. "We should have never done what we did, *Brother.* If we'd have left things alone, none of this would be happening."

"Left it alone? She killed our father."

"Father died from typhus. She did not aid in that, and you know it."

Silas hated their father as much as his brothers did. Castor Monroe had been a brute with large hands and wide shoulders. He had stood over six feet and could fight up to five slaves at a time. No one crossed him, and if they did sure-fire hell came their way.

"She placed a spell on him. Used her magick to spawn the disease," Silas spat.

"That was no magick, Brother. That was luck, and father deserved what he got."

"Damn you!"

Jude was between the brothers, holding them by their collars.

Their chests heaved as Silas and Hiram glared at one another.

"Calm the hell down. We will rectify this. We will hire more men. Send two or three out at a time." He pulled the brothers close. "We will find the child, and we will kill her."

Hiram shoved Jude from him.

"No. I want no more of this."

Silas laughed a pitted and piercing sound. "There is blood upon your hands, Brother. Therefore, you cannot walk away."

Hiram pointed his finger at Silas.

"The evil has taken your soul. It has caused the lines upon your face to hang, your mouth to droop and your lips to spew rancid sentences."

"The child must die," Jude said. "We haven't a choice."

Hiram shoved his fist within his mouth and bit down hard.

Silas saw him only as a broken link to the chain they'd formed. He needed to be removed.

"Hiram, you cannot expect us to stop until our daughters breathe life."

Without another word Hiram spun on his heel and walked from the room.

CHAPTER FOUR

Kade opened his eyes. Twilight blanketed the room. He turned his head and was stopped by the discomfort ringing in his ears. *What the hell happened?* The last thing he remembered he was in the gypsy's wagon. He could recall nothing afterward. He scanned his surroundings. He wasn't in a cabin, but instead a wagon.

A rope, a rake, two small shovels, and a hammer hung on the wall to his left. He shifted on the bed and realized his arms were tied down.

"Ah shit."

Had they found out who he was? Did they know he searched for the child or perhaps the child was here? If it were true, he could finally put the endless hunting to rest and finish what he'd set out to do.

The letter was still sewn into the seam of his coat. He'd memorized every word; the child with the mark behind her left ear and the urgency in the written words to find her. If his head didn't hurt like bloody hell, he'd yell like an Indian warrior. His nostrils flared, and each breath burned straight to his lungs.

He kicked his foot, but the effort was for nothing as his legs stayed where they were. He needed to escape and shook the bed, rattling the walls. Tools clinked together, and a glass jar fell from a shelf to shatter on the floor. The scent of honey filled the wagon, and he licked his lips in hunger.

He hadn't eaten since this morning. No light came through the boards. He figured it was past dinnertime or close to it. The air held a chill, and he wondered if they'd leave him here all night.

He used all his strength to sit up—to force the bonds to break, but instead was met with an intense ache at the back of his head. The room spun, and his mouth watered with the urge to vomit. Had she hit him with something? He searched his mind for any recollection of the afternoon. His mind was blank. *Damn it.* He yanked on the ropes once more. He was stuck—bound to whatever the gypsies had in store for him—and utterly useless.

Pril shoved the tweed satchel and burlap sack into the bench beside the bed. It had become clear that she and Tsura would have to leave the clan. She stood back, hands on hips and blew out a long sigh. With Galius' warning of Milosh, she'd not be caught unaware if they needed to flee. *It was better to be prepared than not.* A soft knock startled her. She closed the lid on the bench softly before going to see who was there.

Galius stood outside—grim and commanding.

"I've come to take you to Mr. Walker," he said.

She released a slow breath thankful it'd not been Milosh. The fear of seeing her brother—of speaking to him—haunted her, and she knew it was from the guilt she felt.

"Let me grab my shawl." She hurried inside and took a quick peek at Tsura, still asleep in their bed. Hand on the bench she lightly patted the wooden top. She couldn't afford for Galius to be suspicious. He'd surely try to stop her, and she didn't want to deal with him. It was easier this way.

He raised his hand to help her from the vardo and escorted her across the lawn. Fires burned among the clan as they prepared their evening meals, and the smell of roasted venison wafted throughout the camp. The corset was uncomfortable, and she shifted her hip to relieve her skin from the tight confines. The bones pressed into her side, putting pressure on her broken rib, and she pulled her arm from Galius' to wrap around her middle.

"It will take some time to heal."

She ignored him. She was tired of being told as if she were a child.

She spotted Finn and Radu as they ran in between the wagons. She quickly swept the camp for the boy's sister, Callie. The blonde haired little girl was nowhere to be seen. Heart in throat, she placed a hand to her chest and stopped, forcing Galius to do the same.

"What is it?" he asked, concern creasing his brows.

"Callie? Where is she?"

Galius followed her line of vision, to the children playing ten feet in front of them.

"Ivan and Lena struggle to let the girl play outside of their vardo."

She nodded. How could she blame them? There had been three girls, and now two remained. She swallowed past the lump in her throat and willed her legs to move.

Galius cleared his throat.

She turned toward him. "Say what needs saying, Brother."

He was never one to keep things from her, and she knew the signs when a truth needed to be told.

"Milosh watches us from his fire."

She didn't dare look and instead dipped her head from the shame she felt.

"You are not to blame."

"But, I am," she whispered.

There were many things Pril needed to confess, and her stomach churned from it all. How could she have thought raising a child would be easy—one with magick and hunted no less? Vadoma hadn't thought of her. She hadn't thought of anyone when she laid the blood curse upon the Monroes—a curse that had the clan running for the lives of their children. Resentment straightened her spine and thinned her lips.

Their life would never be the same again. The pendant had been lost, another betrayal of the sister she loved.

She peeked at Milosh through her lashes. His back rounded as he hunched forward. No longer tall and strong—the man she'd always known him to be was gone, and she was to blame for it. Magda sat on a tree stump by their fire, pale and weak. Her hands shook as she lifted a piece of bread to her dry lips, and Pril stifled the urge to run to her sister in-law.

When Magda saw Pril, her face distorted, and her eyes shot daggers.

Their hate slammed into Pril, crushing her heart and triggering her throat to spasm for air. Pril worked her fingers within her skirt. Her ribs screamed. How could she ever forgive herself for the agony she had caused? She blinked back the tears and dropped her chin. She would not let Galius see her cry. He'd want to help, offer reprieve from the torment she felt, but there was nothing he could do. Pril faced her heartache—her betrayal—alone, and today she was sure she'd die from it.

"We must speak with him," Galius murmured.

"He wants nothing to do with me."

He placed his hand on her chin and lifted it up toward him.

"Sister, you cannot be afraid. He is your brother. He will remember this and come around."

"How can you be so sure, when he stares at me with such disgust?"

"I will talk with him before we have counsel together."

He placed his arm around her shoulders, and they resumed walking.

Sorina idled up to them. Her long black hair, braided to the side, brushed Pril's arm.

"Good evening," she said, smiling. "My sister sits with Tsura."

Pril nodded, returning the girl's smile.

Galius cleared his throat, a common occurrence when Sorina was around.

"While walking past the supply wagon I heard the man. He has woken, and he is not agreeable," Sorina said.

"Agreeable to what?" Pril asked.

Sorina looked at Galius, and Pril turned to see her brother's black eyes flash with anger.

"What have you done, Brother?"

"I am keeping us safe." He scowled at Sorina. "Do you have something to calm him down?"

"I do," Sorina said as her cheeks flushed crimson.

"Then go and fetch it," he snapped.

The girl jumped, and Pril didn't miss the way her eyes, moist with unshed tears, fell from Galius' face to the ground.

She glared up at her brother. "Sorina, I thank you for helping us so." She grabbed her hand and gave it a light squeeze.

"I will go, and do as you wish," she whispered before hurrying toward her wagon.

"Honestly, Brother. Can you not see she cares for you?"

"I haven't the time for such things."

Galius had always been the practical one of the family. When Vadoma had betrayed them, he saw reason and helped Pril raise Tsura. He dealt with Milosh's anger and sharp tongue, smoothing things between the brother and sister. He'd never forgive Vadoma for what she'd done, but he did see hope in the child. He believed in Pril, and in turn she leaned on him for support.

She peeked at him, strong jaw, trained eyes and lonely heart. How had she not seen it before? Milosh had Magda, she had Tsura, and Galius had no one. He'd been the leader of the clan; too busy helping others, her included. He'd put his own happiness to the side for the sake of them all.

They came to the supply wagon. *I am second daughter to Imelda the great enchantress.* She stepped in front of Galius and climbed the two stairs into the wagon. The room was small, and with Galius' size it seemed to shrink right before her.

Mr. Walker lay on the cot at the end of the wagon, and she inched closer. His eyes were closed. She watched the rise and fall of his chest. The even rhythm told her he slept.

"How is his wound?" she asked Galius.

"I do not know. Stefan and I put him here but did not stay."

"You did not bandage the wound?"

He was silent.

"Sorina did not attend the gash when she came to see him?"

"She has not come."

She glared at him and shoved him out of the way. He knocked his large shoulder into the wall behind them. The tools rattled as they fell onto the ground and echoed in the small space.

"Where are you going?"

"To get bandages and salve for his wound."

She'd need something else as well. Because of Galius' lack of attention to Mr. Walker, he could be suffering from infection by now. Pril hurried toward her vardo. She ignored the pain as it vibrated up her side. She grabbed a needle, thread, cloth, bucket and her herbs. She tossed a peppermint leaf into her mouth and waited for the minty taste to coat her insides. She often used the leaf to stop her stomach from convulsing as she mended bloody wounds.

"That lamp is not going to be bright enough," Pril said to Galius. "You will need to light another."

Mr. Walker lay sleeping on his side. She inspected the wound. The blood had stopped flowing and had dried in a mess of matted hair. She dunked the cloth into the water and gently dabbed the cut, pulling the blood from his scalp. Mr. Walker didn't move, and she worried infection had set in. To be sure, she placed cattail on the wound once it was cleaned. Taking the thread she dipped it into a bottle of whiskey before she threaded the needle. She poked it through the scalp at the back of his head and sewed up the torn skin. Still Mr. Walker did not stir.

"Where is the beeswax?" she asked.

Galius handed it to her. She opened the jar of wax and herbs. She scooped some of the thick salve onto her fingers and covered Mr. Walker's wound. She placed her palm over the wound, feeling the energy flow into her mind and heart. She pushed it into her fingers and whispered, "Mend thee now whilst one day past. Heal thy wound, ever last."

The wax would keep infection out, and the herbs would kill any contagion wanting to start, but the spell would fix it all.

"What in hell?"

She jumped and dropped the jar of wax onto the floor. "Mr. Walker, we are here to help you." She glanced at Galius. Did he hear her say the spell?

He rolled onto his back, eyes narrowed, lips grim and unchallenging. "I find that hard to believe."

"It is true. We mean you no harm."

He lifted his arms until the chains tightened.

"My apologies."

"Bullshit."

She was silent.

"Where are my dagger and horse?"

"Your horse grazes with ours," she said.

"And the dagger?"

"It will be given to you soon," she said.

He scowled.

"Why am I tied to this bloody bed?"

Galius stepped forward.

She raised her hand to stop him.

"Sir, you fell from my vardo and hit your head."

He spat onto the floor and turned a pointed glare toward her.

"Yet, you feel it necessary to chain me?"

"You will be released as soon as you tell us why you've come."

"To hear of the days ahead of course." He smirked, and she knew he was mocking her.

"We both know that is not the truth."

"You damn gypsies know nothing of truth. You make a living from lies."

"It will suit you best to answer the questions instead of handing out insults," Galius said.

"And you best hope I don't get free from these chains."

Galius growled.

"What is your given name, Mr. Walker?" she asked.

He tried to sit up, the chains clinked, and she felt sorry for him. There was no need to keep him tied down.

"Brother, release him."

"Not until he speaks of why he's come."

"Kade. My name is Kade Walker."

"Why have you come, Kade?" Pril asked.

"To hear my bloody future. Why is that so hard to understand? You have people coming from all over the damn place to hear their past or present. Why am I any different?"

She sucked in a breath and let it out in a loud whoosh.

"You did not want to know the days ahead of you, sir. You came for another reason."

"If you are so sure, then what is the other reason?"

"I do not know."

He pulled at the chains, shaking the bed, and winced when his head came down onto the cot.

Pril leapt forward to help him when a strong hand reached out, grabbing her shawl and pulling her close.

"Remove these damn chains," he said through clenched teeth.

There was something in his eyes. A flash of agony, betrayal, hurt?

She didn't know, and when she looked again it was gone.

"I...I cannot until you speak the truth."

He shook her violently. The walls vibrated, and she closed her eyes.

A loud thud silenced the wagon and loosened the grip on her shawl.

She opened her eyes and regarded Kade, unconscious and bleeding from a cut above his right eye.

Galius leaned over them.

"What have you done?"

"What I always do."

"He wasn't going to hurt me. He was confined to the cot."

Galius shrugged.

"Out!" she shouted. "You have done enough. Now I need to mend another wound."

She waited until Galius left before blotting the cut above Kade's eye. Why had he come? He didn't believe in what she did, and she could see the lie in his eyes clear as the morning sun. He searched for something. She swept his blond hair from his forehead and stared at his handsome face. Dark brows framed even darker eyes. A somewhat crooked nose and square chin gave him a rugged appearance, but it was the clean-shaven cheeks that had her wondering where he'd come from.

Most men in her clan kept a beard during the colder months, and only those of wealth shaved often. She spotted a ring on his right hand and lifted it to see the jewel better. Large hands with callused palms told her he worked hard wherever that may be. The gold ring housed a round emerald in the center, and she couldn't help her gasp. It must've cost a fortune. She leaned closer. *Who are you?*

She dabbed the wet cloth over the cut above his eye, cursing Galius and his hot temper. She sunk her finger into the jar of wax and slathered the slash. The brow had begun to swell, and a light shade of purple colored the skin.

Mr. Walker wasn't telling them the truth. He wasn't here to harm them, but possibly another. *Tsura.* Her child needed protection from the world outside of their clan, and she couldn't do that. Galius had tried, but Milosh disagreed on every matter concerning the child. He'd been held against a stone wall far too long. Now things had become worse. Milosh's child was gone, and he blamed hers.

She'd have to face her brother sooner or later, and the thought frightened her to no end. She'd not allow herself any comfort. Her niece died because of her hand—because of her selfishness. She released the tears waiting on the edge of her lashes. How could she have not protected them all? What good was the magick she held if she couldn't help those in need—her own family?

She knew the spells by heart, she'd said them often enough, but she didn't know how to save her only child. She wasn't strong enough. When she was younger their mother concentrated on Vadoma's gifts. She was the Chuvani, the one with the most power out of the two sisters. Pril was self-taught. She felt the light in her, the heat as it moved from her soul to her fingers, and spoke the words. She'd made mistakes, but Vadoma had tried to help her when she wasn't busy studying her own magick.

After their mother died, Pril leaned on her sister for comfort but was met with a resistance she'd never felt before. Vadoma had placed beams around her heart, and no one could get close.

CHAPTER FIVE

The fire rose high, reflecting off of the concerned faces of the Peddlers gathered around. Pril held Tsura upon her lap while waiting for the clan's counsel to begin. She didn't want to be here, but like all the times before, Galius insisted. She searched the familiar faces for Milosh and Magda. She exhaled when she saw no sign of them.

She should feel more relieved than she did, but instead her chest was heavy, and her hands fidgeted. She yearned for a word, an embrace, or even a smile from her sister in-law. They'd been close, and now a boulder stood between them. Milosh had never been accepting of Pril's decision to raise Tsura as her own, and even though he hadn't said so in the last year, she knew his defiance and anger were coming soon. She squeezed her daughter to her chest as fear turned her blood cold, and she shivered.

Galius stood in the center of the circle, the fire behind him. She knew he'd be by her side through anything, but this battle was hers to fight. He cleared his throat to summon everyone's attention.

"Tonight we hold counsel to answer your questions, and calm your fears," he said.

Pril's hands shook, and she rubbed Tsura's back for something to do. She knew what her people dreaded, and Milosh was mixed up in their doubt.

"We've been told Tsura is of special blood. She is the reason for the hunts," Ivan spoke, clutching his daughter Callie to his side.

"This is untrue," Galius said in low even tones. Pril knew he would only give short answers, refusing to divulge more.

"Your own brother, Milosh, has said these things. How can we be certain she is not the one the Monroes want dead?"

The faces of her clan stared back at her and Tsura. Pril bounced her daughter on her lap to hide the fact her legs were trembling.

"Milosh is grieving the death of his own child. His words cannot be taken as truth."

"We want to see behind the child's left ear," Emmett said.

Often quiet during clan meetings and ensconced in his vardo most days, Emmett didn't seem at all the man he'd portrayed himself to be these past years. His wide shoulders stood out, daring any person, Galius included, to decline his request.

She was having none of it. She was not afraid to stand up for her child. "What will that tell you?" she asked, her voice pitched as she glared at the other man across the fire.

"It will tell us if she is branded. The Monroes hunt the marked one."

"Of course they do, but would you not have seen way of this mark on my child long before now? She has frolicked among you for three years."

Emmett snickered, and she didn't miss the muscles twitch in his neck.

"I do not go about checking behind little girls' ears."

"But you have need to now?"

"Yes, we all do."

She addressed the crowd. "You're all wanting to see behind Tsura's ear?"

Some nodded while others turned away, refusing to acknowledge the question.

"Sister, show them," Galius said from beside her.

She inhaled expanding her chest and stood with Tsura in her arms. Placing the child's head to her chest, she ran her fingers through the thick curls to pull back the hair behind her ear. With careful steps, she walked around the fire. Every muscle in her body tense, she prayed the light from the fire, the herbs and powder covered the mark she knew was there.

It'd been Galius' idea to hold the counsel in the evening. He knew they'd ask to see the child's ear, and with just enough powder and firelight it could be hidden. The mark was small and sat in the crease behind her left ear. Vadoma had the same one.

Sorina refused to look, showing she trusted her friends and didn't believe what Milosh had said. While others nodded in acceptance as she passed. Once back at Galius' side, she tucked her head into Tsura's neck to blow out the long breath she'd held.

"Who is the man in the supply wagon?" Ivan asked.

"His name is Kade Walker, and we will make sure he holds no threat to us before we release him," Galius said.

"He is injured, and when he is well I am sure he will be on his way," Pril added.

Milosh burst into the circle, hair disheveled and eyes wild. He pointed a long finger at her.

"That child is a spawn. She is the reason we all have been running."

Pril caught Galius' eye. Heart hammering in her chest, she placed Tsura on her hip and turned to shield her daughter.

"You have been grieving, Brother." Galius placed his hand on Milosh's shoulder.

He shoved the gesture from him and took two large steps toward Pril.

Galius stepped in between them.

"No, Milosh. Not like this." Galius' voice was low, but the warning within the tone could not be missed.

"You've all gone mad to believe these two," Milosh addressed the clan. "They're liars protecting the devil's child. Give her to me."

"No," Pril said.

"I will show you the mark," Milosh shouted at the clan.

"We have seen," Ivan said. "There is nothing."

"That is because they've hidden it." Milosh stepped toward Pril. "Hand her to me."

"That is not going to happen, Brother," Galius spoke, and Pril stood taller knowing he was there.

"You all have heard stories of Vadoma, the great Chuvani."

Gasps surrounded her, and she blinked, trying to steady herself. She bit down hard on her lip to keep from shouting at Milosh. Vadoma had been known for her ruthless behavior and vengeance if crossed. She peered at Galius—her eyes pleaded with him to end this.

"Enough," Galius growled.

"You know Tsura brings death."

"My brother has become delusional because of his grief. Please, ignore him."

Milosh laughed, a chilling sound that struck the back of her throat and made it difficult to swallow. He bent over, throwing his hands up as he continued to carry on. The clan grew quiet, and she stepped back.

Milosh shot up, his black hair sticking out in all directions, eyes wild and mouth turned down. He spat at her. "I despise you."

"Why would you say such horrible things about your sister's child?" Sorina asked.

"Because that child is the reason mine is dead!" Milosh went for Tsura, and Galius jumped on him.

Tsura cried into Pril's chest. She could feel the child grow warm. *Not now.* She wanted to stay—needed to. She had to see what transpired between her brothers. The skin beneath her blouse heated. Without a word she raced to her vardo, holding Tsura tight, her flesh screaming.

Tears streamed down her cheeks as she hurried, praying no one saw the smoke from her shawl and blouse. Once inside the wagon she dropped Tsura onto the bed and reached for the bucket of water she kept on the floor. She cried out as she dumped it onto her chest.

She dropped to her knees as pieces of her shawl fell to the floor. The smell of burning flesh permeated the room, and she gagged from the intensity of her wounds. Tsura's whimpers faded as she ignored her child and tried to figure out how to fix what had just happened. She'd never been burned this badly before. The skin on her chest above her breasts oozed, and the cool air stung the open sores. She wheezed. A pang in her side reminded her of the broken ribs, and she leaned to the left to relieve the pressure.

Her hands shook as she slowly removed the blouse. The corset had saved her breasts and stomach from being burned. The white chemise had singed holes, but otherwise was in good shape. Her blouse and shawl could not be salvaged. She stood on trembling legs and reached for the jar of beeswax on the counter. Her hands shook as she tried to grab hold of the lid and open it.

Her chest stung, the skin still smoldered as the room dipped before her. She reached out to steady herself. The jar fell from her hand onto the floor and rolled under the table. Black dots danced in front of her, and she blinked as her vision blurred. She sunk to the floor and lay on her side. With the remnants of her blouse, she covered her burned flesh. The skin throbbed with the beat of her heart. The pain was so powerful her teeth chattered, and she bit down hard to stop them. She couldn't halt her body from shaking and soon was in full convulsions.

Kade spit the key from his mouth onto his lap. The gypsy, Galius, hadn't thought to check his pockets when he let Kade relieve himself earlier. Working on a vessel his whole life he'd acquired certain talents. Pickpocketing was one of them, fighting the other. He pressed his fingers into his pant leg, pulling the fabric so the key slid down and into his palm. He glided the key into the metal lock. In one turn, he heard the click. Every muscle in his body sighed.

He stretched his arms above his head and inhaled a deep breath. It felt good to be free of the chains. His fingers skimmed the cut on the back of his head. Whatever the gypsy had put on the wound was working. The ache had all but disappeared.

His dagger gone, he took an ax from the wall, opened the door and peered out into the blackness. He expected a guard to be standing outside the wagon and was surprised to see no one there. Shouts in the distance brought his head up toward the large fire a hundred feet away. Two men wrestled around the flames. The shorter man flailed about. No rhythm or beat to his punches; he'd lost all control, fighting with anger rather than a clear head. He'd lose because of it.

His opponent was Galius. Kade's palms twitched with the urge to beat the other man into a bloody state. He didn't care for the big gypsy and owed him for the knot on his forehead.

Galius let his opponent pummel him without so much as a flinch. He was a thick mass of muscle, and Kade felt he'd met his match in the gypsy. It'd be interesting to see who would win if the two of them went at it.

Two more punches struck Galius before he puffed out his barrel chest. Eyes full of remorse, he lifted his meaty fist and, with one blow, clipped the shorter man under the chin, sending him through the air to land awkwardly on the ground. The crowd gathered around the fire fell silent. Galius fell to his knees beside the fallen man.

Branches broke to Kade's right. Someone was coming. He observed the area on his left. A short distance away was the wagon where he'd met the gypsy, Pril. The steps drew closer. With no time to wait, he fell back into the shadows and headed toward the wagon.

He leaned against the wood structure, his back firmly to the wall he inched toward the door. Voices could be heard across the camp, but they were more concerned with the man who'd been knocked out instead of their escaped prisoner.

He peeked around the wagon. No one was there, so he ducked inside. He halted at the doorway. Pril lay on the floor, her small body trembling. He closed the flap and dropped to his knees to help her, when he saw the small boy with big green eyes and black curls sitting beside her.

The muscles in his chest tightened, and he inhaled through his nose. His stomach dropped, and his soul cried out. Memories assaulted him of a boy with blond hair, brown eyes and of the man who raised him. *Damn it!* He sat back on his heels and pushed his face into his hands. He'd put it all away, tacked it down tight. Forced upon his own hand, he'd given his word to do the unthinkable.

He groaned. *I have no choice*. He set his jaw, ignored the constant ache within him and considered the boy.

The child moved away from him to lie across the gypsy, protecting her.

"I won't hurt you," he said. "Please, let me help."

The boy gawked at him, and Kade didn't know what to do. He'd never had anyone gaze at him so intently. It was as if the child could read his mind, or see into his soul. After what seemed an eternity, the boy moved to the side and off of Pril.

Kade lifted the blouse from her chest and gasped when he saw the blistered skin above the charred corset. He moved to the bucket on the floor, dunked the blouse inside and swished it around the little water that was left. He gently laid the fabric over her wounds. It wasn't enough. He needed to do more and pulled her onto his lap while she shook.

"Is this your mother?" he asked the boy.

He nodded, one black curl dropped over his eye.

"Is there any medicine in the cupboards?"

The child stood and went to the last cupboard on the right. He reached up, taking a small jar with herbs and handed it to him.

"What do I do with these?" He held the jar up gazing at the green and brown crushed leaves inside.

The boy crawled under the table, pulled out another jar and gave it to him.

He opened it, and inhaled the bee's wax.

"Do I mix them together?" He loosened his hold on Pril, still shaking, and dropped the jar.

The boy picked it up and opened it. He placed his fingers inside, scooped some out, placing it in the palm of his pudgy hand, and pointed at the jar of herbs beside Kade.

"Here." He watched as the boy dumped the herbs into the wax and worked it between his hands.

"What's your name, boy?"

The child ignored him, still molding the wax within his hands. He motioned for Kade to remove the wet blouse covering his mother. Then very carefully he smothered the open blisters with the concoction.

Pril moaned and tossed her head. Her petite body had slowed its restless shaking. Kade reached for the blanket on the bed to cover her legs and torso.

The child crossed his legs and grabbed his mother's hand, holding it within his own.

Kade could see the bond between them. He cleared his throat as memories of the past, and the reasons he was here, slammed into him. He stole a peek at the kid and wondered again if the child he searched for was among these gypsies.

Loud angry steps came through the doorway, and he wasn't shocked to see Galius standing before them.

"Release my sister," he growled and wiped at the cut on his lip, missing the other one above his right eye.

Kade smirked. His opponent had gotten in a few good ones.

"I could've escaped without you or the others knowing, but instead I am here tending to your very sick sister," he said with an air to his voice that told the other man he wasn't going anywhere.

"Boy, go."

The child gazed at his mother and back to his uncle.

"She'll be fine. I'll see to it," Galius said.

"Actually, I've seen to it. With the help of the child of course."

The man growled low in his throat, and Kade never moved.

The boy stood. His green eyes locked with Kade's, and he couldn't pull his gaze away. What was it about the boy that had him in some sort of trance? His head snapped to the side, when Galius struck his cheek.

"What the hell?" he mumbled before he fell over unconscious.

Pril woke with Tsura curled up next to her like a cat. Without turning her head she knew Galius was in the room. His loud breathing sounded like the ox outside.

"You have no need of your own vardo, Brother?" she asked.

He was at the table, reading their mother's spell book. She sat up, pausing halfway because her ribs hurt. She slowed her movements to ease the pain. She placed her hand to her chest. The burn? There was no pain. Where had it gone? She inspected her chest covered in a white night shirt and lifted the fabric. There was nothing. The skin appeared the same. Had she imagined it? Had it been a terrible dream?

"The child healed you," Galius said quietly.

She shifted Tsura from her and covered the girl with the thick blanket before she crawled out of the bed.

"How?"

Galius held the book up.

"A spell? She used a spell on me?"

"Her hands."

"I beg your pardon?"

"The child can heal with her hands."

Pril peeked back at her daughter curled into the blanket and snoring softly.

"Were you here? Did you see?"

"I did."

Shocked at the news, she moved about the vardo in a daze. Tea she needed tea. She filled the pot with water and placed it on the burner to heat while Galius stoked the fire. Once the tea was made she sat down across from him.

"Tell me all of it."

"I found the healing spell and read it to her while she placed her hands over your wounds. The flesh healed right before my eyes." He shook his head. "I still cannot believe what I saw."

"Which spell was it?"

Galius flipped through the book and showed her the healing spell. This was the same spell she used when applying herbs to a wound. It was to keep infection and pain away. It was not for removing the wound in its entirety.

"This cannot be. The spell you have pointed to is to aid in healing, not vanish it as if it never happened."

"I assure you this is the one."

Galius' eyes spoke the truth but it didn't make sense. How could the child heal without words, without a spell?

"Vadoma could not do such things. Cast spells, throw a beam, yes, but to heal the flesh with her own hands she could not."

"Her child can."

"But how?"

He shrugged, a sentiment she felt as well but one best kept a secret.

"Her powers are far more than what we thought," Galius said, and he didn't seem happy about it.

"Yes, all the more reason to protect her."

"We are to have counsel with Milosh at midday."

Her stomach flipped, and she shook her head.

"Yes."

"You saw him last night. What good can come of this?"

"There is need, and you will be there if I have to drag you kicking and screaming."

Galius stood and without another word exited the vardo.

Pril wrapped her hands around the cup. How could Tsura heal without the words? Without the knowledge and aiding of a Chuvani? Pressure built on her chest when she thought of what could come of the gift the child had. People would hunt her—kill her even. She lifted the mug to her lips and held it there, allowing the warmth to heat her skin. The need to protect her daughter even more than she already had filled her soul and dripped from her eyes. *I must prepare to leave soon.*

"Milosh is waiting for us in the field."

Pril tilted her head. She could not meet Galius' eye for fear she'd burst into hysterics. *I will not let him take my daughter.* Milosh suggested it years before, and she'd begged him to let Tsura stay.

The set of Galius' shoulders, and the grim look upon his handsome face spoke volumes. He turned, and Pril had no choice but to follow. She knew what Milosh wanted, and she knew she'd fight him on it.

They walked into the thick of the woods. Tall pine and elm trees shadowed them from the sun. She stepped over gnarled roots and broken branches. The shaded forest was a reflection of what she knew was to come.

Relieved to be exiting the woody confines, they stepped into a lush field of green grass. She inhaled the fresh clean scent and the sweet fragrance of dandelions.

Milosh stood in the tall grass, his once strong body now frail and thin from grief. A black eye and swollen lip were evidence of his fight with Galius the night before. She hadn't spoken to her brother since the death of his child. He'd avoided her, but in truth she'd made no attempt to comfort him. She stared at the ground too afraid to look at him now. How could she after what she'd done?

Galius stopped, and they stood facing each other.

"She has to go," Milosh growled.

"No," Pril gasped, and when she met her brother's eyes she stumbled backward from the hate evident there.

Galius sighed beside her and placed his large arm over her shoulder. Rather than calm her, the gesture did nothing but alert her senses and caused her back to go rigid.

"Pril understands we cannot have any more disasters," he said.

"The child is evil and must be taken from the clan," Milosh argued.

Galius nodded.

She gaped at him, shocked at his behavior. "You agree with him? You'd take my child?"

Galius averted his eyes and nodded.

"I asked you if I should go. You said no."

"Yes, and you shouldn't."

"But the child must," Milosh growled.

"I will not have it!" Pril shoved Galius' arm from her and turned to Milosh. "Brother, I am sorry, so sorry that Alexandra is gone." Her voice quavered.

"I cannot seem to find one reason why the child needs to stay," Milosh said.

"She is my daughter. That is reason enough."

"I will take her somewhere safe," Galius said.

"She is safe with me."

"No one is safe from the girl, not even you," Milosh snapped.

"The child is your niece," Pril spoke, and anger spiked her words.

"She is of mixed blood, a reaction to Vadoma's betrayal."

Pril would die before she'd allow them to take Tsura. Anger resonated inside her and swirled to rage.

"She is mine."

"She is a curse!" Milosh yelled and stepped toward her.

Pril stood her ground. He may be taller than her, but she'd fight him on this. "You will not touch my daughter."

Galius slid his strong arms between them.

"You hide her. That is not the solution," he said.

"Of course I hide her. They will kill her otherwise."

"The very reason she has to go," Milosh shouted.

Pril could not believe her ears. She bent, arms wrapped around her stomach as the truth of their betrayal slammed into her. Tears filled her eyes, and she squeezed them shut.

"We love Tsura as much as you do, but she has put our clan in danger far too many times," Galius said.

"You have betrayed me, Brother. You spoke words that I thought honest and true." She spat at his feet. "You are a liar."

Galius hung his head.

"I cannot allow this." She straightened and glared at her brothers. "I will not allow it."

"You have no choice," Milosh said. "If you do not agree to rid the clan of the child, I will go to the Monroes myself. I will tell them of Tsura."

"No," Pril gasped.

"I forbid that, Brother. We cannot turn the child over to her death," Galius reasoned.

"But you will take her from her mother, the only one who loves her?"

"I love Tsura," Galius spoke.

"Lies! They spew from your mouth causing my eyes to water," Pril hissed.

"She will go," Milosh growled.

"She is but a child. She is innocent."

Milosh shifted his weight from one foot to the other, his pitted cheeks sunken in, and his full lips shifted downward into a permanent frown. It was clear he couldn't stand her presence.

"And since the Monroes have made no attempt at hiding the fact they're searching for a child with a mark behind her left ear it will be easy to tell them of yours."

Pril frowned at Milosh. "The Monroes do not care about the mark. They are killing any gypsy girl-child they find."

Milosh groaned, and his face twisted.

The sound sliced through her, cutting away a small piece of her soul.

A thick tear dropped onto his cheek, and she went to him. He slashed at her arms with his own. "Do not comfort me."

She tried to be brave, to be honest and loving, but the agony she saw within his gaze knocked the air from her lungs and bowed her head in shame.

"It is because of you my daughter has died. Bile rises within my throat, and fire scorches my insides when I think of you and your child."

Pril sucked in a sob as her body shook from his horrible words.

"Milosh, that is enough," Galius growled.

"I despise you," he went on.

A sob escaped her pursed lips, and she covered her mouth with a trembling hand.

"Look at me, Sister," Milosh screamed. "Look at me damn it!"

She mustered all the courage she had left from his brutal assault of the truth and lifted her eyes to his.

"I want nothing from you, but to never see your child's face again."

"You cannot get those words back. You've said too much." Galius stepped between them.

"I have not said enough." Milosh shoved Galius aside. He grabbed her chin and forced her face upward. His fingers dug into her skin as he squeezed. "The only thing that is saving you from my pistol is the blood that runs through your body." He spat into her face before walking away.

Pril fell to her knees within the tall grass and wept.

"He still mourns," Galius said as he knelt beside her.

"He speaks the truth, and I cannot gaze in the mirror without seeing what I have brought upon us."

He sighed, and she knew he felt it, too.

How could she stay, knowing that her own brothers blamed her and Tsura for Alexandra's death? She wouldn't abandon her child, and so she must abandon them.

"Leave me, Brother," she whispered.

"Pril—"

"Leave me to weep for all the wrong I have done."

He placed a light kiss on the top of her head. "I will take Tsura tomorrow when the moon is bright. I will keep her safe, Pril. I promise." The grass rustled as he walked away.

She watched him go, knowing it would be the last time she'd see him.

CHAPTER SIX

Kade woke tied to a chair.

"Shit."

He was in the same wagon he'd been in earlier. He whipped his head back and shook the chair. The wooden legs creaked and shifted, but the ropes wrapped around his limbs didn't budge. He growled low in his throat and gnashed his teeth together until his jaw ached. This was the thanks he got for helping the gypsy.

Damn it. He should've headed straight into the forest, and to hell with the lot of them. He spat onto the floor. Disgust bubbled inside of him and turned the cauldron of fury brewing within his gut.

The wagon was black. He couldn't see a foot in front of him. Which direction was the doorway? He sighed. What did it matter? He was stuck here for now. He tapped his fingers on the armrest. None of this made sense. Why were they determined to lock him up especially after he helped Pril? He shuddered. The burns on her skin were atrocious, and he could only imagine the agony she'd feel when she woke.

Thank the saints he still had his coat, the navy blue fabric with the woolen liner inside, the note sewn between them. He'd been searching for the child for four months—four long, endless months. He'd visited every gypsy camp this side of the colonies. He even ventured onto Spanish land and still nothing.

He was tired, exhausted really, but this was important. He gave his word. A life depended on him. He was bound to his promise, and there was no turning back. He missed the sea, the smell of the water, the wind in his hair and the hint of salt when he licked his lips.

He'd spent most of his life on the large vessels, traveling from port to port, docking on the shores of Spain, London and the Africas many times. His life was full—charming and risky, and he loved every minute of it. Once he found the child, he'd return her to the Monroes. Soon he'd get back what was his and be on his ship sailing the deep blue seas once again.

The wagon shook. Boots scraped the steps. Kade waited. The door opened. A woman's silhouette stood in the moonlight. *Pril.* She closed the door quietly behind her and came toward him.

"Mr. Walker?" she whispered.

"What do you want?"

She shuffled her feet across the floor until she knocked her knee into the chair and collapsed on top of him. Her hair tumbled onto his face, and he sputtered, trying to remove the long strands from his mouth.

She shoved her hand into his cheek and pushed herself from him.

"My apologies."

The scent of rosemary lingered in the air. Out of all the herbs she worked with this one clung to her skin like a whore's cheap perfume. He decided he liked the herbs much better.

"I'd have helped you, but I'm tied to this damn chair."

"Why are you not on the cot?"

No one told her he'd come to her aid the night before?

"I tried to escape but you were injured. Somehow you burned yourself, and I helped your son by placing herbs on your wounds."

He didn't miss the sharp intake of breath or the scrape of her shoes as she rocked from side to side.

"How did you end up here then?"

"Your brother thanked me by knocking me out when I wasn't looking." It still got his blood hot when he thought of how Galius had duped him. He was never caught off guard. He was the captain of his own ship damn it. He knew the rules. Always face your opponent, never turn your back, and be prepared for anything to happen. He'd fought in many brothels with men twice his size. Sometimes he won, sometimes he lost, but he never backed down when challenged. Galius was a coward. He'd attacked him when he was unaware, and he'd be sure to settle the score.

"Blast."

"Not quite what I was thinking."

"Mr. Walker—"

"Kade. Call me Kade."

"Very well. Kade, I need your help, and in return I will set you free."

"I'm listening."

"I need you to take me and my son to Charleston."

"What for?"

"That is none of your concern."

"I'd say it is if I'm to take you there."

She was silent, and he could feel the irritation pour from her body to settle at his feet in a pool of anger.

He opened his mouth to tell her that he'd not help her when something struck the side of the wagon. The smell of smoldering wood filled the room.

"What was that?"

"Untie me."

"Not until we have a deal."

"There will be no deal if we burn to death."

"I do not understand."

"The bloody wagons on fire!"

"Oh…oh dear!"

She made quick work of loosening his bonds enough so that he could wrench his hands free. He grabbed her hand, pulled her toward the doorway and outside into the cool night air.

The sky lit up as Pril took in the scene before her. Several vardos were on fire, and she watched horrified as her clan raced about with buckets of water trying to put out the flames.

She gasped. Her own wagon blazed as red and orange flames danced high into the sky. *Tsura.*

"No. No. No!" She clawed at Kade to release her. She needed to save her baby. *God, no, please not Tsura.* When his arms slackened she wiggled free. She bunched her skirt in both hands, lifted it high off of the ground and took off running. Her heart hammered inside her chest, wanting to break free of the flesh. The commotion around her faded, her ears rang, and she couldn't think past saving her daughter.

She raced up the steps and burst into the room. Smoke filled her lungs, clinging to the inside of her cheeks, and she placed a palm over her mouth. Her eyes watered, and she blinked several times to clear her vision.

"Tsura! Tsura!" She went to the bed and frantically slapped the mattress for the girl's body. She pulled at the empty blankets and tossed them onto the floor. The fire licked at the quilt, quickly smothering it in bright orange flames. She turned and ran into a hard chest.

Kade.

"I cannot find her." She coughed, trying to suck in clean air.

"You need to get out of here."

"No." She twisted out of his embrace, dropped onto her knees to look under the table and bed. Tsura wasn't there.

Panic clawed at her soul, and she pushed it away determined to find her daughter.

"The child isn't here," Kade shouted.

She ignored him.

"Come out baby. Mama's here."

A fiery beam slipped from the roof of the wooden wagon and landed on top of the bed. Pril jumped back.

"Tsura!"

A muscled arm wrapped around her waist, lifting her feet from the floor and out into the night air. She clawed at him to let her go.

"What is the matter with you?" She shoved him from her.

His square jaw was smudged with black soot. His long hair had come undone from the tie he used to secure it and hung past his shoulders.

"I need to find my child."

"You will not find him in there!" He motioned to the wagon engulfed in flames. The roof whined as it collapsed, shooting debris and sparks into the black sky.

Pril wanted to scream, to drop to her knees and sob, but instead she set her shoulders against the hopelessness that wanted to consume her. She would not fall apart. She needed to find Tsura.

Sorina ran by with a bucket in her hands.

"Tsura? Have you seen her?"

The other woman looked at Kade, her blue eyes round with worry, and shook her head.

She ran her hands through her hair and pulled at the long strands. This was not happening. Who had attacked them? Was it the Monroes? Had they taken Tsura? Her stomach flipped. Did her daughter lay under the smoldering debris injured or worse, dead? She shook her head unable to accept any of it. She scanned the chaos around her, searching for black curls and a white night shirt. *Please...please.*

Galius and Stefan ran toward her. She raced to meet them. She needed her brother—his strength, his calm rational thoughts, but most of all his love.

"What is it?" Galius asked, his large hunting bow at the ready in his hand.

"Tsura, I cannot find her."

He peered behind her for his niece.

"Brother, I have searched." She wiped the tear on her cheek. "She is not here."

"Stefan, go to the south side of the forest and look for Tsura. Kill any Renoldi you see."

Without question, the man took off toward the tree line.

"Renoldi?" she asked.

His eyes shifted from hers, and she knew he didn't want her to know.

"The gypsy clan has attacked us."

"Tsura?"

"They know she is here."

"But...oh no." Tears flooded her eyes. "Not Milosh?"

He nodded.

Panic kicked her heart into spasms and pushed the breath from her lungs to lodge into her throat. She bent, clutching her stomach and moaned.

He knelt in front of her. "We will find her."

She threw herself into his arms, and together they stood.

"What can I do to help?" Kade asked beside them now.

Galius flexed his jaw, and his hold on Pril tightened.

"Brother, we need his help. We need to find—"

"Head to the east side of the forest," Galius said.

Kade nodded.

"Wait. You're going to need this." Galius handed him a pistol and a pouch containing a black powder flask and some lead musket balls.

"Thanks."

An arrow whizzed from the darkness and struck Galius in the back. Before he could retaliate, two more drove into the skin beside the first. He groaned and fell forward. Pril grabbed the bow from his hand and two arrows from his quiver. She rolled to the left, positioned an arrow within the string and released it into the night sky. Another arrow flew through the air to lodge into the ground between her and Galius. She glanced at her brother, quiet and breathing hard, as blood seeped from his back.

"Hold on, Brother."

Kade fired the gun from behind a burning vardo. It'd take him longer to load, the pistol only able to hold two lead balls at a time. Pril waited. Most of the Peddlers ran to the unburned vardos to gather their weapons. An arrow dug into the ground two inches from her right side. She inhaled and waited.

A war cry echoed from the forest followed by the trampling of feet. Men burst through the tree line, torches, arrows, knives and pistols pointed at the Peddler camp. Arrows lit up the sky as the Peddlers fought to keep their clan safe and charged toward the intruders.

Pril ran to a vardo that wasn't on fire and readied her bow. She peeked around the corner, aimed and released. The arrow struck its mark, and the man fell onto the ground. She ducked back around the wagon ready to do it again when she was yanked backward against a hard chest. A thick arm wrapped around her neck.

She tried to push against him, but his arm only tightened. There was nothing in front of her to anchor her feet onto and push into him. Unable to move her head, she couldn't see what was to her side. With no other choice, she took her bow and slammed it into the top of the man's foot, pushing the pointed end through his flesh.

He howled, and when his grip loosened she spun to face him, brought her knee up and slammed it into his groin. He bent, and she kneed him in the nose, finishing with a kick to the gut.

The pop from a pistol rang in her ears, and she turned to see Kade standing a few feet from her, another Renoldi dead on the ground beside her.

She met Kade's eyes for a mere second before she took off toward Galius' vardo and more arrows. *Tsura. Where are you?* She scanned the camp. Vardos smoldered pushing smoke high into the starless sky. Bows released, knives clashed, pistols fired filling the night air with their raucous disregard as the clan fought off the enemy. She shoved the fear, the agony of what may be from her mind and ran. She'd find Tsura…if she died this night, so be it.

A wooden chest sat underneath Galius' wagon. She opened it and pulled out five arrows. An extra quiver lay on the ground beside the trunk, and she slung it around her arm to rest against her back. She shoved the arrows into the quiver and ran back toward the center of camp where the fighting still took place.

A horn blew from the east, and she watched as the Renoldis retreated back into the forest.

She ran after them.

"Cowards! Come back!" She couldn't let them go. They had Tsura. She pulled an arrow and aimed it at the back of a Renoldi when she was knocked to the ground. The bow flew from her hands to land a few feet from her.

Kade lay on top of her.

She kicked, punched and bit his forearm until he cried out and released her.

"What the hell is the matter with you?" he asked, holding his arm.

"You let them get away!"

"You're insane." He stood and brushed his pant legs, throwing small bits of dirt and twigs onto the ground.

"They have my child!" She reached for her bow.

"You're not sure."

She went to walk around him when he grabbed her arm.

"Your brother is injured."

She'd forgotten about Galius. She stared past him into the dark forest. *Tsura.* Her brother needed her, but so did her daughter. She stepped toward the trees.

Kade placed his arm on her shoulder. "He's lost a lot of blood."

She pushed past Kade and went to her brother.

Galius lay on the ground, face down. Three arrows protruded from his back. Pril knelt beside him and laid her head next to his.

"Brother?"

He moaned.

She observed the clan gathered around their leader, clothes torn, dirt and blood splattered upon their faces, weapons clutched within scraped hands, and sweat glistened off their brows from the battle they just won.

"We need to remove the arrows." She glanced at her vardo, nothing left of it but a heap of smoking wood. She'd need to go into the forest and find the correct herbs. "Is there any wax left?"

"Yes, my vardo is still intact, and I have wax, herbs and my teas," Sorina said.

She didn't miss the tremble in the other woman's voice or the tear she quickly wiped from her cheek.

"Please, bring me what you have."

Sorina nodded.

"We've searched the debris of your vardo and the camp itself. Tsura is not here," Emmett whispered.

"Thank you. Are the other children safe?"

"Yes, they are all accounted for."

She dipped her head so they wouldn't see the torment as it sliced across her face. Desperation grabbed hold of her soul and squeezed. The air within her lungs grew stale, and her vision blurred. She locked her shaking hands together, clenched the fingers between her palms and squeezed the limbs until they hurt. She wanted to expel the anger—to kill the bastards who took her little girl. The need to drain the horrible thoughts tormented her mind and rounded her back. She placed her head onto her knees. She released one sob—one pitiful, heartwrenching sob. With it she sucked in the ache, the fury and every piece of fear that clawed at her insides wanting her to fall a part. She gathered them, grabbed hold of any strength she had left and buried them deep within her. *Tsura. I will find you.*

She straightened, tipped her chin, and her eyes sought Kade.

"I will need you to hold Galius while I break the arrows on his back." Unsure of why she asked him and not another from her clan, she dismissed the thought and shifted to the side for Kade to kneel at Galius' head. He placed both hands on her brother's large shoulders and waited.

His eyes met hers, and he nodded that he was ready.

She grabbed hold of the first arrow and broke the wood in half.

Galius pushed up against Kade's hands and let out a guttural cry that tore at her heart. She'd never seen him injured like this before; he'd had his fair share of scratches and burns but nothing to this extent. He'd always been the strong gentle one out of the three siblings.

"I am sorry, Brother."

She broke another one. This time he didn't move just growled low into the ground.

"One…" SNAP "more." She wiped the sweat from her brow and tossed the last piece onto the ground beside her.

Sorina returned with her sister, Sabella. The quiet girl held a bucket and ripped sheets while Sorina carried the herbs and wax.

"Emmett and Ivan, I will need light. Please bring your torches near," Pril said.

The two men stepped forward, holding the fire sticks away from Galius but close enough for Pril to see what she was doing.

Her stomach dipped. She'd need to do this without her peppermint leaves and without a spell. She exhaled slowly, the act calming her nerves and stomach.

"Let me know when you're ready to begin," Kade said while he hovered over Galius.

She rubbed her hands briskly together.

"Give him this. It will help him to sleep." Sorina handed her a small bowl with crushed berries.

She lifted the bowl and sniffed.

"Opium paste?"

"I have not put in very much, but enough to knock him out for the better part of an hour."

"Have you tested this on anyone?"

Sorina eyed Kade.

"You drugged me?" he growled.

"I am sorry. I was only doing what I was told."

"I don't give a damn—"

"Please, we need to concentrate on the task at hand." Pril nodded toward Sorina.

The other woman put some of the paste on a spoon and fed it to Galius. Once the contents were ingested, they waited a few minutes before loud snores rumbled from his chest.

"Who has a blade?" Pril asked.

"I do," Stefan said from above her.

His shaded eyes caressed her face.

Irritated, she frowned, and for a mere moment the thought of lashing out at him appealed to her.

"Heat it within the flames of Emmett's torch. Do not give it to me until the tip glows orange," she said without looking at him.

The urge to chant a spell for Galius moved over her. Too many ears and eyes watched her, and she clamped her lips shut instead.

The blade was handed to her. The harder she gripped the handle the more her hand shook. *Steady...steady.* She tried to gain control, but the shaking increased until the knife fell from her hand onto her skirt to singe the fabric.

Kade was quick to grab it.

"I will do it."

"Have you done this before?"

"Yes."

With the blade still orange he dug it into Galius' flesh beside the first arrow. A few minutes passed before he pulled the arrow free, and Pril placed a cold compress over the bleeding wound.

He did this two more times, removing each arrow. Once the bleeding had subsided, Pril took two Achusa Strigosa leaves from the jar and crushed them within her palm. She placed them over the open wounds and sealed them with the wax from the jar.

"I will need to stitch these wounds closed."

Kade nodded.

"He needs to be moved to his vardo."

Kade stood, and with Stefan's help they carried the large man to his wagon.

Pril watched them take her brother, thankful the arrows hadn't gone in deeper, or he would've died. The weight of the past events pulled her chin down, and she hung her head. How was she going to fix this? Tsura was missing, her clan needed explanations, and Galius was injured.

One person's name came to mind. *Milosh.* Hot anger scorched her stomach, and her face heated. She needed to find her brother. He was the reason her daughter was gone, and Galius was hurt. She stood. Determination set her shoulders, and she frowned as she marched toward his vardo still intact.

"Milosh," she yelled outside his wagon. "Milosh, you coward! Come out, and face me!"

A few minutes had passed when she heard footsteps coming from inside. Magda pulled back the curtain and cast evil eyes toward her.

"What do you want?"

"I want to speak with my brother."

Magda's black hair hung in matted knots, and dark smudges circled her eyes. Her skirt and blouse were soiled with dirt, and the night breeze carried the stale scent toward Pril.

"He is not here."

"Where is he?"

The other woman shrugged.

"Tell me where he is, Magda."

"Why should I?"

"Because I ask it of you." She stepped toward her. "Please, I beg you."

"Pril, sister to the mighty Vadoma, begs?"

She glanced around them, mindful of the others.

"You have kept this secret far too long," Magda said.

"Vadoma is passed. I am not what she was."

"You are worse."

"Please, Magda, this is important."

"Important you say? Well, dear sister, isn't that a horrible dilemma? Vadoma would've admitted her wrongdoings. She would've dared us to judge her. But you have not come to my vardo since the death of my only child to offer condolences." She choked up, her voice wavering. "To offer your love. Instead you stayed away. You fooled our clan into pitying you. Poor Pril. You never cared about our dear Alexandra. All you cared about was Tsura."

"No, that is not true. Oh, I feel horrible." She blinked the wetness from her lashes. "I cannot sleep for the anguish I have caused you and Milosh. I am sorry...so very, very sorry."

The edges of Magda's eyes softened for a brief moment before contempt, betrayal, and pure raw hatred filled the black depths. "Sorry you will be, *Sister*." She smiled and let the curtain fall between them.

Pril knew without a doubt that Milosh had taken Tsura. The Renoldis had come in hopes of finding her daughter, but Milosh had already vanished with her. What did Milosh want to accomplish by having the Renoldis attack their camp, especially with his wife still here? Something was amiss. Milosh adored Magda. Why hadn't she gone with him? An uneasy feeling settled at the back of her neck, and the urgent need to find her daughter grabbed hold of her soul and squeezed.

CHAPTER SEVEN

Kade was tired. He'd worked for hours helping the Peddlers clean up their camp, and he didn't think he could stay awake much longer. He kicked at a mug covered in soot; the tin clinked as it knocked into a cracked jar of honey. He'd picked up unbroken ornaments, jars and dishes stacking them into a pile most of the night.

Once Galius had been mended the clan went about picking up the wreckage and building shelter for those who'd lost their wagons. They hadn't begun to build anything yet. Charred wood, arrows, clothing and buckets still littered the ground.

The sun crested the east hills giving light to the once ashen land. The warmth from the sun's rays pushed out the shadows and cold the night had brought. He shivered into the woolen sweater he'd been given to keep warm. It'd been a long night, and he hadn't slept in more than two days. His mood was sour, and he was famished.

His last meal was yesterday while locked in the wagon. The gypsy girl had given him some sort of root soup with bread. He'd been so hungry he hadn't thought, much less cared, if there was any drug or poison within the delicious fare. After he'd eaten the soup, he could not keep his eyes open and fell asleep. The fact that he was poisoned did not sit too well with him.

He brushed away a long lock of hair that clung to his whiskers. He'd lost the rope he used to tie back the wild mane. He didn't like wearing it down. The hair got in the way, but he wasn't about to cut it either. The mane was a symbol of what he'd become—what he'd worked hard to achieve. He thought of his father, Samuel Walker. The tall, brawny, rough around the edges captain had taught him everything he knew about the sea. He'd shown Kade the business of a merchant, taught him how to fight and most importantly to never trust anyone.

He smiled. The old man had gotten him into a few tussles over the years too, but he always came out the victor. He wondered if Sam's motives were deliberate, and the gleam in his eye when Kade finished a fight told him so. Old Sam was a codger. An educated man with a giving heart.

He picked up a child's handmade doll. The feet on the toy were singed from the fire, but everything else was still intact. He turned the doll in his palm, saw a name stitched on the back...*Tsura.*

The child, whose hair had been cut short, donned trousers and wore a knit sweater. He frowned. He hadn't missed the terror in Pril's voice as she searched for her child, when she called Tsura's name and as she begged for her daughter's life. He picked up on the words—the meaning, and he'd known Tsura was the child he searched for. Relief and angst filled him. After months of hunting, he'd finally found her. He could make good on his word. The stakes would be high to get her back from who ever stole her, but he didn't have a choice. Another life counted on him.

He scanned the camp for Pril. She knew the Renoldis had taken her daughter. Soon she'd go in search of them, and he would follow. He hadn't seen her since she left Galius' wagon hours before. Her own wagon had been destroyed so he didn't bother looking for her there. He didn't know where the Renoldi camp was, and he needed to stay close to Pril in case she left. He ran his hand through his hair. He'd trail Pril, steal back the girl and head home.

A commotion caught his attention, and he turned to see three of the Peddlers tossing destroyed furniture, pieces of their wagons and other household items into a burning pile at the center of camp.

He stuffed the doll into his pocket, picked up a long piece of singed wood and walked toward them. It was a shame the peddlers had to start over. When he'd come into their camp two days before he was shocked to see how charming it was compared to some of the other gypsy camps he'd entered. Theirs resembled a small village. Gardens and bushes, placed into long wooden boxes, grew fruit and vegetables. Wood was neatly stacked, furniture in its place, and flowers hung from windows and doors. It was inviting and warm. Now as he stood in the center of the camp it resembled a war torn village with little left to continue on.

Had they known the child was among them? Had they been aware and made a pact to protect her? And why was she so special? He groaned. There were no answers to his questions, and he was too exhausted to think on them any longer.

"There is still so much we need to clear," Ivan said beside him.

The high flames from the fire warmed him, and Kade stepped closer to rid the chill in his bones. He tossed the wood he'd held onto the pile and watched as the fire ate it up.

"It will get done."

"Yes, but it won't fix the devastation within our hearts."

"You can rebuild. It will take time, but together you can do it," he said.

Ivan's eyes reflected a deeper emotion, more than broken and burned wagons.

"We've lost another child. I fear this one will have the same fate as the last."

"The last?" Who was the last, and what had happened to them?

"Milosh's daughter was killed nigh on thirteen days. We found her body over the hill."

He pumped his fist. Children should not die. There were a lot of awful people in the world that needed to meet the Almighty, and he'd helped a few get there, but not children. Never children. He thought of the reasons he was here. Why he'd trekked through every bloody town for miles. Why he was so desperate to find the girl with the mark.

"Have you seen Pril?" he asked.

Ivan turned and pointed toward her wagon, now a pile of rubble. On the far side, and away from view, Pril sat on her knees sifting through the debris. Her wavy red hair, pushed from her face, cascaded down her back where the ends dipped into the dirt on the ground. A green shawl draped across her arms and tied in the front. Determination thrust her shoulders back and set her jaw.

"She is strong...but this will kill her," Ivan said.

The other man walked away, and Kade stretched his arms to rid the heaviness within his chest. He prayed no harm came to the child. He was desperate to bring her back—to receive what was his.

He needed information, and he shouldn't feel guilty about asking. He'd given his word damn it; therefore he couldn't let the emotions of a gypsy stand in the way...even if it was the mother of the child he was going to steal.

Pril tossed a hunk of wood to the side and cringed. The tips of her fingers stung, burned from touching the too-hot wood. She'd searched for hours and still hadn't found the spell book. Her heart sank as the reality of what had happened to it began to settle over her. The spell book had been in her family for more than a hundred years, and now it was gone. How would she teach Tsura about the gift if she had nothing to help her do so?

She'd memorized most of the spells, even though she could only count a handful of them, but it was the information within the ancient pages that Pril required to aid in raising her daughter. Tsura was still so young that Pril hadn't begun to explain things. Tsura had healed her without the words...instead using only her own hands. How was it possible? She'd hoped to read it in the book for she hadn't seen it yet, and she'd not finished the thick tome.

She slammed her hand down into the dirt and yelped. The burned flesh screamed as the skin throbbed. Her head ached, and every time she blinked pain shot across her forehead. The disappearance of Tsura pressed into her shoulders, and the urgency to find her daughter caused her lips to tremble. She didn't know what Milosh would do with her, but she was sure it would not be good.

My baby where are you?

Her brother had become a stranger to her—a ruined soul that housed bitterness and hatred, and she mourned the loss of him, even though his presence she felt everywhere she went. She yearned for his forgiveness, for his love and acceptance, but it had never come. He pitied her for taking Vadoma's child, for being stuck with a curse until he realized it would affect them all. His pity turned to anger, and soon their relationship had been strained. Neither willing to sacrifice their beliefs for the bond they once had.

The blame lay with Vadoma, with the blood curse and her acts as Chuvani before she died. She'd left them with nothing but a legacy of evil doings. She understood the anger her brothers felt toward their eldest sister, but she could not hate Vadoma and raise Tsura at the same time. She had to put tainted thoughts aside and concentrate on her daughter. But even now after so long the words were at the tip of her tongue to lash out at her dead sister—to speak unkindly of her—to hate her. Instead she bit the inside of her lip and refused to give into the anger she felt.

"What are you searching for?"

Kade stood behind her, and she tensed. She thought he'd be long gone by now, leaving the clan to deal with their mess.

"Why have you not gone?"

"Help was needed."

"How kind." She dismissed him. Her heart was empty, drained of all emotion. She was unable to hold a conversation with him. She had more insistent matters that took refuge within her mind. She'd have to leave soon if she thought to have a chance at catching Milosh and Tsura.

"I can see you really think so." He turned to leave.

"Wait."

"Yes, Gypsy?" He glared.

"I need your help. I can pay. I—"

"First you throw insults, and now you're begging. That is not an attractive quality."

"I need not this quality." She bristled. "I need to find my son."

"Son?"

"Yes."

"Do you know who took him?"

"Of course I do."

"Who?"

She inhaled and paused.

"Who?" he repeated.

"My brother, Milosh," she whispered.

"You have two brothers?"

She nodded.

"No one else will help you find your child?"

"I cannot ask if of them."

"Why not?"

She bit the inside of her cheek. "The clan has just been devastated. I cannot expect them to help me in the midst of such chaos."

His black eyes searched her face for any hint of deceit she may try to hide.

"Stand so that I may see you."

She pulled the shawl tight around her shoulders and did as he asked.

"How are your burns?"

"They…they are well," she lied.

He nodded.

"Truth. It is a word I value above all else. And, it is what I'd like from you."

She averted her eyes and nodded. He did not know of the burns, and she'd keep the act to herself at all cost.

Kade took her chin within his fingers and lifted it so he could look at her.

"I will not put my life in danger for a liar."

"I am not a deceiver."

"Yes, well that is to be decided now isn't it? You will answer my questions with the truth. If I feel you're misleading me in any way I will not help you."

She nodded this time, keeping her eyes on his.

"Tsura is your daughter."

How did he know? Had someone told him?

"Answer me."

With no other choice but to tell him the truth, or part of it, she whispered, "Yes, she is."

"Why do you dress her as a boy?"

"Because bad people have hunted our children, killing many of them. They search for a little girl. We decided to keep our children safe and dressed them as boys."

"Why are they hunting gypsy girls?"

"Some say because of a curse, but we do not know."

"Why would Milosh take his niece?"

"I do not know."

"I say you do."

"I do not."

"I wish you well on your journey," he said and walked away.

"Wait."

He stopped.

"Milosh's daughter was killed not long ago. He must be angry that my child lived when his did not."

She watched as his brows rose, and she prayed he believed her. She gave him half of the truth. To give it all could mean destruction far worse than she was ready to face. The Monroes hunted Tsura, and right now they were the least of her worries. What Milosh was going to do with her daughter was more important.

"So he wants revenge?"

She nodded.

"What will he do with the child?"

"I do not know."

He reached behind him and handed her a doll. She recognized it as the one she'd made for Tsura months ago. The girl always slept with it.

She ripped it from his hands and clutched it to her chest.

"Where did you find this?"

"Over by one of the dilapidated wagons."

"Was it close to the forest?"

"Yes. Why?"

"Tsura slept with this doll. She wasn't allowed to take it from the vardo."

"She had it last night."

"Yes, and where you found the doll is the direction I must go to find her."

He regarded her for a long while, and she twisted the doll within her hands. The only man who'd ever shown her any attention was Stefan, and she kept a safe distance from him. She was about to ask him why he was so forthcoming when he turned and walked away.

"Where are you going?"

"To eat and rest. We will leave at dusk."

She let out a loud sigh, relieved she wouldn't be going alone and hopeful she'd find her daughter. She watched him, wide shouldered and tall. He reeked of arrogance—of privilege. He challenged everyone around him. She scanned the scorched and smoldering pile that used to be her home and squeezed Tsura's doll to her chest.

Uncertainty of where her child was tore at her soul. How was she going to stay sane when her insides were a bloody mangled mess of emotions? One minute she wanted to weep, the next lash out at anyone who came near, and she struggled to contain every bit of it. She needed to stay strong—clearheaded. To behave like a crazy person wouldn't help find Tsura.

Oh, how she missed her daughter. She wanted to hold her and kiss her. To tell her that everything would be okay. She promised to chase the bad men away and keep her safe. She tipped her chin. She'd failed. Her vision blurred, and she dropped to her knees. She clutched the doll to her cheek and inhaled. *I will find you. I promise.*

CHAPTER EIGHT

Silas stood over the grave of his newborn daughter. There were three other graves to the left, each marked with a small wooden cross. He reached for Beth's hand, cold and clammy, only to have her pull it from his grasp and tuck it back within her cloak. He'd known this last time would torture her, be her undoing, but he'd hoped she'd hold on for a little while longer. Wait until he'd killed the girl.

She'd put on a strong face for the others, but this time was different. This time he'd promised the curse was broken, and she believed him. She'd given herself to him, trusting that all would be well, and now she hated him for it.

He gnashed his back teeth together. How had he failed for so long? He'd sought out every well-known marksman within his reach to find the child, and still nothing. He'd resorted to using his slaves, and when met with resistance, he blackmailed them with their family as ransom. Yet, the bloody girl still hadn't been brought to him dead or alive. The mark was the true-tell sign, and he wasn't sure his hired guns had seen the brand on the child, instead killing any gypsy girl they found. All had been unsuccessful, and so he'd done them in.

He peered at Beth, thin and frail. She'd not bothered to put on a day dress, instead keeping her nightgown on underneath her coat. The priest said a few words, blessing the infant and her family. He went on to chant in Latin, and Silas couldn't understand him. All he could think of was the girl and killing her as he'd done her mother.

He had one last hope, one more chance to rid the world of the wicked child. His eyes surveyed the barns, the longhouse where the tobacco dried and the slave's quarters. On the west side of his land, as far from the slaves as possible, stood the Monroe Mansion. The large two story home with a veranda, twelve bedrooms, massive kitchen, ballroom, lavatory and two libraries. Within the walls, hidden from view, was all the hope he had left.

He inhaled a cold breath that froze his insides and crystalized his heart.

He'd held his daughter this morning before he dressed her in a white gown and laid her in the tiny box. She'd not lived long enough to take even one breath before she died. Blonde hair and blue eyes, she looked different then the last three. This one resembled Beth.

Jude and Ilsa stood on the other side of the small grave. Jude's arm lay protectively across his wife's shoulders, and she leaned into him.

Irritation flooded his senses, and his head ticked to the left. Beth couldn't stand to be near him. She'd pushed him away, cast blame in his direction with every stare, mute answer and dejected stature. She'd given him reason to seek lust elsewhere and not feel guilty about it.

The priest ended the sermon. Beth released a sob and flew into his embrace. Silas bit back the cuss words he wanted to let fly and left the cemetery. Hiram and Jude were soon by his side. A rough squeeze to his shoulder offered in comfort did little to ease the hatred he felt growing within him.

"We will find her," Jude whispered. "We have to."

"It has taken too long already. I need to know the girl is dead. I must see it myself." He stopped and turned toward them. "Send a telegram. Ask if he has located her."

Jude nodded.

"Tell him with each day that passes we remove one limb, starting with the fingers."

"Silas, you cannot be serious?" Hiram said.

"I am very serious, Brother. This needs to be finished."

"There must be another way."

He stepped into Hiram, his hands around his throat. He wanted to kill the bastard. Watch as the life faded from his ruddy face.

"Your children live while mine have all perished. Do not tell me to find another way when there is only one."

Hiram stood before Silas, arms to the side, not showing one ounce of fight within his brown eyes.

"I will not fight you, Brother," he whispered.

"You are no better than our poor excuse for a mother. Soon you will turn to the opium and other aides to get you through the day, too. All because you cannot deal with reality and the life you've chosen to live."

"Do not speak ill words of the woman who bore you."

"I will speak what I desire. She was a waste of human flesh who could not be bothered to get out of bed for the last fifteen years of her life."

"You know why, Silas. You know why!"

"I have lost four daughters, and still I run this plantation. I've kept things going. I have not fallen to the sin in which she did. I have not given up on my family—on my life."

"Yet, you seek to kill a child," Hiram said.

Jude stepped closer.

"A child that you should've killed four years ago!"

"You bastard. How dare you put this on me? I will not kill a child. Not the girl or any other."

"You forget one thing, Brother. You already have."

Hiram's lips thinned. He spat onto the ground between them and walked away.

Silas' chest heaved, and his nostrils flared. He peered past Hiram to see Beth still in the priest's embrace, and rage boiled within him.

"He is not to be trusted."

Jude nodded.

"Send the letter."

CHAPTER NINE

Pril sat beside Galius' cot. The long narrow bed barely held his large frame, and she found herself sitting close so he didn't fall onto the floor. A thin blanket covered him, and she felt his forehead to check for fever. He was cool, and she brought the blanket up to his chin, tucking it underneath him.

"You are leaving." Galius' voice was rough, his eyes still closed.

"I am."

"Can you not wait until I am well?"

"No, I cannot."

He shifted on the cot, and she didn't miss the clenched jaw or pursed lips when he inhaled.

"I need to find her. I cannot wait for another hour to pass. You must understand."

He knew her better than anyone. She would not wait for him.

He nodded and reached for her hand before he opened his eyes.

"The Renoldis out number you. Sneak into their camp and steal Tsura. That is the only way."

She nodded. Now was not the time to tell her brother that Milosh had taken his niece.

"Be careful of Pias. He is ruthless and will stop at nothing to have the girl."

"What does he want with her?"

"I do not know, but Tsura is safer with the Renoldis than the Monroes."

"I will do as you say, Brother." She placed her lips on his forehead. "I love you."

He squeezed her hand.

"Be careful, Sister. Remember all I have taught you."

She nodded.

She exited the vardo without another word. She'd not glance back; it was a sign of weakness. Galius would sense it and find a way to go with her. He'd been the one who had always fought for her, helped her when she needed it and cared deeply for Tsura. She'd miss him.

Kade waited in the alcove surrounded by bushes behind the vardos. Two ropes wound carelessly around his hands; one tied to her gelding, Athos and the other to the biggest horse she'd ever seen. She didn't recognize the animal and knew that it must be his.

"Have you packed all that you'll need?" he asked as she drew near.

"I have."

She'd slung the brown sack over her shoulder and carried it with ease.

"Then let us get to it shall we?"

She reached out, touching the nose of the brown and white spotted horse.

"Hello my friend," she whispered to Athos.

The horse whinnied and shook his muzzle.

She smiled, resting her cheek against Athos, and peeked at Kade.

"I've never seen such a large animal before."

He patted the horse's rear.

"Goliath is a Spanish stallion. I brought him back from one of my trips to Spain."

Spain? He'd been halfway across the world? She knew nothing of the man who stood before her—the man she placed all her hopes upon. She squinted. She'd question him on his past later. Tsura waited.

"Thank you for preparing Athos."

She tied her sack to the side of the worn leather saddle and pulled Tsura's doll out. She wanted to keep it close. The detail within the oiled leather saddle always stopped her. Deep carvings of vines with thorns and roses adorned the sides. The saddle had been her mother's. It was the only gift she'd passed on to her second daughter. Pril cherished it.

"Have you any news as to where your brother might have taken Tsura?"

She shook her head.

"I've told you all I know."

He sighed.

"It will be a long day."

"Yes, I assumed. How will you know where to go?"

"I will track them."

"I wasn't aware that you knew how to track. I assumed we—"

"You should never assume to know the past of those around you…or their future."

She didn't miss his last words and sent him a chilling glare.

"After you, Gypsy." He bowed.

Pril wanted to kick him in the shins, but settled for a saucy smirk instead and climbed on top of Athos. She straddled the horse, tucking her skirt under her legs. Her long red tresses hung in waves down her back, and she was careful not to sit on them.

"I am in charge. I say when and how long we travel. What time we eat, sleep, and when we come to Milosh's camp I will determine how we attack."

Every part of her wanted to lash out at him. She would not take orders from anyone especially someone as bigheaded as him. She sat up straight and stared past him into the Peddler's camp. No one there would risk their lives to help her, and she couldn't ask them. She needed Kade. Pril bit down hard on the inside of her cheek. *Damn him and his rules. I will decide what is best.*

She nodded.

"I have your word?"

"You have it." She scanned the forest, misery drenching her soul, and she wanted to weep. She squeezed the doll between her hands.

He climbed on top of his horse. The dagger, the body of a lion engraved into the blade, sat within the sheath which hung from the right side of his hip. She wondered if he was accomplished with the weapon, or wore it simply for appearances. She chewed on her bottom lip, said a silent prayer that Kade Walker knew what he was doing, and soon they'd find Tsura.

They'd been riding for hours in the hot sun, and Pril had removed the scarf from around her waist to wrap her long hair within the fabric, tying it on top of her head. Sweat settled at the nape of her neck. She ran her hand along the damp wisps and wiped it away. She reached for her flask and took a long drink. The leather pouch felt light, and she shook it to judge how much water was left inside. It was almost empty.

She scanned the countryside for any hint of a river or lake nearby. A short stop to refill their flasks was needed, and she wanted to wash her face. She blinked, feeling the dirt scratch her lids, and each time she licked her lips, she tasted the soil upon them.

"Have you spotted water?" she asked.

"There is no need to search for it."

"I have but one drink left within my flask."

"You should have rationed your supply more carefully."

She noticed a change in him after they'd stopped in Riverbend for supplies. He was intent that they made good time and hadn't uttered more than a few sentences to her in four hours. She wanted to find her daughter more than anything, but it seemed Kade did as well, and that made no sense to her. Yes, she agreed to pay him for his help, but he didn't strike her as the kind of person who rushed for anyone, instead doing things at his own leisure. But a reason pushed him now. She could see it in the creases around his eyes when he frowned and in the set of his jaw. Even more she felt it deep within her soul.

"Why are you pressing?" she asked.

His wide shoulders tensed, and she waited for his reply. Nothing came. Not a long sigh or even a groan…utter silence.

"Are we to travel in complete quiet?"

Silence.

"It is rude not to answer when asked a question."

"I do not like your questions."

"What does that matter?"

"It matters a lot."

He frustrated her, and she felt the sun more so now as her temper rose.

"Very well. Have it your way, mewling toad-spotted scum." She whispered the last bit.

"I thought gypsy women had a much better vocabulary range than that of toad spotted scum."

"It is when dealing with the lower class one has to shorten their vocabulary so that they can be understood."

He snorted followed by a raucous, deep from the belly laugh. His shoulders shook, and he hunched forward.

"What, Mr. Walker, is so amusing?"

"A gypsy has deemed *me* lower class." He burst into another fit of laughter.

"Bloody lout." She didn't know what else to say. He thought her a fool. She wanted nothing more than to pull the arrow from her quiver and aim it at the back of his head. "Finish with this foolishness, and take me to my daughter."

This sobered him. He straightened in his saddle, cleared his throat and took a left into the forest.

"Why are we going this way?"

"The trail leads this way."

"What trail?"

"The one we've been following since we left your camp."

"You can see Milosh's trail?"

"What did you think I was doing, scavenging the countryside for a nice place to picnic?"

"Of course not."

He shook his head.

She remembered her bow and the thought she had earlier.

"What do you see on the trail?"

"Horse prints. Your brother didn't bother to hide his trail. Anyone wanting to find him could do so with ease."

"I'm sure he thought me too daft to watch for the signs."

"Well, if this keeps up we should be upon them soon."

"How soon?"

No answer.

Pril flexed her hand. He was vexing, and she needed to remain calm. The desire to unleash her temper would not help in these circumstances, and she couldn't afford to lose him.

Kade stood on the edge of the cliff and examined the valley below. Smoke from a fire could be seen above the trees. He'd bet it was Pril's brother and the girl. It had been easier than he thought to track them, but something in his gut told him there was a reason.

He'd hold off until nightfall when Pril was asleep and sneak down the hill to the camp to check things out. He may even abscond with the child and be on his way with no one being the wiser.

"Are we bedding down here for the night?" Pril asked from behind him.

He wasn't used to the light airy sound of a female's voice, and it caught him off guard. He shook off the loneliness as it crept into his heart and remembered why he was here.

"Yes."

It was better not to engage in conversation. The less he knew about Pril and her daughter, the easier it would be to take the child and get what was his.

"Very well."

She took her bow and arrow from the quiver slung from the saddle and walked toward the line of trees.

"Where are you going?"

"To fetch our dinner."

She wasn't like any woman he'd come across in his thirty-six years. However, most of the women he'd known were of ill repute or wanted him for the money they thought he had. None were at all like the petite redheaded gypsy, and he didn't know why that amused him.

Now was a good time to search through her things. He didn't trust her and wanted to know what she was hiding.

He rummaged through the brown sack she'd placed against a tall pine. He pulled out a jar of wax, some herbs and a few pieces of clothing.

There was nothing else. He placed the contents back inside the bag and propped it up against the tree when she came back. She held a rabbit with an arrow shot through the middle.

"I hope you can skin this," she said as she tossed the dead hare at his feet.

"I am adept in other fineries than sailing the sea."

She shrugged and laid her bow next to her sack.

He went about skinning the rabbit while she washed up by the small ravine a few yards away. Once cleaned of all its fur, he used some leather strips he'd had in his saddle to tie the hare's legs to the long skinny branch and mount it over the fire.

"I am so famished," she said as she watched him turn the rabbit.

The trees swayed from a light breeze, and he gazed up at the sky, seeing the first few stars shine bright.

"Do you wonder what they mean?" she asked.

"The stars?"

"Yes. I've always been fascinated by them."

"Never thought about it."

"I have seen them twinkle."

"Bollocks."

She nodded.

"It is true. If you gaze at them long enough, they wink at you."

He'd seen it before, but was enjoying their light banter and went along as if he'd never known.

"I'd say you're full of it."

She lay on her back and stared up at the night sky.

"Aboard your ship you've not witnessed such glory?"

He was quiet. He'd seen many splendid wonders when the sea was calm, and the sky was black. "I have seen them drop from their place and fall toward us."

"You cannot be serious."

"I am."

"Where did they go?"

"I do not know, but it was amazing. A sight I shall never forget."

"I say not."

He pulled the rabbit from the fire and laid the stick on the rock beside him. He watched through half closed lids as she sat up and nestled around their dinner. Her slender fingers darted out, pulling the meat from the hare and popping it into her mouth. She closed her eyes savoring the flavor, and her innocence had him curious as to where she came from.

Pril pretended to sleep as she watched Kade disappear down the hill from their camp. *What was he up to?* She tossed the blanket from her and followed him.

She was grateful the moon was almost full, and she could see a short distance in front of her. A wolf howled in the distance. She shivered. The ground beneath her feet rose up and down in uneven bumps, and she stumbled. She threw her arms out, balancing herself so she didn't fall flat on her face. Careful not to alert Kade, she waited a moment before she stepped softly into the grass.

She came upon him standing on a flat bluff overlooking the valley below.

"Where are you going?" she asked as she came up behind him.

He spun around, and she didn't miss the shock on his face before it was covered with his usual pompous smirk.

"I could not sleep and needed to walk."

She did not believe him. The way he stood, possibly a little too relaxed had her second-guessing his reply.

"I see."

More wolves howled in the distance.

"Head on back, I'll be there in short time."

"No, I'd rather stay thank you."

He sighed.

She heard branches break to her left and turned. She was greeted with panting and a low ominous growl.

"What was—?"

"Quiet," he said. "Do not move." He grabbed her wrist and pulled her close to him, just as two eyes glowed ahead of them.

She blinked, and four more pairs stood with the first.

A large grey wolf stepped a thick paw forward. His white fangs flashed in the darkness, and he snarled.

"This cannot be good."

"They must've smelled the hare," he said.

"Or the fear," she finished.

The wolf hunched his back, and the fur stood. He pawed at the ground as saliva dripped from his curled lip.

"Gypsy, prepare yourself to run."

She turned back the way they'd come when two brown wolves moved from the shadows toward them and growled. Unable to move, her heart thudded in her chest. She opened her mouth but nothing came out.

"When I say run, you do it without looking back."

"K…Kade?"

"Yeah?"

"There are more on this side."

He glanced past her.

"Shit."

They stood back to back. She could feel the muscles flex in his arms.

"You need to reach within my sheath, and pull my dagger."

She nodded.

The grey wolf came closer, and before she could move her hand the animal howled. She froze, immobilized by fear. No matter what she told herself, she could not move her arm.

"What is taking so long?" he whispered.

"I cannot...I cannot do it."

"You must, otherwise we will be dead."

"They will kill us any way. There are ten of them to two of us."

"I am not going down with out a fight, so unless you can spout one of your harebrained spells, I suggest you find the strength to get my bloody dagger."

"Why can you not reach for it yourself?"

"I am larger than you, and if I move they will take it as a threat and lunge. In which case we are doomed."

The two wolves closest to her growled and snarled.

Her legs trembled.

"You may wound one, but the others will surely kill us."

"Why must you argue?"

"I am stating logic."

"Logic is for us to defend ourselves."

She searched the black ground for a stick or rock, something she could lunge for and help Kade against the wolves, but all she saw were shadows.

The wolf came closer, and she felt his hot breath upon her side. His growl caused the hairs on her body to stand.

Kade pushed his back into hers, a reminder to grab his knife.

She inched her hand along his thigh to his sheath.

"Good girl, Gypsy. Now pull the dagger slowly from the sheath."

She did as he asked, pausing when one of the wolves in front of her snapped at the other.

Something moved in the bushes to her left and drew their attention away from them. The other wolves noticed, too. Soon they barked and snarled at one another, deciding who would go for the prey first.

"They're distracted," Kade said. "Step forward with your right foot now."

She did, his leg against hers moved in the same direction.

"Another step with your left."

He melted into her, and they moved as one, slowly away from the deranged wolves. The bushes moved again, and the animals lunged.

Violent barks followed by the sound of teeth into flesh. A yelp and whine. They were attacking each other for the prey.

"Run!"

Kade grabbed her hand and pulled her back up the hill to their camp. She raced for her bow and arrows. She threw herself onto the ground and faced the darkness ready to defend against any of the wolves that followed.

Dagger in hand, Kade went to his saddlebag and pulled the pistol Galius had given him. He fired a shot into the air, loaded the musket and fired another time. They remained on watch until the moon faded, and the sun appeared.

CHAPTER TEN

Pril massaged her chest to ease the ache within her heart. It'd been three days since she'd seen Tsura. The loss encompassed her whole body, and at times she struggled to even walk. Before the Renoldis attacked, she'd tucked her daughter into bed, kissing her face until she giggled, and her cheeks turned red. Her pudgy arms encircled Pril's neck and squeezed. She replayed the moment a hundred times in her head and could still feel Tsura's hug.

The urgency to know where she was, if she was okay, squeezed her ribs and turned her stomach. How was she supposed to concentrate when all she wanted to do was fall onto her knees and beg for her little girl to come home?

"They departed sometime in the middle of the night," Kade said crouched beside the ashes left from the fire.

She wandered the camp where Tsura had been hours before, searching for any sign that she was okay. A broken branch, a piece of hair or clothing would give her some relief to know she'd been here. *Please let her be safe.*

"Milosh started another fire over here but changed his mind."

She paused.

"Could be that it was too close to the trees."

She raced to where he stood and surveyed the area of charred grass and singed branches. *Tsura.* She knelt in front of the burned sward and ran her hands along the spot where her daughter had been. She hoped for an extra beat of her heart, a jolt to her side, or a sensation over her skin—anything to tell her she was still alive. She waited. All senses alert, she yearned for a sign, but all she experienced was the tightness in her throat.

She paused, hands buried deep within the grass. *Milosh would not kill her would he?* He couldn't possibly harm his only niece? She didn't know, and it tortured her beyond anything she'd ever felt before. How would she go on living if her daughter perished? She blinked back the tears and shook her head unable to think of a reality so harsh. She needed to concentrate. She closed her eyes and pressed her hands into the grass around the tree.

She felt the rope the second it touched her finger and pulled it up out of the sward. It was singed—burned off. Milosh had tied her here. She'd been scared, and her body temperature rose and burned the grass around her. The girl's power was uncontrollable. Without Pril's help she could harm herself or someone else.

She gasped.

What if Tsura hurt another person? What if someone saw the power she held and wanted to use it for evil? She'd be hunted, or worse, hanged just as her mother was. The Monroes would no longer be their only worry.

"What have you found?"

Kade came toward her, and she dropped the rope back into the tall grass.

"I've found nothing."

He brushed her shoulder as he passed her, bent by the tree and retrieved the rope.

"Nothing?"

She shrugged. She was hoping he'd notice her indifference and leave the rope.

He examined it, and she busied herself with searching the rest of the camp for more clues.

"The rope is burned."

"Hmmm?"

"I said the rope is burned. Milosh tied Tsura with it, but it is burned."

"Milosh wouldn't tie her with a burned rope. What good would that be? It'd hardly hold her."

"Maybe the rope was burned after she was tied."

"Well, that does not make a lick of sense. Are you suggesting he burned my daughter?"

He didn't answer, and she knew that was what he thought. She was sure Tsura had enticed the flames and burned the rope herself, but if Kade wanted to think otherwise she wasn't going to correct him.

"We've wasted enough time here."

She grabbed Athos' reins and climbed up into the saddle. She glided her hand along the red-brown mane.

Kade stood, rope in hand, and stared at her. Sadness reflected in his eyes, and she looked away, refusing to acknowledge it.

"What are you waiting for?"

He tossed the rope onto the ground.

"Not a damn thing, Gypsy. Not a damn thing."

They came to a small village not far from the Chesapeake River. The sun had sunk below the Appalachian Mountains, and smoke billowed from the chimneys of the nearby homes. Short fences leaned inward beside the cottages to corral the chickens and pigs.

Kade steered Goliath left down a path with a brothel and mercantile on one side and more homes on the other. He stopped in front of the brothel, dismounted and tied Goliath's reins to the hitching post in front of the saloon.

"What are you doing?" Pril asked still saddled.

"I need a drink." He wanted to see if Milosh had passed through here, but he wasn't going to tell Pril that. He enjoyed riling her.

"We haven't the time."

He pulled his leather money holder from his saddlebags.

"We have to keep going."

A long strand of hair dropped onto his cheek and tickled his chin. The errant hair had escaped the rest which was tied at the nape of his neck. He smirked and tucked it behind his ear.

"We are losing daylight," she said.

He gazed up at her still on the horse. Long red hair flowed down her back, metal bracelets jingled on her wrists, and the green shawl he'd seen used for so many things was now wrapped around her shoulders.

"We are staying here for the night."

"I beg your pardon, but I am not staying in there." She pointed to the one story shoddy building with no glass on the windows and the front door hanging by one hinge.

"Suit yourself." He turned and went inside.

Kade stepped over a man lying just inside the door and walked to the bar. It was a long slab of wood propped up onto two barrels. A reedy fellow stood behind it with a bottle of brown liquid in his left hand and a rag in the other.

A quick scan of the room told Kade the local farmers were the only customers, most of them were piled sideways and probably seeing two of him.

"All I got left is one bottle of whiskey," the man said.

"Drank you out of the rest did they?"

He nodded, pulled a short glass from the shelf behind him and placed it on the bar.

"You get a lot of business in these parts?" he asked.

"Just locals mostly."

He poured the whiskey into a glass and slid it toward him.

"Must be a sight when newcomers pass by."

"We don't care much for newcomers. Most everyone knows it, too." His eyes narrowed as he scrutinized Kade.

"Well, you should consider placing a sign of some sorts on the outskirts of town. It may stop that problem."

The bartender shrugged.

"Has anyone come through lately?"

He shook his head, but Kade could sense a liar when he saw one, and this scrawny bar man was one.

"No one?" he asked again.

"I believe I already said that."

He threw down some cash. "Thank you for your time. I'll take the bottle."

The front door slammed against the wall shaking it, and he turned to see Pril standing there. He took a long swig of his whiskey feeling it burn all the way to his stomach and put the glass back on the bar for the bartender to refill it. He watched as she lifted her skirt and stepped over the man passed out on the ground.

"Nice of you to join me," he said.

"Do not flatter yourself, Mr. Walker. I've come inside to tell you we must get back on the trail."

He reached behind him to grab his glass.

"I believe I am quite comfortable." He brought the glass to his lips and realized it was empty. He spun around to ask the bartender to fill his glass and was met with the barrel of a shotgun.

"Have I had my fill already?"

"We don't serve her kind here." The man pointed the gun at Pril.

Kade stiffened, every muscle in his body firm, and his hand closed tighter around the glass.

"What kind is that?"

"I'll be outside," Pril said.

"No, Gypsy, you stay," he said without taking his eyes from the bartender. "What kind are you referring to?"

"Her kind."

"Care to explain?"

"It is fine, really, Kade. I can leave," Pril pleaded.

"Do not move," he commanded and turned back to the man behind the bar. "Now, why don't you tell me what kind she is?"

His voice left no room for challenge, and he didn't miss the man's eyes shift behind him as the other men sobered.

"Her kind are thieves, filthy mongrels who prey on innocent people to sell their wares," a rotund man said from two tables over.

"They delve into black magic, Satan's work," another protestor spoke from a table in the back.

"That is absurd," Pril hissed.

"Well, you got me there. She is all of those things," Kade said as he leaned back against the bar.

He didn't miss the glare Pril shot him. The only way they were getting out of here was if he pretended the gypsy was crazy. At first he'd thought to set them straight on Pril and her lifestyle. Even though he didn't agree with it, she should be welcome where he was. But as the rest of the bar roused, he'd had second thoughts. There was no way he could take them all, and Pril would be of no help.

"She spouts off from time to time but if you ignore her she hushes up."

"If yer agreein' with us why are ya travelin' with her?" one of the drunkards asked.

"That, my friend, is a great question. You see, I'm taking her to jail."

He heard Pril gasp and prayed she'd see through his fib long enough for them to get out of here.

"I caught her stealing from some farmers back west."

"You sayin' there's a warrant for her arrest?"

Shit.

Three men stood close to Pril, and he didn't miss the flicker of terror in her eyes.

"I wouldn't touch my prisoner if I were you."

"You must be stupid, mister, cause there's only one of you and ten of us," a short man closest to him said.

"You may be right, however I am sober, and you my friends, are not." He pulled back and punched the short man in the nose, sending him over the table.

"Get out of here, Gypsy!"

He tried to see if she made it through the door when two men jumped on his back. He spun around, knocking over chairs as he tried to fling them from him. Hard punches to the side of his face blurred his vision and had him banging into walls. He reached behind him, grabbed the nearest man and threw him over his shoulder. He picked up a chair, ready to hit the man coming toward him, when an arrow whizzed by and stuck in the man's arm.

A shot rang out from behind the bar. There was no time to see if Pril was okay as more punches flew at him.

An arrow flew by and embedded into the bartender's arm, causing him to drop the shotgun and howl in pain. More arrows flew by one after the other as men screamed around him. Kade spun and caught the man that had been wailing on his kidneys in the chin. The drunk stumbled backward, caught his balance and came back fists flying.

The man clipped him above the eye, and he felt the skin break. Blood poured from the wound and onto his cheek. Another blow to the left side of his face snapped his neck back and made the room spin.

An arrow stuck in the man's knee, and he dropped to the ground before Kade. He turned to see Pril, cheeks glowing, eyes full of anger and red hair disheveled.

"I had him," he said.

She swept the room with her loaded bow.

Kade walked toward the bartender, lying on the ground. He reached across the makeshift bar and yanked him close.

"Now, why don't you tell me if anyone has passed by in the last few days?"

He remained mute.

Kade shook him. "I don't have all damn day."

A bang came from the door to their left, and he released the man to go see what it was.

"What in hell?"

His stomach dropped. The last sip of whiskey turned in his gut. A boy no taller than Kade's elbow huddled in the corner of the closet. His clothes, torn and threadbare from wear, hung from his skeletal frame. The sour stench of his unwashed body wafted toward Kade, nauseating him. Matted black hair hung in his eyes and to his shoulders. The boy shook so violently that Kade thought him ill.

The boy looked up, one eye was swollen shut and oozing with yellow puss while his bottom lip was split in two. Anger coursed through Kade's veins, pumping into his fists as he flexed them. In two strides he was behind the bar, and without another thought he punched the bartender, busting open his nose.

The man slumped over, and Kade grabbed his collar, bringing him up to meet another blow of his fist, this time in the stomach. He hit him again, and again and again. With each punch he thought of the boy with the bruised face.

The bartender slumped to the side. When Kade released him, he crumpled to the floor.

"I should drive my knife right through your black heart, you rotten bastard." He spat on him and walked back over to the closet.

"Where did he go?"

"Where did who go?" Pril asked.

"The boy that was in the closet." He pointed. "Right here."
"I cannot know."
He raised a brow.
"I saw no one."

He scanned the room; men groaned from the floor, arrows stuck in their backs, arms and stomachs. Pril stood by the entrance bow ready to fire at anyone who moved. She'd been too busy standing guard to see a child escape.

He hoped the kid was okay and well on his way to safety. He took one last look around for any sign of the boy. He wasn't in the room. Kade went back to the bar, grabbed the whiskey and the money he'd left on the counter.

"You do not need spirits. Put it back," Pril whispered as he came close.

"My ribs, kidneys and face hurt like hell. I'll be taking the damn bottle."

He walked past her and outside.

"You're welcome," she said taking up the rear.

"I'll not thank you, Gypsy, so forget it."

"I just saved your life." He pointed the whiskey bottle at her.

She mounted Athos.

"That may be, but you did so only because you need me. " He saddled Goliath the whiskey still in his hand. "Had I been a stranger you would've walked away."

"Is that what you think of me?"

"Not think, Gypsy. It's what I know."

She moved her horse next to his and handed him a handkerchief. "Hold this to your face until we get somewhere safe."

He took the blue fabric and placed it gently above his eye. Damn, his face hurt. He couldn't deny she'd saved his life. He was out numbered and hadn't stood a chance. He was a skilled fighter, but skill didn't matter when there were ten to one odds. His only concern had been her. Had she not been here, his task would be much simpler.

As it was, he still hadn't figured out how he was going to steal the child from her once they found Tsura. He flexed his jaw, and the bone ached. He had no choice in the matter. Pril wouldn't see the child again once he took her.

Guilt pressed against his sides, and he fought to take a breath. As much as the gypsy annoyed the hell out of him, she had come in handy. Her talent with the bow and arrow was remarkable. He'd never seen anything like it.

Over the years aboard his vessel he'd come across some talented riflemen, swordsmen and fighters, but he'd never seen one as proficient as Pril with the bow.

"Where did you learn to shoot?" he asked as they traveled south.

"Galius."

He nodded.

"I started when I was four, Tsura's age."

He didn't miss the hinge in her voice or the way she fidgeted with the reins.

"Tough weapon to learn."

"I have tried others, but I was always good with the bow, and it was the one I felt the most comfortable with."

He wanted to know more, but stopped himself. Too much information about the gypsy may cause him to falter in his plan. He couldn't afford to get soft on her. He needed to bring the girl back. He'd made a deal.

Pril dug inside her bag for the beeswax she'd brought. Her hand closed around the glass jar, and she sighed. She thought she'd lost it. The one ingredient she needed to perform most healing spells. She placed her hand over the jar and said the words loud enough for her to hear.

"Blend together to bind thy mess, heal thy flesh upon caress."

The spell had been cast on the wax in the jar and would mend Kade's wound without her reciting the words for him to hear.

If she had the book she'd be able to find a spell to search for Tsura. She closed her eyes and allowed the loss to sweep over her. It'd been burned, and she'd not found one page left from it among the rubble. The most valuable family heirloom she had, trusted to her after Vadoma died. She shook her head. How could she have been so reckless as to keep something so important in her vardo? She should've buried it, created a spell that would keep the book from anyone's eyes but hers.

Vadoma kept the book with her at all times. The people were frightened of the evil Chuvani and never came near her. She lived most of her life alone, and Pril believed she liked it that way. People came to her for balms, advice and even childbirth, but they wouldn't allow her within their circle of friends or inside their homes. She was an outcast.

Pril was content to be with her family and the Renoldi clan. She didn't need simple folk to make her happy. But Vadoma did. She needed to belong. Pril often thought this was because of her powers. They pushed her away from society, and instead of being accepted they turned her away. Soon Vadoma grew black to all things that were good and concentrated on getting revenge to those around her. She reveled in their fear, giving her immense pleasure.

Pril walked toward Kade. He sat on a tree stump, holding the handkerchief she'd given him earlier above his eye. The cut needed stitches, but she had no thread so she settled for a healing spell instead.

"About bloody time," he growled when she drew near.

"I needed the wax."

He examined the jar and raised a brow.

"It seals the skin, and since I don't have any thread it will have to do."

He blew out a long breath and removed the makeshift bandage from his brow.

She took the blood soaked fabric from him and dumped water from her canteen onto it. Slowly, and with sure hands, she dabbed at the dried blood from the gash above his left eye.

"I'm sure it feels worse than it looks," she said.

"Cut the small talk, Gypsy, and get to it. I've got a bottle of whiskey to drink."

He yanked the rag from her and dumped some of the whiskey on it.

"What are you doing?"

"Clean the wound with this. Water won't get infection out."

"I know that." She grabbed the cloth. "I was ridding the wound of all the dried blood first."

He shrugged and took a swallow from the bottle.

She watched as he made a face, and his body gave a slight tremble.

"If it tastes so awful why drink it?"

He stared at her, his eyes glazed and bloodshot.

"Who said anything about it tasting awful?"

"I cannot imagine it tasting like berries."

His face really did look horrible. The skin around his eye was swollen and blue. He had a cut on his chin, and the cheek was bloated.

"Not berries, but rather pure ecstasy."

He winked at her, and she knew the alcohol was influencing him.

"Hmmm."

"There are many things in life that will give a man such ecstasy, Gypsy."

"I'm sure there are." She opened the jar and scooped out a healthy portion of wax. She gently rubbed her thumb over the cut.

He flinched.

"Apologies."

He frowned.

She pulled some herbs from the pocket on the inside of her skirt and dabbed them into the wax-covered wound.

He moved back.

"Do sit still," she said.

"I am still, but the earth is not."

"Oh, dear."

The bottle in his hand was empty. He'd had all of four drinks from it. How could there be nothing left?

He swayed to the side, and she caught him before he would've knocked his head on a rock.

"Thanks, Gypsy."

He swatted the air, and she ducked so he didn't hit her. She left him to go retrieve his blanket and saddle. When she came back he was out cold, his loud snores fit to raise the dead.

She sighed, propped his head against the saddle and covered him with the blanket. She inspected the wound one last time, making sure she'd covered it good, pleased to see the skin already closing.

The sun dipped behind the hills and an array of colors lit up the horizon. Soon it'd be twilight; she needed to get a fire going for warmth and a meal. She gathered wood, stacked it and found Kade's flint and steel. She struck the two together until the sparks fell onto the dried leaves and twigs. She leaned in and blew onto the smoldering pile until an orange flame licked the air.

Pril sat on the ground next to the fire, lost within the dancing flames. She missed Tsura more with each passing hour. *Where could Milosh be?* She hadn't asked Kade if they still followed her brother's trail or if they'd lost it. They'd been so close the night before, and she wondered now if Kade had known Milosh was at the bottom of the hill all along.

She didn't believe he'd gone for a stroll. He was going somewhere, she just didn't know where. Kade's loud snores mingled with the growling in her stomach, and she reached for her quiver a few feet from her. She better hunt their supper before nightfall when she'd be too frightened to go anywhere.

CHAPTER ELEVEN

Kade folded the paper and tucked it back inside his shirt. He flexed his jaw. Too much time had been lost, and he was no closer to finding the girl than he had been a month ago. As each day passed the pressure in his chest built, and he was sure his heart would explode. They were still at least a day behind Milosh. He worried they wouldn't find the girl before time ran out. He rubbed his eyes, refusing to think of the consequences that lay ahead. His stomach turned and bile rushed up his throat.

They needed to move. Determination pushed his shoulders back, and he stood taller. He went about the camp, gathered their supplies and shoved them into the saddlebags. He glanced at Pril, curled up on the ground fast asleep. He hadn't the time to sit here and wait for her to wake. He stood above her, long red hair barely visible, the blanket covering her whole body.

He nudged her with the toe of his boot. "Get up."

An owl hooted from somewhere above, and wolves howled in the distance. She didn't move, and he bumped her again.

"Wake up, Gypsy." There was an edge to his voice, a pitted, grated sound that he didn't recognize, and he set his shoulders against it.

She rolled over, flipped her hair out of her eyes and glared up at him.

"Why are you waking me in the middle of the night?"

"We must travel. Time has been wasted."

"Is that so?"

"Yes, now move." He pushed her with his foot again. "Get up."

"I am not a dog." She flung his foot from her. "Do not kick me again."

He raised a brow.

She stretched her arms above her head and threw the blanket off.

"Time has been wasted due to consumption of liquor," she said under her breath as she walked into the forest to relieve herself.

He folded her bedroll and tied it to the back of Athos. He'd woken with a pounding headache and sore muscles, the bottle of whiskey empty on the ground a reminder of how much he'd drank the night before. He was thankful Pril had left some cooked salmon wrapped in a dry cloth beside the low flames of the fire. Had it not been there, he'd be heaving into the bushes. The whiskey numbed the pain from the beating he'd taken, but also the memories of the past. He shook his head to lessen the guilt he felt over why he was here and what he was going to do. He watched Pril as she came closer, a scowl fit to scare the devil himself on her face.

"Brighten up, Gypsy. Morning is only a few hours away."

She tipped her nose and tied her shawl into a knot around her shoulders.

The night air was brisk, and the dew dampened their skin. Clouds of fog formed around their mouths. He shivered and pulled his coat tighter around him. Lack of sleep made it difficult to keep warm. He'd known this from years upon his ship. There had been many evenings where sleep eluded him while he kept watch for pirates and thieves out across the waters. He missed the sea and yearned to go back to the life he loved.

He was stuck here, bound by blood, by obligation. He couldn't give up now and go home. He'd never forgive himself. Honor had kept him here, searching for months for a child with a mark behind her left ear. Devotion pushed him beyond reason—beyond any sense that taking a child was wrong. Duty was the one emotion outside of anything he'd ever felt before where he'd sacrifice himself to end it all.

These things were rooted within his heart, the breath within his soul and the blood pumping within his veins. And, he experienced it all. He ached deep within the core of his being where pain obeyed no rules. Where memories lingered to haunt his dreams, pushing past a resolve he knew was uncertain. It was not a choice. *It was not choice*.

"Let us leave," she said from on top of her horse.

He'd watched her sleep during the night, lost in her red hair and pale complexion. She was an anomaly to him—a mystery he fought hard not to concern himself with. But he wondered where she came from. Who was she, and why at her age did she not have a husband? What was so special about the child that the Monroes, Milosh and others hunted her?

He mounted Goliath and headed in the direction he'd seen the tracks.

"Do you know where we are going?" she asked irritation in her voice.

"Not a morning person, Gypsy?"

"This hardly qualifies as morning."

She yawned.

"Milosh's tracks are just past the tree line. I'd seen them yesterday when we left the village."

"And Tsura's?"

"There is one set."

"How then are you sure we are following the correct ones?"

He sighed.

"Because they are the same ones we've followed since the beginning of this Godforsaken trip."

"Oh."

She was silent, and with Pril that either meant he'd pissed her off somehow or she was contemplating her next question.

He waited.

"How is your head?"

He hadn't thought about the wound at all. She'd placed the wax on it, and when he touched his hand over the skin all he felt was the sticky lotion. No pain or discomfort of any kind.

"Remarkable. There is no pain. Your wax must really work. That is the second wound you've healed with it."

"Do I sense your belief in the healing methods of my people?"

"No. I still have my suspicions, and from yesterday, I can tell I'm not the only one."

"Yes, well, those people, you included, are daft. You know not what the earth can offer you."

"Listen, Gypsy, I don't need a lesson in the healing elements found within the soil as you like to say. I am well aware that there are benefits to plants and herbs."

"How so?"

"I've lived at sea all my life. When my crew got sick the doctor on board always used such things."

"You lived at sea?"

"I do."

"Oh...what is it that you do aboard a ship?"

He hadn't thought she wouldn't know. He was used to being recognized within the small towns and villages by the sea where he'd port for an evening or two. Most of society lived by the wharfs and shipping yards, but the gypsies had gone deep within the bush to hide the child.

"I sail it."

"You're a Master?"

"I prefer Captain."

"Do you own the vessel?"

"I do."

"What do you transport?"

"Sugar, cotton, tobacco." He heard her gasp and knew she was thinking of the Monroes. They were the wealthiest tobacco farmers in the south. He'd taken their tobacco aboard his ship many times, carrying it to London and Bristol. It was where he'd become acquainted with Silas Monroe and his brother Jude. Both offered him friendship among the docks, and Silas always had a whore waiting for him when he ported from a long journey. Had he known what would come of the friendship, he'd have killed Silas then.

"Was your father a Master, or Captain rather?"

"Samuel Walker was the captain of the S.S.W merchant ship before I." Saying his father's name sent a wave of emotions up his spine causing his face to heat and his head to spin.

"S.S.W?"

"Solomon Samuel Walker, my grandfather's name. The vessel was named for him."

"You lived aboard a ship all your life?"

"Yes."

"What about your mother?"

"I didn't have one."

"Surely you had a mother. Did she pass when you were young?"

He never spoke of the woman who bore him, knowing little to nothing about her. All Sam had told him was that she came from wealth. He knew nothing more and didn't care to. Had it not been for Sam he'd have been cast into the sea swallowed by the waves, forgotten forever.

"Did you have any siblings?"

"No."

He didn't like the turn the conversation had taken and was anxious to stop it. He didn't care to know of his lineage or bloodlines. All he cared about was the here and now and the task he'd set out to achieve.

"I find it odd that you know nothing of your mother."

He flexed his jaw.

"Was she of ill repute?"

"Gypsy, if you keep pushing me about my past I'm going to push you from that horse."

"You wouldn't."

"Try me."

She was silent, and he could tell by the way she fidgeted beside him in her saddle she had another question but battled whether to speak it or not.

"Do you know where she came from?"

Her curiosity won out. Without another thought he reached over and shoved her from Athos' back.

She fell, landing in the river with a splash.

He stopped Goliath and waited while she flailed about. The river couldn't be more than a foot deep on the edge. What was she making such a ruckus over?

He walked Goliath closer and pushed Athos out of the way. The red-brown horse backed up to allow the massive stallion passage. The water danced around Goliath's hooves coming inward and outward.

She stood off to the side, dress soaked and dripping. Her hair was disheveled, the ends wet.

"You bastard!" She came toward him and slapped Goliath's rump.

The stallion reared, throwing his front legs up into the air and sending Kade backward off of the horse and onto the ground.

He took a moment to catch his breath. Goliath whinnied and stomped back and forth.

"Goliath stay," he said in a calm voice.

The horse shook his muzzle before standing still.

He pushed himself up and wiped the dirt from his pants.

"That was not very ladylike."

"Ladylike? Ladylike you say?" She pulled her thin arm back and punched him in the jaw.

He stepped back and gaped at her.

"I think I broke my hand," she yelped as she hopped up and down throwing her fist into the air.

"Serves you right," he said rubbing the tender spot on his cheek where she'd hit him.

"Why did you throw me from my horse?" She held her hand close.

"You were warned not to ask me another question."

"I thought you were bluffing. What man throws a lady from her horse, into the river no less?"

"I never bluff."

She assessed her skirt, sopping wet, and shivered. The cold night air seemed more frigid than before. He felt sorry for her. He hadn't known the river was that close. He took off his coat and handed it to her when he saw it on her neck.

"Uh, Gypsy?"

"Yes?"

"Do not move."

One arm in his coat, she eyed him. "Beg your pardon?"

"Cease your movements." He spotted another one on her collarbone.

He gave an uncontrolled shake. He hated the damn things, always had. Their slimy, squishy bodies disgusted him. He shook again.

She froze, her eyes wide.

"What is it? What's wrong?"

"Are you familiar with leeches?"

"Oh no, oh no, tell me you jest."

"I wish I was."

Her face glowed white in the dark. He watched the play of emotions slide across her face. Fear. Disgust. Anger. Fear.

"Get it off," she shrieked. "Get the damn thing off!"

He didn't know if he should tell her that there was more than one.

"Where is it? Where is it?"

"On your neck, collarbone and left arm."

He wasn't prepared for the high-pitched scream that blew past her mouth.

"Please, please get them off," she begged, bouncing from one foot to the other.

"I don't fancy them myself," he said, trying to figure out the best way to tackle the situation.

"You have to remove them. Oh, please, please."

He'd never seen her like this before. The longer he waited the bigger her eyes got, and her whole body vibrated. She was going to lose her mind. He could see it in the way she bounced around, fidgeted and chewed on her lower lip.

"I need you to stand still."

"Please, just hurry."

He came close enough to smell the river on her skin and see the panic in her eyes. He reached out with his forefinger and thumb, skimming the bloodsucker before he snapped his hand back.

"Damn, they're slimy."

She hummed and stared up toward the stars.

He tried again, but once his finger touched the leech it shot back to his side.

"Get it off," she growled between clenched teeth.

"I'm trying, but I hate them as much as you do."

"I do not give a damn, Kade Walker. Get the blasted thing off!"

Goliath neighed and shuffled his hooves. He never did like loud noises.

Kade inhaled. With accurate speed, he grabbed the bloodsucker pulling it from her neck and flicked it into the bushes.

"Two left," he said more for himself than her.

She nodded and held still.

He blew out three puffs of air before he latched onto the second one, yanking it from her chest and flinging it into the river.

They both exhaled.

"One more."

She held up her arm. The leech pumped up and down, sucking her blood.

He blocked it from his mind, knowing it was the last one he'd have to pull. He worked his fingers before he ripped it from her skin sending it into the trees.

"Thank you," she murmured, and her shoulders sagged with relief.

He needed to sit down. His head was spinning, and he had to regulate his heartbeat before he passed out.

She searched the rest of her body for any more, and he sighed when she declared all was well.

He leaned against a tree, inhaled slow and easy until the fog left his head. He'd battled angry seas, tidal waves and pirates, but none left him defenseless like the tiny leech.

The sun broke through the trees casting thin lines of light into the forest. He grabbed hold of Goliath's reins. He paused, allowing the warmth to caress his face and chase away the chill in his bones. He needed to move, to continue with one foot in front of the other until he found Milosh. He glanced at Pril. She'd wrapped her shawl around her head tying it at the back to hang past her long hair. Soon he'd rip her world apart, and he wondered if she'd ever recover.

Remorse and dishonor filled his mouth with bitterness, and he glanced away, blinking past the anger.

"We've wasted enough time. Mount up," he growled.

She climbed on top of Athos, pulled Kade's coat tight around her and waited for him to give the signal.

On top of Goliath, he kicked his heels into the horse's side, and they continued through the forest.

CHAPTER TWELVE

Pril crouched beside the lake and dipped her hands into the cool water. She splashed it onto her cheeks and sighed. She rubbed her face with the palms of her hands trying to rinse the dirt and grime away. Her tresses were in need of a rinsing. She bent forward and dunked her head into the lake working her fingers through to the scalp. She massaged the tired skin, pulling the water through the long strands to the ends before she wrung it out. Refreshed, she tipped her chin up letting the afternoon sun dry the remaining droplets of water left on her face.

She hadn't seen Tsura in five days. The time tore at her insides. Was she healthy? Was she scared, lonely and missing Pril? All these questions gnawed at her. With each passing hour, she fought to stay sane—strong in mind and body. She needed answers, but knew there were none to give.

She peeked at Kade giving oats to the horses. He'd been a moody companion with lack of propriety. He was harsh, overbearing and commanding; three attributes she despised. He held no regard for her emotions or the urgency she felt to find Tsura. The travel was on his time, whether it meant tracking in the middle of the night or all day long. He moved at his own leisure, on his own schedule. There was no more she could do. She needed him.

If Milosh was only a day's ride ahead of them, they should be riding all night. Sleep would come once she had her daughter safe in her arms. Kade was not open to her suggestions, ignoring her inquiries.

She felt the scab on her neck from the leeches yesterday and trembled. Had it not been for Kade, she'd still be in the marsh, screaming at the top of her lungs and possibly drained of all her blood.

She sensed he didn't like the suckers any more than she did, and she was thankful he had removed them just the same. She'd gotten a small glimpse into the life he'd led before meeting her and was delighted to know he was a sea captain. She yearned to hear more about where he'd sailed and where he'd lived, anything to make the time go faster.

Her clan had lived by the sea all her life and when Vadoma was at her worst. Thinking of those times brought tears to her eyes. Pity and resentment melded together, and she didn't know whether to laugh or to cry at the consequences of Vadoma's actions. Life had been simpler; their cares consisted of food and the wares they sold. Pril had been a happy girl with hopes and dreams.

When she'd found out Vadoma carried a child, and as there was no husband or lover to claim, she'd asked her sister to tell her whose it was. Vadoma refused. She found this odd and terrifying at the same time. Two months later she had her first and only premonition. Vadoma would die—hung and then burned by the man who planted the seed within her.

Pril knew without a doubt it was Silas Monroe. He'd been captivated by Vadoma and her beauty, coming to call often. Her sister wasn't one to turn her chin up at affection whether it caused her shame or not. She'd go off with Silas unchaperoned and not return until late in the evening. Galius and Milosh warned her not to get comfortable with the wealthy plantation owner, but Vadoma was her people's Chuvani and would not be ordered about. She refused her brothers' advice and cast them from her cabin.

Pril had witnessed the change in her sister as her stomach grew. She became softer, but still defiant in her defense of Silas. Vadoma had found love, and Pril was happy for her. As her pregnancy progressed Silas showed his face less and less until months passed, and he never came. Vadoma grew angry, casting spells on those who angered her and becoming a recluse. She grew more devious, more threatening and more evil than before. The clan became terrified of her. The people of Jamestown feared the great Chuvani and begged the clan to stop her. But there was nothing they could do. Vadoma was more powerful than Pril. She knew the spells, taught by their mother since birth. She'd been born with the gift of magick which surpassed anything Pril would ever possess.

She ran her fingers through the tangled wet hair. The edge of her skirt was torn, and she ripped a piece of the fabric, placing it in her mouth. She gathered her hair in sections, and weaving it together, she tied it with the fabric she'd held between her lips.

What purpose did Milosh have for taking Tsura? She understood his anger and sadness, but to take another's life—especially a child's— because of a loss of your own was foolish. She was desperate to see him—to convince him in some way to let Tsura go. Maybe she should try the finding spell again. She never understood how some spells worked for her, while others did not, and often thought it was because she was second born. She'd have to try the spell when the moon was bright. Most spells worked by the light of the moon and the difficult ones not at all, unless the moon was round.

"Here," Kade said from behind her.

She turned to see him holding a piece of dried meat, and her stomach growled.

"Thank you."

She bit into the food, grateful for his generosity. Although tough around the edges, Kade Walker was kind when he allowed himself to be.

"How close are we?"

"They're still hours ahead of us. If we have no more stops we should be on them sometime tomorrow."

"Good."

They mounted, and she brought Athos to walk beside him through the pasture.

"What is it like being on a ship?"

He gazed straight ahead, and for a moment she wondered if he was going to answer her.

"It is the most wonderful thing in the world."

Taken aback at his comment, she watched as his eyes glossed, and he swallowed.

"You miss it."

"Every day." He sighed. "It is all I've ever known. Land seems foreign to me. I do not fit in here."

She understood. She'd never fit in anywhere, and fleeing from place to place didn't allow her the opportunity to make friends. If it hadn't been for the Monroes invading every gypsy camp, she'd not have met Sorina and many of the others that made up the Peddlers. They'd become her family, and thinking of them now intensified how much she missed them.

"When we find Tsura will you go back?"

He hesitated before nodding.

"Do you take passengers aboard your ship?"

"Rarely."

"If I paid you, would it be possible to take me and Tsura to the other world?"

He turned toward her, his charcoal eyes surrounded by thick lashes, framed with jagged edges and a square jaw. The sun had tanned his face and brightened his blond hair softening his features. The white shirt and cotton tan trousers were that of a sailor, and she wasn't sure why she hadn't noticed them before now. His attire reflected his carefree attitude.

He was rogue, handsome and dangerous all at the same time.

"No."

The word slapped her in the face, and she gaped at him. She was sure he'd say yes.

"Why ever not?"

"I owe you no reason."

"You've taken passengers before but you will not take me and my daughter?"

"Correct."

"Even if I paid you?"

"What will you pay me with, Gypsy? The beads that hang from your ears, or the silver around your neck? How about the bracelets on your wrists? I am in no need of your baubles."

"I have other riches I could offer."

He peered at her out of the corner of his eye. "Unless you're offering me what's underneath your skirt, save your breath."

She gasped.

"You are unbelievable. What kind of woman do you think I am?"

"I believe we've had this discussion already."

"Yes, right. You think me a thief and liar and now a whore."

"I never said you were a whore."

"I have told you countless times I am none of those things."

"And I have told you I do not care."

"Why, if all you see me as is a thief and liar, are you willing to help me find Tsura?"

"It is the right thing to do."

"But taking me and my daughter across the sea to safety is not?"

"Once I find your daughter you are of no concern to me."

"Your beliefs and constitutions are blurred."

He ignored her, which fueled her rage.

"Silence? You become silent when asked for the truth? How convenient."

"I owe you nothing."

"You owe me the truth."

He stopped Goliath and turned to face her. Fury lined the edges of his face.

"That's where you're wrong, Gypsy. I answer to myself and no one else."

She curled her lip. Why wouldn't he tell her?

"Lies," she spat.

She watched as his face changed.

His mouth twisted, and he glared at her. "Do not call me a liar again."

"Or what? You'll push me from Athos? Perhaps you'll throw your dagger through my side?"

"Sarcasm does not suit you."

"This coming from a man who spouts to be wiser then most, but when pushed to the edge will not own his end. You, Mr. Walker, are a fraud." She kicked Athos sides and raced off ahead of him.

She heard the rumble of Goliath's hooves behind her and urged her horse to go faster. Before she knew it he was beside her and had pulled her from Athos, plopping her down in front of him.

"What are you doing?" she yelled.

He tugged on the reins and slowed the stallion to a trot.

She wiggled in his embrace and felt the muscle in his forearm tighten.

"Let me go, damn it."

He ignored her, his breathing forced and jaw clenched.

She dug her elbow into his stomach, but his hold on her waist only strengthened.

"Release me."

She didn't miss the lust in his eyes. Fear clawed at the back of her throat, and she squirmed even more desperate to escape him.

He pulled her close, squishing her to his chest and, without a word of warning, brought his lips to hers. She pummeled his chest pushing away from him, but he continued to kiss her. His tongue caressed the edges of her lips urging them to open. She wouldn't do it. She shook her head. He combed his fingers through her hair and yanked her head back. When she yelped he drove his tongue into her mouth. He tasted of pinecones, earth and desire, and she slowly sank into his embrace. She pressed her breasts into him, and he groaned into her mouth.

Their tongues battled, her nipples hard and crotch wet. She rubbed her thighs together to ease the want she felt there. She didn't know it before, but she needed this—needed him, his hands, his mouth and something more, something unexplained that only he could give her. She yearned for a way to release the anxiety inside of her. She moved her lips over his and hummed her enjoyment. She didn't stop his hand as it moved toward her breasts. He felt good—right. She'd take his acceptance now and deal with his rejection later.

Kade pulled his lips from hers just in time to see her horse canter toward the forest ahead, a rider on top.

"Ah shit." He tugged her close, dug his heels into Goliath's sides and held tight to the reins. The horse sprinted forward, chasing after Athos.

They raced alongside when he noticed it was the boy from the other day.

Determination spread across the youngster's dirt smeared face.

A loud offensive whistle shrilled from beside him, and Athos slowed before coming to a stop.

Kade peered at Pril.

"Why didn't you do that a few minutes ago?"

"I couldn't catch my breath while being jostled about. I am not used to sitting sidesaddle."

He climbed down and assessed the situation. He sensed the kid wanted to flee and would do so at any minute if he weren't careful.

"Easy," he said holding out his hands as he stepped toward him. "We will not hurt you."

The boy's black eyes darted about, and Kade's heart sunk. The kid was terrified. He'd been beaten most of his life, and the affect it had on him was clear as water. His lip split, the eye red-rimmed and swollen from two days before when Kade had seen him in the closet.

Now that he was getting a better view of the kid, he could see the tanned skin, black hair and high cheekbones. The boy was Indian. He'd been a slave. Kade's muscles pulsed when he thought of what the boy had gone through at the hands of his master.

"Do you speak English?" he asked.

The boy didn't answer, instead he flexed his scrawny legs around the horse, urging the animal to move, but without Pril's command Athos stayed put.

"Are you hungry?" Pril asked, walking past him toward the boy.

"Gypsy, don't startle him."

She held out some of the hard tack they'd chewed on earlier.

His eyes darted about as he peered from Kade to Pril and then back to the meat she held.

"Here, take it."

He snatched it from her hand and shoved the whole piece into his mouth.

Kade's gut clenched, and he shook his head.

"Can you come down, and I'll offer you some water?" Pril said, reaching out her hand.

The boy didn't hesitate and slid from Athos. He went to Pril and wrapped his skinny arms around her waist. Kade witnessed the unshed tears within her eyes. She hugged him back, kissing the top of his unwashed head. For the first time since they left the Peddler camp, he'd seen how much she missed and worried for her daughter.

The emotion tugged at his insides, and he turned from them. He couldn't think past the display behind him and wanted some space. Time was short, and he needed to find the child. He glanced back at the scene again. How was he going to take the girl from Pril? He ran his hand across his tired eyes. He must. There was no choice—a life waited for his return. If he didn't follow through, the life would be taken—a repercussion he wasn't willing to let happen.

He walked into the forest, leaving the boy with Pril. Distance was best for now—before he broke down and spilled all his apprehensions to her. He sat down on a log and pulled the letter from the inside pocket of his trousers. It told of the child and her mark. He ran his hand through his hair, pulling the tie that held it back and off of his face.

He thought of the messenger he'd spoken to before they left Riverbend. He'd told him of the threat with each day that passed if the girl wasn't brought to them. A day hadn't gone by where the words didn't replay in his mind. They were a reminder of what the future held if he did not find the child.

He hoped it wouldn't come to fruition—that by some force of nature things worked out. But it had already been five days, and he feared what he'd find in the next town. He brought the worn paper to his lips and inhaled. He'd been pushed into a wall, and there was no way from it without hurting Pril.

He never asked what did the Monroes wanted with the girl. He'd had no time, and he doubted they'd tell him. Thrust into the situation without being told all truths was not how he conducted business, but then this wasn't business. This was bribery.

CHAPTER THIRTEEN

Silas stood on the harbor away from all the commotion. Sellers and buyers lined the wooden walk, waiting anxiously for the merchant ships to anchor and display their products.

He was relieved the ship transporting the slaves was the first to dock. He stood among men of all esteem waiting to cast their bid. The smell of unwashed bodies and sickness wafted toward them as the slaves filed off the boat. Men shackled with metal chains around their wrists and ankles shuffled down the wooden plank onto the wharf.

Silas pulled the handkerchief from his pocket covering his nose and mouth. Even though he was careful to position himself down wind, the smell made its way toward them. He hated the stench—the rotten state the slaves came in was nothing short of vile, and he refused to be anywhere near it.

The peruke he donned this morning was made of goat's hair and smelled of orange flower. He'd had it freshly powdered the day before. He was careful not to move his head too quickly and leave small deposits upon his face. Had it not been for propriety, he'd have ripped the wig from his head just to inhale the orange flower and drown out the stench from the slaves.

Jude stood beside him, tall and rigid. His long wig tied at the nape curled down his back. His brother hated this as much as he did. Neither of them cared for the process, more so because of the unkempt state the slaves came in. He and Jude demanded the slaves be bathed before they arrived at the plantation.

He motioned to Isaiah and waited for his foreman to amble toward them. The heavyset man wore no wig. Instead, he chose to keep his greasy black hair long and loose around his shoulders. It wasn't a fashion Silas cared for, but he elected not to address the man's appearance on many occasions for the mere fact of him dealing with the slaves directly.

Isaiah nodded to both Jude and Silas as he came to stand in front of them.

"We will take three and no more. Be careful who you choose. I desire none that are related," Silas said.

"Right, boss."

"Do not bring them without a bath and clean clothes."

"Yes, Sir."

Finished with the foreman he walked away, and Jude followed.

"Did you send it?" he asked.

"I did," Jude said.

"Which slave did you chose to deliver it?"

"Malachi."

He nodded.

"He knows what will happen if he does not deliver the message?"

"He does."

"Very good."

Jude was the second oldest of the three brothers and always did as asked. He never wavered or defied Silas' demands. Instead, he agreed to even the most absurd ideas. Hiram was nothing like Jude. He was defiant and needed to see just cause for everything even when there was none to give. Silas had begun to despise him. The youngest brother had proved to be more of a nuisance when it came to the capture and death of the girl.

He would not be stopped, not by the gypsies or his own brother. He'd be sure the child held no life within her if he had to drive the knife through her heart himself.

He spat.

"Troubled, Brother?" Jude asked.

"I cannot condone Hiram's way any longer."

"What are your thoughts?"

He stopped, turned toward Jude and with evil eyes that held no hint of mercy or empathy growled, "He will soon expire."

"Why wait? I myself have grown tired of his relentless whining and reluctance to get rid of the child."

"I do not know all of Hiram's secrets, and until I do he will live."

Jude nodded.

"Now let us slip into the goldsmiths. I'd like to buy something nice for Beth."

CHAPTER FOURTEEN

It'd been seven days since Pril had seen Tsura. She was so close to holding her baby she couldn't contain her excitement. They'd been tracking Milosh for a week, and the last two days they'd rode with short breaks just to catch up to them. She hadn't slept in twenty-seven hours. The insides of her legs ached from sitting on top of Athos for hours, and she longed to stretch them. Soon all the tiredness and hurting muscles would pay off.

She wanted to know her brother's reasons for taking Tsura. Kade had mentioned yesterday they were heading south. She knew they were close to the Monroe's place. Had Milosh intended to take her daughter there, to the enemy—the very men who killed so many gypsy girls and possibly his own? Had he no love for his niece at all? The answer came quick and without shock. He'd despised Tsura from the moment Vadoma placed the blood curse. He'd wanted nothing to do with the baby or Pril for raising her.

She missed the days when they were young. Milosh had been her best friend. They had explored the land around their home, pretending to fight off evil sorcerers while Pril threw spells, and Milosh used his sword. She smiled. Their imaginations kept them busy for days. Galius hadn't stepped in to help Pril until Milosh had disowned her and Tsura. Being the leader of their clan, Galius commanded Milosh to keep the family secret once they left the Renoldi clan.

When Magda became pregnant and Alexandra was born, his resentment toward Tsura seemed to fade. He concentrated on thinking of ideas to keep the girls safe from the Monroes. As more families joined their clan, Milosh made it his job to find new ways to protect the children.

When Alexandra was killed, his anger came back tenfold. He was filled with rage, hurt and resentment. She wished she could've helped him, but her shame would not allow it. It had been her job to create a protection spell—one that would shield the girls from harm. There wasn't enough oil, and she'd been selfish. She protected Tsura instead. The ache in her chest resonated down her back and into her sides compressing all her emotions. She'd live with the consequences of her selfishness for the rest of her life.

She was anxious for answers. She wanted to talk with Milosh. Too much time had passed, and she needed to make things right between them. Her legs tightened around Athos' sides as she sat in her saddle. The valley was shrouded in darkness except for the flicker of a campfire below. Kade sat beside her on top of Goliath, the boy asleep in front of him.

"What will we do with him?" she asked.

It'd taken two days for the boy to talk, and neither of them could understand him. He was Indian, but of what descent or tribe they didn't know. He'd not divulged his name, not that they could understand, or if he even knew what it was, and so they continued to call him boy which bothered her.

"We take him. If a fight breaks out I'm sure he will scramble."

She sighed.

"It is only my brother."

"Precisely."

She glared at him. He had a tendency to convey too much sarcasm, and it got on her nerves. This was a serious situation and shouldn't provoke one's arrogant side. There was no time for such foolishness.

Athos whinnied and shook his head.

"Ready, Gypsy?"

She sat taller in the saddle, inhaled the cool night air and fixed her gaze on the glowing embers a few hundred yards away.

She nodded.

Kade clicked his tongue, and Goliath made his way down the hill. Athos followed a short distance behind.

As they drew near, Pril's stomach rolled, and her hands shook while she held the reins. She stared at Kade's wide shoulders and broad back to keep from falling off of her horse. Soon she'd see Tsura—touch her hair, kiss her cheeks and hold her tight. The light from the fire outlined his body, and she knew they were close. Anticipation built within her, and she found it difficult to swallow.

Kade stopped suddenly, and she pulled on the reins to halt Athos from bumping into them.

"What is it?"

"Something's not right."

"What do you mean?" She yanked Athos' reins to move beside Kade and scanned the deserted area.

The fire glowed bright in the middle of the camp. Milosh's horse was tethered to a nearby tree, the saddle on the ground and some blankets strewn about the grassy floor.

"Where is Tsura?"

"The better question to ask would be where is Milosh?"

Anxiety crept in to steal her breath and squeeze her ribs. She slid from Athos, letting the reins fall from her fingers.

"Tsura?" she whispered as she walked toward the blankets on the ground. "Tsura?"

The camp was deserted. Left as if someone were coming back. Where could they have gone? She picked up a blanket, holding it to her lips and nose. She inhaled trying to draw any scent of Tsura that she could.

"There are other tracks here," Kade said.

She spun to face him as he knelt, inspecting the ground.

"Whose?"

"I do not know."

He stood and walked the perimeter of the camp while she rummaged through Milosh's saddlebags. She pulled out dried food, wax and the charm she'd made to keep Tsura safe from the Monroes. He must've taken it before the Renoldis attacked them. *Tsura. My baby, where are you?*

"Pril?"

He stood on the edge of the trees, his face pale. She looked into his eyes and didn't miss the remorse and pity there. *Tsura... Tsura.*

"No. God, no."

She scrambled to her feet, dropping the charm. She ran past him into the woods. She wasn't sure what she'd find, but she knew by the look on Kade's face it would be devastating. She didn't know where to go once she'd passed him. The blood rushed through her body making her lightheaded and dizzy. She struggled to catch her breath as the realization of finding her daughter dead struck her in the gut and knocked the wind from her lungs. She was anxious and at the same time full of dread at what she'd find.

She stopped, bottom lip trembling. She turned slowly toward Kade. She was unable to go in alone and see the image that would change her life forever. She waited, frozen by nature, by the existence of living a life without her precious child. She swallowed, the tears hovered within her lashes, and she blinked them away.

He went to her, placed an arm around her shoulders and squeezed.

"It is not Tsura."

Any ounce of courage she had left dropped to her feet, and she collapsed in his arms. Relief gave way to her sanity, and she released a loud sob.

He held her and rubbed her back as she leaned into him.

"Pril?"

She pressed her face into his chest. The smell of leather, pine and horse surrounded her, and she inhaled slow even breaths using him as her leverage—strength.

"Pril?"

She tipped her head up.

His face solemn, he whispered, "It is Milosh."

She shook her head not wanting to believe what he'd said.

"It cannot be. He has Tsura, and she is fine like you said."

He held her away from him, and she witnessed the regret flicker in his eyes.

"Tsura is not here."

"But their things—they left everything here."

"Gypsy," he said giving her a shake, "Milosh is dead."

"Impossible."

Kade closed his eyes, and she wasn't prepared for his next words.

"He hangs from the tree to your left."

She stiffened. *No. No. No.* Fear crept up her spine. The forest walls spun around her. She hunched her shoulders forward and groaned. She couldn't contain the shock of what he'd just told her—of what he'd been trying to tell her. Every muscle in her body went numb, and she fought back the urge to scream. She felt his arms around her—strong and protective. She wanted nothing more than to lean into them, but instead she shook him off. She needed to see Milosh, to be sure.

She flew from Kade's embrace.

"Gypsy, wait."

He tried to stop her, but she had to see—had to know Milosh had left this earth.

She cried out as she ran toward her brother. His legs dangled three feet from the ground, a rope around his neck, his head tipped to the side at an awkward angle—eyes open. She grabbed a hold of his feet and pushed him up, holding his legs on top of her shoulders.

"Kade, Kade! Help him. Get him down. Help him," she cried.

"He's gone, Gypsy."

"No. No. No." She wrestled with Milosh's cold legs, trying desperately to push him up and bring life back within him. "Help him! Help him, damn it!"

She couldn't see for the tears in her eyes, and she didn't care. Her cheeks were drenched, but she refused to let him go to wipe them. She needed to hold Milosh to beg for his forgiveness—to hear him say the words. She had to know he still loved her.

"Please. Please help me," she wailed.

She struggled to stay on her feet and pressed up onto her toes to loosen the rope that hung from his neck. How could this have happened? Why had he hung himself? She couldn't comprehend, didn't understand, and the one thought passing through her mind was to tell him she was sorry…so very, very sorry.

She watched as Kade climbed the tree and sawed at the rope holding her brother. The full weight of Milosh came down upon her and buckled her knees. They both tumbled to the ground. She crawled to his side and cupped his face within her hands.

"Wake, Brother. Wake up."

She shook him.

Milosh's lips were blue, and his lifeless eyes stared up into the black sky.

"Bring me my bag. I need my wax and the charm by the fire. I need the charm!"

Kade placed the dagger he'd used to cut Milosh down back into the leather holder on his waist. "He's gone, sweetheart."

He placed a hand on her shoulder, and she shoved it off.

"No." She shook Milosh again. She rubbed her hands over his cheeks and into his long hair. "I can save him. I can work a spell. I can bring him back."

"No, Gypsy, you cannot."

"Leave me!" she screamed. "Go away. I will fix him. I will bring him back."

"It is too late."

"Lies." She placed all her anger, all her guilt into her next words. "You're nothing but a liar. Go from me!"

He crossed his arms.

She flew at him with helpless rage. Her body yearned to expel the emotions swirling within her. She shoved him.

He didn't budge.

"Damn you, Kade Walker." She shoved him again. "If we had been here yesterday my brother would be alive. I could've talked to him. Shown him I was sorry. Told him—begged him—anything. But you kept us from getting here on time. This is your fault."

He was silent while she pounded her fists into his hard chest.

Tears streaked her cheeks and fell from her chin. She was powerless to it all, not an ounce of what she did would matter. Alexandra had been murdered. Milosh was dead. Tsura was still missing, and no amount of praying could fix the past. She couldn't bring them back. She dug her fingers into her scalp and pulled on her hair. *I cannot bring them back.*

She fell onto her knees. Oh, how she'd tried. She'd prayed Alexandra had found peace. She apologized a thousand times over in the middle of the night, and she'd shed countless tears, but it didn't change a damn thing. It didn't make the hurt, or guilt go away. It was there when she'd risen and when she lay down to sleep, haunting her like the vile demon it was. She felt the claws dig into her spine. She fell forward, pressing her hands into the grass and moss on the ground.

Helplessness compressed her lungs, and she gasped. Each breath she took was like a knife to her back—a reminder of her betrayal—of her selfishness. She looked at Milosh, cold and still, and she reached out her hand to him. He was gone, and there would never be reconciliation. He'd never know how truly sorry she was. How each day she lived with her shame. He'd never know that after everything he'd done, the words he'd said and taking Tsura, she still loved him.

She crawled toward her brother, placing her head onto his chest, she wept.

"I am sorry, Brother. Please, please forgive me."

Kade watched with a heavy heart as she lay over her brother weeping. Her desolate sobs tugged at his soul causing his own eyes to water. Unable to survey the scene any longer, he left her to grieve.

He walked the campsite one more time. He searched for anything that would tell him who took the girl and why her uncle would hang himself. It didn't make sense. He frowned. Why would Milosh do himself in if he had the girl? What benefit would come of that? Pril's brother was taking Tsura to someone, he was sure of it, so why would he end his life before doing so?

He walked back to where Pril lay with Milosh and stood over them scanning the area with careful eyes. Something wasn't right. He examined the tree Milosh had hung from. It would be impossible for him to place the rope around his neck then throw it over the branch ten feet above and hoist himself up.

He bent over Milosh's body and inspected it for any signs of a struggle. He spotted the bruised and chafed skin around his wrists.

He'd been tied.

Kade went to Milosh's head where he ran his hands across the sides then to the back of the skull and felt the large bump.

"Your brother did not kill himself," he said.

Pril wiped her eyes and peered up at him.

"He has a lump the size of a mountain on the back of his head, and his wrists were bound. He did not die willingly. My guess is whoever killed your brother took Tsura."

"But why?"

"Only you know that answer."

"Why would I know such a thing?"

"Someone, other than Milosh and the Renoldis, wants your daughter."

She looked at her brother, and her lip trembled.

"Who is it?"

"I do not know."

"Bullshit."

She tipped her chin.

"Who hunts Tsura because of a curse?"

"I know of no such thing."

"Tsk, tsk, Gypsy. Your lies are catching up to you."

She shrugged.

He hooked his finger under her chin and forced her to face him.

"Before we left your clan you mentioned the curse."

Recognition flickered in her brown eyes.

"Ah there it is. You remember."

"The curse is a myth."

"I care nothing of the curse but those that hunt her."

She sighed, blowing the hair from her wet cheek.

"They are of three."

He nodded.

"Brothers."

"Who?"

"They call themselves Monroes."

He hid any reaction to the name and asked, "Are these people similar to the Renoldis?"

"No."

"What do they want?"

"I do not know."

"I say you do."

"I care not of your thoughts."

He studied her—poised with cold tears left on her cheeks, defiant yet broken at the same time. She didn't' make any sense. The child had something the Monroes, Renoldis and Milosh wanted, and she knew what it was. He regarded Milosh, dead between them, and without saying another word he walked away from her.

She held the truth from him, and he couldn't be angry with her for it. How could he expect her to be honest when he planned on stealing

Tsura? He was no better than her. In fact, he was worse. He'd abscond with the one thing that kept Pril alive for reasons he had no control over, and it would kill her. He flexed his hands.

He knew this and yet he couldn't seem to see past the threat that lay over his head, sinking him deeper and deeper with each day that passed.

Time was short, and he felt the pressure like a dozen horses trampling him. Where was the girl now, and who the hell had taken her? All he knew was one rider had been here but that didn't mean there weren't more waiting on the perimeter of the forest. He'd need to find the tracks and follow them. He peeked back at Pril. He should leave her here. She was becoming a distraction, one he didn't need. The boy had crept to her side and placed his head on her shoulder. Thoughts of leaving Pril left him.

He was responsible for them both whether he liked it or not. He wouldn't turn his back on those in need, and the boy needed him. Pril would get by without him, he knew that, but maybe it was possible that he needed her?

He shook his head. What in hell was the matter with him? He ran his hand through his long hair. He was to find the girl, steal her back from whoever took her and trade her for another. He must remain focused. Sam was counting on him.

CHAPTER FIFTEEN

Kade flexed his tired muscles. They'd been traveling for most of the day, and he wasn't about to stop until they reached the next town. His backside ached, and his right hip tingled from time to time, but he pressed on—he had to.

He tightened his grip on the reins. Fear picked away at his sanity. He was restless, and he didn't know how to calm his rigid nerves. The pressure built within him making even the simplest of conversations difficult. He was like a rabid dog, quiet, yet skittish. Lightning flashed in the distance, and he searched the grey clouds ahead. They were riding into a storm.

After they buried Milosh, he'd found the tracks and followed them southwest back toward the mountains. He knew it wasn't the Monroes, but was curious of the Renoldis and if they'd come across the clan on their travels. Pril hadn't given him any information and over the last two days. She hadn't spoken more than three words. Dark circles shadowed her eyes and contrasted with her pale complexion. She refused dinner last night and hardly touched the fish he'd caught this morning. He was growing concerned, and it pissed him off.

He'd always known who he was and what he stood for, but lately he wasn't sure anymore. He glanced at Pril beside him on Athos, the boy wrapped in her arms fast asleep. The kid didn't want to ride Milosh's horse, instead choosing to sit with her. With each day that passed the kid grew more and more affectionate toward her.

The wind picked up, blowing the hair from his face. Goliath shook his head and stepped backward. Grey clouds formed over the mountains, and he watched as they rolled toward them. He needed to find shelter.

"Make sure that horse is tied tight to your bridle," he said to Pril.

She turned mute eyes toward him and nodded.

They were in the middle of the field, tall stalks of yellow and green grass swaying in the wind. A few hundred yards to their right was a stand of trees. He surveyed the treacherous clouds again. Could they make it? The bluff wouldn't keep them dry, but instead defend them against the wind, and right now that's all he could find.

"Are you ready to ride, Gypsy?"

She nodded, and he wanted to shout at her to say something but as the wind pushed him forward in his saddle, he decided against it. He walked Goliath to stand beside her and without warning pulled the boy from her lap and onto his horse.

Her mouth gaped open, and fire shot from her eyes. He waited, but she remained silent. He shook his head, bit down hard, and nudged Goliath's sides with his boots. The horse took off toward the trees. The boy woke and clung to Kade's shirt, his fingernails digging into his skin. There was no time for comfort; the clouds were closing in on them. A loud clap of thunder echoed across the land, and the boy jumped.

He stole a quick peek at Pril to see if she still followed and saw the flash of red hair whipping in the wind. Lightning crackled, and he leaned forward, urging Goliath to go faster. He felt the first few drops, a pleasant kiss to his cheeks before the clouds opened up, soaking them from head to toe.

The trees came closer as the horses raced toward the bluff. The wind picked up, howling across the prairies. He shivered and squinted against the rain. He couldn't see a damn thing and hoped to hell Goliath would lead them to the trees. The boy cried into his chest, frightened of the storm, and he hugged him closer. The rain pelted his face, stinging with each drop. Water ran down his cheeks and dripped from his chin.

They flew into the forest, the downpour not as torrential under the cover of the large trees. The leaves rustled, the tops of the trees bent back and forth dancing in the wind. The scent of wet grass, soggy moss-covered ground, and damp bark filled his nostrils. The earth had been cleansed. He loved the smell of rain. He thought of the sea, and his chest tightened. The rain bounced from the leaves and onto their heads.

He led Goliath further into the bush until they came to three pine trees standing close together. Their bulky needled branches melded with one another and offered shelter. He dismounted before removing the boy from Goliath's back. The lad's teeth chattered, and his little body shook. He pulled his blanket from the horse's back, wet on one side; he had nothing else and offered it to the child.

Pril's hair hung sopping wet down her back as she tied Athos' reins around the trunk of a tree. She turned toward Kade, her blouse soaked through to her skin exposing her corset and the tops of her rounded breasts beneath it. He swallowed unable to turn from the sight of her.

"Uh, Gypsy? Cover yourself...please."

She peered at him, and he knew she had no idea why he'd asked such a thing. Although soaked through the temperature was warm.

He couldn't take it anymore. Her breasts begged for his attention, and he wanted nothing more than to give it to them. He yanked his coat from the back of her horse and tossed it at her.

"Cover yourself, damn it."

She glanced down and gasped when she saw what he was suggesting. She crossed her arms over her chest.

"The coat would do better."

He searched the ground for dry kindling for a fire, desperate to put some space between him and Pril's breasts. It'd been way too long since he'd been with a woman, and this was a reminder of how much he missed it.

He tossed the damp bits of wood onto the ground and pulled his flint and steel from his pocket. He ran the metal rock along the steel. No spark. Both were wet. He dried them on his pant leg before trying again. The rock still wouldn't spark.

"Damn."

"Use this," she said, standing over him.

He took the small magnify glass and thought of Sam. He used one to read and always carried it in his front pocket. He closed his eyes and inhaled.

"The glass might work if the sun was out, but it's covered by the clouds." He handed the glass piece back to her.

He slumped down onto the wet ground and placed his head into his hands. Thoughts of Sam, the girl and how the hell he was going to make things right filled his mind.

"Mother earth dry thy land and lend heat to this wood to warm our hands."

The wood crackled and sparked.

He looked up to see smoke coming from the pile of wood he'd placed beside him.

"What in hell?"

She turned and went back to the boy, grabbed his hand and brought him to the fire. He watched as she sat down beside the child and wrapped the blanket back around him.

"How did you do that?"

She met his eyes with her own, and he saw the sorrow within them. He knew how much she'd suffered over the death of her brother and missing child, and for the first time since he'd met her he inhaled her grief. He let her misery pour into him—into the parts he'd kept hidden and untouched—into his soul.

"A spell," she whispered.

He frowned. He didn't believe in such things.

"I am the second daughter to Imelda the great enchantress."

He'd heard of enchanters and sorcerers. On his many years at sea he'd never witnessed such a person and figured it was nothing but a myth and still did.

"My mother was a powerful Chuvani."

"What does that mean?"

"It is our people's queen. She has the ability to do many things."

"Light fires?"

She nodded.

"My mother used her magick for good. She sampled the earth to help heal the sick, mend a wound, or aid a woman in labor, but her talents did not end there."

"Your mother was a midwife."

"No, she was a Chuvani."

"To your people I suppose, but to mine she was a midwife."

"My mother did more than deliver babies. She had what my people call seeing dreams."

"Is this like your ability to read palms?"

She disregarded him and went on. "She'd throw a beam, harming the most powerful of men."

"Interesting. A beam you say?"

There was no way any of what she said was true, yet she'd started the fire with a few words, or so it seemed. He didn't actually see it.

"Must you poke fun at everything I say?"

"When you're speaking of beams and magick then, yes."

"You saw me light the fire."

"I did not actually see you." Denial was his only defense at what he refused to believe.

"My mother taught me to count the spells, performing the most difficult ones by the light of a round moon."

"So you do all the things your mother could?"

"No, I am not my mother's first born."

"Galius can?"

She shook her head.

"The magick lies within the daughters, and the first born receives her mother's gifts."

"So you have a sister?"

"I did," she whispered, and her eyes clouded.

He waited wanting to hear more of her past.

"My sister, Vadoma, was not like my mother." She played with her skirt. "I loved her very much, but I could not save her just as I could not save Milosh. She was killed nigh on four years back."

A single tear ran down her cheek, and his fingers itched to wipe it.

"Your brother's death was not your fault."

"It was."

"You did not murder him."

"Had I placed the protection spell on all the children his daughter would've lived, and we would not be here. I did not have enough of Vadoma's blessed oil...I only had the amount to perform one spell. I used it for Tsura."

"You protected your own child. I see no harm in that."

She hung her head as more tears fell from her eyes.

"That night my niece was murdered."

He understood her regret. He saw it in the way her shoulders hunched forward, how her eyes bled tears, and her voice trembled. He wished there was something he could do.

"I refused to look into my brother's eyes. I could not allow myself to see the anguish he and his wife felt. I pushed it all away. I...I was a coward." She wiped her cheek. "I should've dropped to my knees and begged their forgiveness, but instead I stayed within my vardo away from the agony and pain—away from Milosh."

"Pril..." He didn't know what to say. He'd never had a brother or a sister it had always been him and Sam.

She met his gaze with her own tortured depths.

"Have you ever experienced a love so powerful you'd do anything to save it, even if it meant you had to die?"

He thought of Sam and the journey he'd been on for the past six months. He cared for the man who raised him more than any person he'd ever met, and yes he'd die for him, but something told him this was not the kind of love she was referring to.

"I have not."

She glanced at the boy snuggled into her side, and the corner of her mouth lifted. "I would die for Tsura."

He knew she would, had seen the fight in her many times since they'd left her clan, and he wished he could help her. He tore his gaze from hers and stared into the trees around them. What did the Monroes want with the girl? He debated whether to ask Pril again, but figured she wouldn't tell him, or even if she knew the answer.

He leaned against the tree. The fire, now larger than before, was warm. He listened as she yawned and had to stifle one of his own. Grief exhausted her, and she propped herself against the child. The two supported one another. A yearning he'd never felt before settled over him. There was no one special in his life, no wife and no children, only Sam. He was all Kade had, and without his guidance and love, he would never have made it past his adolescent years. He'd do anything to keep him safe and out of harm's way.

The last message he'd received had been a threat, and he was anxious to get to the next town to make sure Sam was okay.

He prayed the old man was still alive. He'd been ill for a long time, suffering from a heart condition no doctor understood. Kade had taken him to every physician in England, and none had answers as to why Sam's body couldn't keep up the way it used to. No one could explain the sudden onset of tremors Sam had two or three times a week, leaving him exhausted and frail.

The last time he'd seen him was when he docked the S.S.W in Jamestown. Sam hadn't gotten out of bed the whole month long trip from England. Crowley, the ship's doctor, had tended to him keeping a watchful eye on his symptoms. Two days later Sam had vanished from the hospital, and Kade had searched everywhere for him. A week passed, and he figured Sam for dead. Drunk in one of the brothels on the wharf, he'd been approached by Silas Monroe.

He'd remember that night for the rest of his life. The plantation owner's devious smile, his ruthless eyes and prominent chin cast Kade into a whirlwind of trouble and forced him to do the unthinkable.

Pril and the boy were cuddled into one another, and he wished there was another way. He expelled a ragged sigh. He'd take her daughter, forced beyond his own will—a double-edged sword with both ends pointing toward him. When he swapped the one for the other, no amount of alcohol would numb his deception and guilt. He'd come out the victor, but forever he'd be the loser.

CHAPTER SIXTEEN

Pril woke with a start. She opened her eyes and gasped. The butt end of a musket pressed into her cheek, squishing her face. The leader of the Renoldi clan stood over her.

"Hello, Pias," she said.

She shoved the gun from her, reached for the boy and pulled him close. She glanced at her quiver a few feet to her right.

"What the bloody hell is going on?" Kade grumbled from across the fire.

"Nice to see you again, Niece," Pias said and motioned with his gun for her to stand.

Pias married her mother's sister, but she refused to see him as anything other than a conniving bastard. She positioned herself in front of her bow and quiver, covering it with her skirt.

Bavol and Cato, Pias's guards pulled Kade to his feet, each holding onto one of his arms. She held the boy tight to her and watched as Kade struggled against their grips. Together the men were stronger and held him still.

"Cease, Mr. Walker, or I will be forced to make it so," Pias growled.

Kade spat onto the ground. "Go to hell."

Pias laughed and walked toward Kade. He threw the handle of his musket into Kade's stomach once, twice, and Pril thought he'd hit him a third time, but he stopped and turned toward her.

"Tell your friend to stand down, or I will kill him."

She knew he would. Her family had been Renoldis for many years until Vadoma's curse. Pias had been their leader and challenged Vadoma for all her wrongdoings. He ruled his people with a strong hand.

"Kade, please do as he says."

"Are you well, Gypsy?" he asked his eyes searched her face.

"I am." She prayed he would give her a distraction so she could grab her bow.

He relaxed, but his stature didn't last long. He flung his arms out, tossing Bavol to the ground and turned in time to connect his fist with Cato's chin. He lunged, and jumping on top of the Renoldi, he drove his fists into Cato's sides and face.

She leaped for the bow, and wasting no time she loaded the arrow. On her knees she twisted ready to fire when it was knocked from her hand by Pias. He threw his boot into her ribs, and she fell to the ground. Her ribs were still mending, and she grit her teeth together as the bone ached.

Pias went to the trees and tossed the bow among them, leaving the quiver where it was.

She went to the boy. Her side ached but it was the least of her worries. Kade was still on top of Cato, and Bavol had jumped onto his back. She cringed at the sound of flesh pounding on flesh. The thud of knuckles as they crunched against bone sickened her. She grabbed the boy's shoulders and turned him toward her.

"You must run," she whispered.

He shook his head.

He'd understood her. He knew what she'd said. He peered up at her, onyx circles surrounded by the brightest shade of brown she'd ever seen. He'd been playing her and Kade all along. A loud crack spun her around in time to see Pias drive the end of his gun into Kade's head knocking him out.

"Tie his hands and then gather their things," Pias said.

"What do you want?" she asked.

"To fetch you, my dear."

She crossed her arms.

"I am in need of counsel with you." He glanced at Kade, unconscious on the ground. "And your friend."

"Did you kill Milosh?" She needed to know if the clan leader had hung her brother.

"Of course not."

"I do not believe you."

"I do not care." He went to her and ran the tip of his finger down the side of her face. "I never liked Milosh, but kill him I did not."

"Do you know who did?"

Pias gazed at her, and the corner of his mouth lifted before he turned and walked toward his horse.

"Let us have council within the clan walls."

"No."

"No?"

"We can speak here." She stood tall, not willing to be taken by her enemy.

"I believe it is I who gives the orders, hmmm?" He nodded toward Bavol The other man hoisted Kade over his shoulder and tossed him onto Goliath, his feet and head dangling over either side.

"Come, Pril of the Peddlers." He held out his hand.

She didn't trust him and rightly so. He was a devious devil by nature. She refused to be taken by him and his men.

"No," she said again.

Cato and Bavol mounted their horses and waited for Pias's direction.

"Where did the boy come from?" he asked, acknowledging the child for the first time since they'd arrived.

"He is a slave. We came upon him in one of the villages we passed through."

Pias went to the child. He looked him up and down before he reached out to flip his long black hair with his finger. The boy flinched and cowered into Pril's side.

"Leave him be, Pias."

He turned his attention toward her and smiled. His long features curved upward making his face appear lopsided.

"You are very demanding for someone who has been in hiding for the last four years."

"And you, Pias, haven't changed a bit. You are still the same coward I used to know."

He dropped his head back and laughed, a low devious sound. His head snapped up, and the back of his hand shot out, catching the side of her face.

Pain shot across her cheek, and she dropped her head. His ring had caught her lip, ripping the skin. The flesh pulsated, but she refused to wipe the blood as it seeped from the wound. Determined to stay put, and not be taken by the ruthless bastard, she lifted narrowed eyes toward him wishing she had the power within her to kill him.

"You are not Vadoma," he said reading her mind.

"You are lucky I am not."

"Hmmm."

"What is it you want, Pias?"

"If I remember correctly you've been blessed with the counting of spells."

She didn't answer.

"Amara and Emine have been blessed with a similar gift."

She remembered Pias's daughters—her cousins. Both had been

given the ability to cast spells, a gift from their mother who could do the same. It was the Chuvani that held the most magick. The lineage lay within Pril's mother Imelda and passed through her onto Vadoma and so on to Tsura. Pril remained the same, blessed with the magick of a spell, and even then she was limited.

"Get on your horse, and take the brat with you."

"No," she growled.

"I am growing tired of your insistence to stay…I will not ask you again."

"I am not leaving."

His hand was quick, a snake attacking its prey. He grabbed her around the throat and walked her backward into the tree.

"Do not test me any longer," he yelled as spittle spewed from his lips onto her face.

The trunk of the tree pressed into her back. The uneven wood pushed through her thin blouse and into her skin. Pias squeezed the muscles on her neck together, cutting off her air. She gasped. Her mouth worked as she tried frantically to draw in air. Black dots flashed before her, and she searched for the boy. Cato held him upside down in the air. The boy cried out, kicking his leg and arms in the air trying to fight off the bigger man.

She'd never forgive herself if something happened to him. With no other choice she nodded her co-operation. Pias released her, and she fell to the ground coughing. On her knees, she wheezed and gasped for air as she strained to inflate her lungs. Her throat ached, and she rubbed her palm across the burning flesh.

He grabbed her arm and dragged her toward Athos, shoving her into the animal.

"Get on your horse."

She knocked Pias's arm from her and faced Cato. "I will kill you for touching that child," she hissed.

The other man laughed, showing rotten teeth, and she shuddered.

Pias nudged her.

She spun and spat into his face. Her spittle dribbled from his lip and chin. Not prepared for his reaction, she didn't shield herself when he brought his fist up and slammed it into the side of her face. She blinked, her vision blurred, the earth spun, the trees melded together, and she turned toward Kade and the boy before she passed out.

Kade opened his eyes and squinted against the dull ache at the back of his head. His hands and feet were tied to a chair made of woven branches. He inspected the elaborate detail. He'd never seen anything like it and presumed the gypsy clan had made them. He pulled on the twine that bound him to the chair. The wood whined, but did not move.

He clenched his jaw and scanned the area. His chair had been propped in between two log structures. All around him were wagons, a few small homes, and behind those were tall Oaks, Pine and Elm trees. The Renoldi quarters were intimidating. The massive trees acted as a wall and secluded the gypsy camp from any intruders. It was a fortress. He searched the forest around them and wasn't surprised when he saw men on small platforms high up in the trees surrounding the village.

Torches burned lighting the night, and he saw the fire in the center of the camp. His dagger gone, he had no way to protect himself. There was no sign of Pril or the boy, and he wondered what the gypsies had done with them.

He watched as three men, the same ones who'd attacked them earlier, walked toward him. The Renoldi leader, Pias was in the middle. He wanted to smash the gypsy's face in, ambushed and tied in the middle of nowhere would be his first reason, the knock to the head the second.

"Mr. Walker, we've been waiting for you to wake," Pias said as they came closer.

He yanked on the twine, cringing when the rope sliced through the skin on his wrist.

"You will not break free. It is the strongest rope ever made."

"What do you want?"

"To talk with you of course."

"Bullshit. Where are Pril and the boy?"

"They are fine."

"Where are they?"

"That is no concern of yours."

As he struggled against the rope, the desire to run his boot into Pias's face overwhelmed him.

"Tell me," he growled.

"Shall we play a game then?"

"I do not play games with scheming bastards. Where the hell are Pril and the boy?"

"I will bring you to my niece and the slave if you answer my questions."

He wasn't sure he could trust him, but with no other choice, he nodded.

"Very good." Pias smiled. His black hair hung in uneven lengths around his high cheekbones and wide mouth.

"What do you want to know?"

"Why are you with Pril?"

"To help find her child."

"The girl?"

He didn't answer. Pril, and her brothers, had dressed the girls as boys, and he didn't know if Pias was aware of their deception.

"You've traveled with her to search for the girl is that correct?"

He remained silent.

Pias's eyes lit, and he snickered.

"Do you think me not wise enough to know the child is a girl?"

He flexed his jaw.

"Mr. Walker, I am ten times smarter than you give me credit for."

"Good for you."

"You have no other reason as to why you've helped her?"

"No. I do not." He met the leader's green eyes and glared.

Pias motioned to Cato, the wide shouldered man to his left. The bruises on his face were still bright and swollen from Kade's fists.

Cato handed Pias a piece of rolled up cloth.

"I will ask you one more time. Why are you with Pril?"

"And I believe I've answered your question already."

"Hmmm."

Kade watched as Pias very carefully unraveled the cloth to reveal a finger. Cut at the first knuckle, the limb was swollen and blue. He lifted the finger to show Kade. A sapphire ring was attached to it and spotted with blood.

He bent forward, the rope pressed into his chest, and bile climbed the length to his throat. He tasted the vomit on his tongue and spat. He wasn't prepared—hadn't even thought the clan leader would have such a thing.

He groaned.

The anguish, torment and guilt rushed through him, depleting his strength. He blinked back tears. His soul cried out, burning his chest and branding his heart. He hung his head and closed his eyes. *Sam.* It was Sam's ring.

"Where did you get it?" he growled, every muscle in his body tense.

"I believe you know the answer."

"I do not, and I will only ask you one more time. Where did you find the finger?"

Pias gave a dramatic sigh.

"We stumbled upon a slave three days ago. What was his name?"

"You bastard."

"Right." Pias snapped his fingers. "It was Malachi, and he was looking for you, Mr. Walker."

Kade shook the chair. Sam needed him, and because he'd wasted too much time, his best friend had suffered. Misery compressed his chest, and with each beat of his heart the pain intensified. He needed to see Sam—to save him. Girl or no girl, he was going to Jamestown. He'd kill Silas Monroe for what he'd done.

"Where is the slave?" he asked through clenched teeth.

"Dead of course." Pias wrapped the finger back up and handed it to Cato.

"Why would you kill him?"

"Because I was asked to."

"By whom?"

"It does not matter."

"I say it does." He was going to kill Pias for holding him here, but more importantly for killing the slave before he could talk with him and ask if he knew how Sam was.

"Very well, if you insist. Silas Monroe ordered the slave's death."

Kade's head snapped up, and he tried to stand but the chair wouldn't allow it. He used all his strength to pull on the twine around his wrists and ankles until his blood ran from the cuts there. His chest pumped with each breath he took, and he squeezed his hands into tight fists.

"You are acquainted with Silas?" Pias asked.

Kade growled. The Renoldi's must be involved with the Monroes for Pias to know of the plantation owner, but why?

"What does Silas offer you in return for such a large favor?"

"Why protection of course."

It all made sense now. Silas had been sending men to find the girl for four years, and Kade knew when he'd met Pril he wasn't the only one out there who searched for the child. He hadn't thought the Renoldis would be involved with the Monroes. The gypsy clan had been offered a deal they couldn't refuse; their children's safety for cooperation when Silas needed it.

"You're lower than a snake, Pias."

"And why is that?"

"You'd help the Monroes by betraying one of your own."

"My niece is not of us any longer. She is one of the Peddlers. They are outcasts. The child is all I seek. She holds a sense of greatness only Pril can understand."

"You want the girl, too."

"Of course."

"Why?"

Pias leaned toward him, and his eyes searched Kade's face. "You do not know?"

"Know what?"

"This has become most interesting. Tell me again, Mr. Walker, what is the reason you are hunting the child?"

He sighed. It didn't matter if he told Pias the truth. All that mattered was getting the hell out of here and finding Sam.

"Silas holds my friend."

"Friend?"

"The finger belongs to him."

"I see. Tsk, tsk. You are in quite a dilemma, Mr. Walker. One life for another?"

He frowned.

"You are aware that Silas will kill the girl, are you not?"

He wasn't. The thought hadn't crossed his mind. He'd never had the chance to ask. His sole purpose for finding Tsura was to free Sam and nothing more. Silas hadn't divulged what he'd do with the girl when he got her, or why he wanted her in the first place, and Kade hadn't inquired.

"Why would he kill her?"

"The blood curse."

The curse Pril brushed off as a myth. She'd never said what it was, and so he asked, "What blood curse is that?"

"Do you know nothing of the woman you are traveling with?"

"I know enough."

"Yes, so it seems."

"What curse?"

"Do you believe in magick, Mr. Walker?"

He thought of Pril and how she'd started the fire. He remembered their conversation afterward, of her mother and sister, but did he believe in something he could not see?

"I do not consider such nonsense," he replied.

"Now, that is a shame. If you do not believe in magick then why are you here?"

"What do you want with the child?"

"I seek nothing but peace."

"You will hand her to the Monroes?"

Pias smiled and without another word turned and walked away. Bavol and Cato followed.

"You bastard!" he yelled after them. "You filthy bloody bastard."

He had to escape. He needed to find Pril and the boy. Something told him Pias knew where Tsura was, and time had stretched enough. The Renoldi leader had Tsura, and Kade wasn't sure if he'd sent her to Silas or not, but he was determined to find out.

CHAPTER SEVENTEEN

Silas buttoned his pants and reached for his waistcoat. The barn reeked of sweat, horses and the honeyed scent of hay. The slave cowered near the short fence that held his horse. Her skirt no longer up around her waist, sat back at her ankles, stained with blood and dirt.

He'd taken his pleasure with Malachi's wife. The whore didn't even fight him, and he wondered if she liked it as much as he did. The scratches and bite marks on her back and neck proved how rough he'd been, but he enjoyed it that way. Torture was what made him hard. He loved being in control, relished the thought of inflicting pain and had often come early when they cried out from his rough hands upon them.

He waved a hand to her and watched delighted as she fled the confines of the barn, shame swimming within her black eyes. He'd have her again, and when she realized her husband wasn't coming back, he'd have to kill her, too. He shrugged. Just one less slave to feed. There were more to be had. They arrived every month from the Africas, and he had his pick of the lot. He'd find another.

He glanced in the direction of the mansion and thought of Beth. He couldn't force himself on her, using his hands in the manner he'd done with the slaves. Intercourse with Beth was slow and tedious. She was a delicate flower. He frowned at the thought. She'd been a rose with thorns that, as of late, withheld any form of intimacy from him.

He didn't care. He'd taken what he wanted from the slaves, showing them he was in charge, and he held no remorse over his actions. He owned Malachi's wife and all the other damn heathens on his plantation.

He frowned.

To hell with Beth and her foolish emotions! What of his? She did not care what he'd gone through each time they buried a child. There was no thought into how he dealt with the devastating situation. She couldn't be bothered. He'd lost sleep, lying awake for countless nights desperate for an answer from the men he'd sent in search of the child. Beth yearned for a resolution to their problem, for the curse to be broken, and still he'd failed her. She'd grown cold, distant, and he hated her for it. He tried to understand her emotions. He bought her gifts—gave her anything she wanted, but it was all for naught. She'd thrown them back in his face.

He drank more. Frequented the slaves and brothels often, and kept a safe distance from her all in the hopes that she'd come around, but she remained the same. Her indifference toward him, and everything he did, turned him black with rage. He'd caught himself many times from knocking her into the wall.

He looked upon her with condensation, with vile and utter disgust. Love? He had none for her. Instead he was filled with bitterness, revulsion and fury when he thought of his wife.

He straightened his wig, flipping the long curls behind his shoulders and walked toward the fields. He wanted to make sure the schedule would be met for this year's tobacco crop. He glanced at his home and reminded himself to pay a visit to the man lying on a dilapidated cot below the stairs.

The tobacco was at his knee, a sign that weekly cultivation would be required. He'd need to assemble Isaiah and give orders for the slaves to till the plants once a week to keep weeds and cutworms from killing the leaves.

He met Jude halfway to the main house.

"We need to speak," Jude murmured.

Silas nodded, and they continued further into the field away from any eyes and ears.

"What is it?" he asked when they stopped.

Jude pulled a folded piece of paper from his pocket and handed it to him.

Silas ripped open the letter and read the words two times before he spat onto the ground.

"He will die for this."

His chest burned, and his flesh lit with fire as rage boiled within him. He gripped the letter tight in his hand.

"What will you have me do?" Jude asked.

He clenched his jaw to remain from spewing profanities.

"Have one of the slaves give it to him. He must not know we've read it."

Jude nodded.

"We will follow him."

He'd known all along Hiram was up to something, and damn it he'd been right. He watched as Jude walked toward the slaves' quarters on the west side of the field. He was sickened at his brother's betrayal and could think of nothing else but to end his life. He gazed at his home. He no longer needed the merchant or the baggage in the cellar, and what he didn't need he got rid of.

CHAPTER EIGHTEEN

Pril opened her eyes. A thick rope wrapped around her chest, through the back of the chair and tied her to the seat. Her hands and feet were bound together. She kicked her legs out, trying to wiggle beneath the rope. She struggled against the constricted twine, the lower she inched the harder it was for her to breath, and she squirmed back up exhausted.

She scanned the walls surrounding her. Heat radiated from the large fire in the hearth, and she shivered. The fire was a welcome sight, and the warmth pushed the chill away from her tired bones. Large logs, one on top of the other, formed the small cabin. Two cauldrons sat near the hearth, another three lined the wall across from it. A wooden table with one chair stood in the middle of the room.

She wasn't surprised to see the glass jars of herbs, wax, roots and oils lined on four shelves behind the table. Her cousins used them for spells. A plant, she suspected to be rosemary, sat on the long counter directly under the shelves. It was here the Renoldis made their balms.

She struggled against the rope again but could not break free. Defeated, her body sagged into the chair when she saw the boy on the floor ten feet to her left. A worn grey blanket was thrown over his body. All she could see were his hands tethered with a rope and tied to a hook on the wall. He lay unmoving, and her heart sprinted as panic set in.

Was he okay? Had Pias and his men hurt him somehow? Did he lay beneath the ragged blanket bleeding, or worse, dead?

"Boy," she whispered.

He didn't move.

"Boy."

Silence.

She wrestled with the chair, pushing it back onto its hind legs. The wood moaned and creaked. She had to get free. She planted her feet on the ground and pressed her back into the wood, using all the strength she had left to force the back of the chair to break. The timber wouldn't budge, and she was too weak to do anymore. She glanced at the boy again. He needed her.

"Damn it," she ground through clenched teeth. "Boy!"

The child still did not move, and her heart sunk. She squeezed her eyes shut praying he was okay, and soon they'd be free. *Please let him live.*

The door opened, bringing with it a nip of evening air, and she shivered. She scowled when Pias walked into the room.

"Ah my lovely Pril. You've woken."

He reached out his hand and took her bound ones in his own.

"Did you hurt the boy?"

He glanced back at the child lying on the floor. "Now why would I do such a thing? He merely sleeps."

She all but screamed for the child to wake, and he never moved. He was not sleeping.

"He will not wake."

"Interesting." Pias walked toward the boy and nudged him with his boot. "Hmmmm."

The child remained the same.

He threw off the blanket, and she strained in the chair to see around him. The boy's chest rose and fell in even cadence, a sign he was at rest, but why wouldn't he wake?

"He will rise soon enough," Pias said and turned toward her.

She peered at the child and prayed the Renoldi was right.

"What do you want, Pias?"

"To speak with you."

"Then speak. I've grown tired of your games."

He clapped his hands together, and his jagged face beamed.

"Wonderful. Tell me, how have you been?"

She glared at him. Pias didn't care about her well-being. He never had. Her uncle had always been envious of Vadoma's gifts. Before her aunt passed, he tried many times to see the spell book, but Vodama refused. He was jealous, driven by greed for the powers Pril's mother had passed on to Vadoma and not onto his own wife and daughters. He wanted something from her, and she was determined to find out what it was.

"You know how I've been. What is it you want?"

"Must you be so pushy? I am simply trying to speak with you about the past. Ask after my niece."

"You said nothing of the past. What is it you want to know?"

His green eyes narrowed, and his full lips thinned.

"Now that you've asked, where might the book be, hmmm?"

"What book?"

"Why Vadoma's book of course."

Pias knew the book would be of no use to him without the talisman. He'd not be able to count the spells if he didn't have it. So why did he care now? The pendant had been lost.

"It is destroyed."

His eyes went round, and he tapped his forefinger on his chin.

"When your clan attacked us. The book was in my vardo, and it burned to the ground."

"Oh my, that is a shame."

"What do you want with the book? You cannot count the spells inside. You do not have the gift."

Pias sighed.

"Yes, so you are right, my dear."

She narrowed her eyes.

"One needs a certain pendant to make the spells come to light, correct?"

Her heart pumped vigorously within her chest, and the room spun. With the pendant she could've broken the blood curse. The pendant held magick all on its own, but with the book any female with the gift of counting spells would be unstoppable, and that included Pias's daughters.

"You're out of luck, the book is gone."

"So it seems."

She smirked, hoping he'd release her and the boy.

"Have you found Vadoma's child?"

She glanced at him, unsure what he was up to. The leader liked to toy with his victims, and she waited.

"Tsura, that is her name correct?"

She nodded.

"You have not found her?"

"No."

"Hmmmm."

"Pias…" she seethed. "What have you done?"

He flashed his white teeth in a brilliant smile.

"A father must try his best to please his children."

"You will reap what you bind, Pias."

"Indeed."

"I am not afraid of you."

"You are not frightened?"

She shook her head.

"What a shame. What a shame indeed."

"I know that without the book you are worthless."

He walked over to a wooden chest beside the unconscious boy and opened it. He reached inside.

"Is this the book you speak of?"

She blinked. *No.* He had her mother's book. The very one she'd thought burned in the fire. Anger hardened all the softness on her face, and she dug her nails into the wooden chair.

"The book belongs to me," she growled.

"Not any longer."

"It is to stay within my family."

Pias flipped the book and studied the outside of it.

"I see no inscription from the great enchantress to make it so." He sighed. "Therefore, my dear niece, *you* are the one out of luck."

"You wretch—ingrate!" She slammed her body into the back of the chair, bringing the front legs off of the ground. "You are worthless without the pendant."

"Right you are." He sat on the trunk, the book cradled within his slender hands.

Silence filled the room. She peeked at the boy, lifeless and still. She needed to get to him, steal the book back, find Kade and resume her search for Tsura.

"Let us go, Pias. You have no need to hold us here. You're after the pendant, and I can assure you it is long gone."

"Can you?"

"Yes. Please let us go. I need to find my daughter."

"Have you searched far?"

She scowled. *Why is he asking me these questions?*

"How do you know the child is not right under your very nose, hmmm?"

Heat resonated from her toes all the way to her head. She gnashed her back teeth together. "Do you know where Tsura is?"

"I may."

"Damn it, Pias, where is she?"

"Safe." He stood and went to her, the book still in his hands.

"What do you mean?"

"I need the child as much as you do, dear Pril."

"You touch one hair on my daughter's head, and I will kill you."

"Oh, I will not harm her, but I cannot be sure they won't." He shrugged. "I shant worry over it."

"Why?" She leaned into the rope around her chest, the twine indenting her skin. "Why are you doing this?"

He leaned in close, and she could smell the deceit on his breath. He stank of arrogance, greed and lust for the power he did not have.

"Why, for the talisman."

"No one has the pendant. It is lost—gone forever," she shouted shaking the chair on the verge of insanity.

"Ah, that is where you are wrong. He has the talisman, and we shall trade."

"Who has the pendant?"

"Hmmm?"

"Who has the pendant?"

"It does not matter."

"Answer me damn it!" Tears filled her eyes, and she blinked releasing them to fall onto her cheeks. "Whom are you giving Tsura to?"

"Now, now, Niece, do not cry." He wiped a tear from under her eye.

"Get your filthy hands off of me you bastard."

He bent and gazed at her. No emotion played out within the green pits. Instead, they were empty, emotionless. She shuddered seeing the lack of feeling there. He came closer, and she pressed the back of her head into the chair.

His lips almost touched hers when he whispered, "My dear sweet Pril."

His tongue slid along her lips. Her stomach revolted, and she twisted away from him.

"Go to hell."

"Tsk tsk. So vile for such a pretty thing." He tipped his head to the side.

"You will bleed for this."

"Nonsense. I will succeed, and you my dear…will not."

She strained against the twine, pulling her limbs as far as she could until the skin tore. She'd kill him for this. She tugged again. The rope still tight, she shrieked—gasping, her chest inflated, and her throat ached. She hung her head. Imprisoned by the blasted ropes and the bastard in front of her.

"Do not worry so."

"Give me my daughter," she pleaded.

"Ah, I do love to see you beg."

"I will do anything, Pias. Please, please hand me Tsura."

He considered her. Minutes passed, and she prayed he'd changed, that he wasn't the merciless man she'd known.

He shook his head and smiled.

"None of this will matter by tomorrow."

"And why is that."

"Hmmm?"

"Why will none of this matter?"

"Because, my sweet girl, you will be dead." He patted her head. With the book tucked under his arm, he walked toward the door.

"Noooooo," she screamed. "Pias, you rotten bastard. Come back. Please, please! I will do anything you ask. I will teach your daughters. Do not take Tsura. Please, I beg of you."

He stopped and turned toward her. "Tsk. Tsk. So sad."

He closed the door behind him and on any hope Pril may have had of finding Tsura.

She cried out. Her flesh burned, and she rubbed her wrists against the twine, feeling the pain bite into the open wounds. She inhaled the anguish and misery into her soul. The emotions festered, too much for her to take. Sorrow filled her, and she gasped, drowning in her own despair. Nothing mattered anymore—not life, not death and not survival. Tsura was gone. Pias had won. She dropped her head and let the tears wash her face.

Her body trembled with each inhale. She fought the pain, trying to remain strong. Anger and resentment covered her, and she couldn't breath—smothered by her own denial—by her own shame. She wheezed, her throat hurt, her chest compressed—her body ached. She'd been beaten by her own cause, by her own hand. Pias had betrayed her, toying with her emotions, and she allowed it. *Tsura.* How she yearned to see her once more. She was to protect her. She was expected to defend her from any harm, and she'd failed. She sniffled. Pias had played her for a fool, and now her daughter would suffer for it.

She glanced at the boy. He'd not woken or even moved from the awkward position. There was something wrong. She skimmed the herbs on the shelf and the plant on the counter again. What was she missing? The plant looked different, when it struck her. The boy had been poisoned. She squinted to try and make out the leaves on the shrub. She assumed it'd been rosemary, a common plant used by the gypsies for its scent, brewed in a tea for stomach ailments and burned to cast off infection. When she looked closer she realized it wasn't rosemary at all.

She gasped. Small green berries flowered on the plant known as Witch's berry. It was used for many things but mixed in the right amounts could cause paralysis, slurred speech, unconsciousness and even death. Pias had given it to the boy, but why?

Tsura was a Chuvani. Pias feared her as he'd feared Vadoma. She looked at the boy again. How would Pias get Tsura to trust him enough to travel? The answer rang in her ears. He'd use the Witch's berry to make it so.

CHAPTER NINETEEN

Pril walked along the windy rooted path littered with twigs and rocks. Her hands tied together hung at her back and swung with each stride she took. Cato walked behind her and held the rope attached to her hands and feet. The Renoldi left no slack in the twine, and if she stepped too soon, he'd jerk her backward. Last time he nearly pulled her shoulder from the socket. She'd not make the same mistake twice.

The boy stumbled in front of her, his legs still weak from the hours of sleep. His steps were slow and clumsy, a sign he was still feeling the effects of the Witch's berry. She called out to him. He did not answer. The child walked alone, no guard held his rope. The boy was not a threat as he was still intoxicated from the berry he'd been fed.

She stepped closer to the boy and was wrenched back. The motion pulled her shoulders toward one another and curved her spine. She lost her footing and stumbled to the left. She tried to steady herself, but with her hands and feet tied together the act was useless. Her ankle bent, the joint rolled onto the ground, and she bit back a scream from the shock as the pain traveled up her leg.

She leaned her hip against the trunk of a tree and inhaled, trying to relax. The ankle pulsed, the ache deep within the bone, and she could feel the injured limb swell. She peered at Cato, a smug smile upon his pockmarked face. She ran her back teeth together and carefully grabbed hold of the rope. She stepped around the tree and tugged on the twine, using the tree as her anchor. Cato's upper body jerked unexpectedly, and he stumbled forward. When he looked at her, she smirked.

"Do you consider yourself smart, Peddler?" he asked.

"Smart, no? Clever, yes."

He wrenched her toward him, and she slammed into his chest. Her ankle screamed from the pressure of her weight, and she chewed on the inside of her cheek to keep from crying.

He grabbed hold of her cheeks and turned her face toward his.

"How *clever* of you to get yourself killed."

She swallowed and tried to pull herself from his grasp.

He hauled her back to face him.

"I will enjoy watching you burn." He released her chin. His laugh faded into the back of her mind as she turned to face the center of the Renoldi camp.

Apprehension sucked the wind from her lungs causing her mouth to go dry and her tongue to stick to her cheeks. Three poles were erected in the middle of the camp, wood piled around each one. This was no hanging. The Renoldis would burn them as Cato said.

Bavol and another man she did not recognize led Kade toward the center pole, his face red with welts, his arms slashed and bleeding. She averted her eyes unable to see what they'd done to him. This was her fault. If she hadn't begged him for his help to find Tsura, dragged him all over the bloody land, he'd not be beaten and facing death.

He lifted his head and gazed at her—raw, bare emotion stirred within the onyx depths, and she couldn't control the tears as they filled her eyes. He'd done all of this for her, and now he'd not see his beloved ship or the sea again. She mouthed her apology to him and saw the flash of remorse when he witnessed her bruised cheek and cut lip.

Bavol and the other Renoldi tied Kade to the pole. They wrapped the rope around his middle several times before they knotted it behind him. He shook the post, his arms taut, the muscles tense as he pulled against the ropes.

They motioned for the boy to come forward, and because he wasn't of right mind the child did as he was asked. They bound him to the pole on Kade's left without any struggle.

"I will kill you both for this," Kade snarled.

Bavol laughed, a deep meaty chortle and slapped the Renoldi man beside him on the back.

She felt the pull of the rope as Cato directed her to the post on Kade's left. She couldn't look at him as she passed, too afraid she'd break down and fall at his feet to beg for his forgiveness.

"You okay, Gypsy?" he asked as Cato wound the rope around her waist, fastening her to the log post.

She inhaled, letting the air resonate throughout her body and calm her nerves.

"As good as ever," she answered.

"What did they do to the boy?"

"Witch's berry."

He raised a brow.

"He's ingested a little too much thanks to Pias."

"Where is the bastard? I've not seen him."

"On route as we speak, delivering Tsura to whomever has the pendant."

"The Monroes."

Her mouth dropped, and she gaped at him.

His face was void of any emotion.

"The Monroes agreed not to attack Pias if he obeys their commands," he said.

"They have the pendant?"

"What pendant?"

There was no time to explain. She needed to find a way out of this. She searched the faces in the crowd and recognized most of them. They'd been her family. How could they kill her without remorse, without a logical reason?

"Please, you must remember who I am," she called out to them.

Mothers turned their children away from her, while men glared from behind them.

"I have not caused you harm. I left to keep you safe."

"You are of Vadoma's bloodline. The child is hers," an older woman said, her wrinkled face showing no sign of regret at what they were about to do.

"Yes, but I can assure you Tsura is not like her mother. She is kind and loving. She is a child—a little girl."

"Just as we believed Vadoma to be," another said.

She saw the frightened faces within the Renoldi clan. The children cowered into their mothers' skirts. The men appeared angry and unpredictable. Vadoma had struck fear into them, and the worry had lasted all this time. They dreaded her child, and rightly so, but Pril was determined to help Tsura do good works instead of the evil ones her mother did.

She thought of her sister. She wanted to believe there was good in her, that somewhere deep down love and forgiveness had flourished, but as she scanned the people before her she could no longer deny what Vadoma was. Time and time again she'd stood up for her, refusing her brothers a vulgar word against the Chuvani. Her desire to see the good overshadowed what had been right in front of her all of this time.

Vadoma was evil—born with a black heart. She'd known what would come of Tsura's birth, of the blood curse, and because of her wrongdoings she'd made enemies in the very clan they'd been raised to be a part of. Pias wanted the power, and Vadoma had shown him what it could do.

Second born, she'd walked in her sister's shadow. The Chuvani, the great enchantress, possessed magick even Pril could not understand. Yet, she idolized her sister. Greed overtook Vadoma's soul and turned it dark. Pril saw it now. She remembered the spells, the slant of Vadoma's face when asked to aid the sick. She heard her screams when rebuked, and she saw the power when Vadoma cursed the Monroes. All this time she thought the evil bestowed upon Tsura had come from Silas when it had been Vadoma who passed the gene to her daughter.

"Vadoma's child is evil and must be stopped," Bavol said.

"No, she is not. How can you justify killing a child? How will you live with what you've done?"

"What of the blood curse? Vadoma cursed the Monroes, casting us all into her threat."

"I understand your anger and resentment, but Tsura is a little girl who holds no traits like her mother."

"The bloodline needs to end."

"You are a simpleton! Do you not see that Pias has mixed your way of thinking?"

"My father has done no such thing." Pias's eldest daughter, Amara, walked to the front of the crowd. Her long white-blonde hair was parted in the middle and hung to her waist.

"Where is your sister, Emine?" The two were inseparable, and she knew the other sister was near.

Amara stared past her.

"I am here," Emine said and came around Pril to stand directly in front of her. Unlike her sister, Emine had mousy brown hair that fell to her knees in thin wisps. She had not been blessed with soft, pleasing looks but instead harsh, sharp features.

"Are you in agreement with your father? Do you wish me to burn along with my friend and a small child?"

The girl's green eyes gazed at Kade, but did not fall upon the boy.

"The two, yes, and you soon after."

Pril fought the rope that held her to the post.

"Do you not remember me?" she asked.

Both girls stared blankly at her.

"You have no memory of the games we played? Of the sewing, the potions?"

"I have no memory of such events," Amara said.

"How could you not? It was but four years past."

"Had it not been for your vile sister, our mother would still live, and we'd not have such horrid memories of our time spent with you."

"Vadoma should've went to your mother that night, and for that I am sorry. I cannot take back what she did to you or anyone else within this clan, but I can tell you she no longer lives, not in me or her daughter."

"Enough!" Emine snarled and nodded toward Cato.

He reached for the torch beside him and walked toward the boy.

"No! Not him. Please!" Pril yelled.

Kade shook the post he was bound to, his face crimson, the veins protruding from his temples.

Cato smiled as he laid the torch upon the wood surrounding the child.

The boy screamed and tried to wiggle up the pole, but the ropes would not allow it.

Fury burned within her, hot anger melted together with boiling rage, and she growled low in her throat. The boy would not die while she still lived.

"Fire! I command thee to burn no more. Cover the earth in blackness until I bid thee to restore!"

The fire around the boy, and every burning torch, snuffed out. Darkness shrouded the camp, the only light coming from the moon.

"Bloody hell," Kade mumbled.

The moon was full, permitting them to see in hues of green and grey. She struggled against her ropes, trying to loosen them. She listened as the men shook the torches. Bavol pulled his knife and flint from his pocket. He ran the blade along the flint, and sparks flew onto the torch but it did not ignite.

Pril heard the arrow right before it whizzed past her and stuck into Bavol's chest. The man glanced down, eyes wide, then he fell forward dead. High-pitched shrieks bounced off of the forest walls as the Renoldi clan panicked. Women clutched their children, disappearing inside their cabins. The sound of men drawing their swords, arrows and pistols filled the night air.

She could hear Kade as he wrestled with the ropes. Another arrow flew between them to strike a woman running past in the leg. There was no time for the Renoldis to find shelter as more arrows struck husbands, wives and elders. She felt the rope loosen around her middle and peered behind her to see Sorina standing there.

"I am so glad it is you," she whispered.

Sorina smiled, and although dark her face lit up the night to warm Pril's heart.

Kade was free and wasted no time diving on top of Cato. The two rolled to the ground, and she prayed Kade would come out the victor. She went to the boy, his eyes glossy, lids heavy and drooping halfway over his pupils. She helped Sorina untie him. Without the ropes holding him up, his knees buckled, and she caught him before he fell to the ground. Lifting him, she turned toward Sorina.

"This way. There are horses waiting," the woman said.

Pril glanced over her shoulder at Kade, still in the throes of battle and ran. She swatted at the branches as she followed Sorina through the forest. Pain shot up her leg from the injured ankle. Each step felt as though the bone had been crushed. The uneven ground did not help her, and she caught herself twice from falling with the child in her arms.

They came to a small clearing, and Sorina stopped suddenly.

Pias's daughters stood waiting for them.

Amara's pasty white skin was translucent and glowed in the dark. Her green eyes flashed against her pale complexion.

Pril knew they'd not let them pass without a fight, and she laid the boy beside a tree before going back to stand with Sorina.

Emine had the same colored eyes as her sister but instead of the pale skin, hers was dotted with freckles.

"I am sorry, Cousin, but you cannot pass," Amara said. Her airy voice reminded Pril of a cold windy day.

"What is it you want?"

"Your blood," said Emine the darker of the two sisters in looks and heart.

She narrowed her eyes.

"My blood?"

The sisters nodded.

"Why?"

"Your line is of Chuvani. Surely there is greatness within your blood," said Amara.

"And if there is, what will you do with it?"

"Drink it of course," the sisters answered in unison.

Eyes wide and mouth gaping, she couldn't believe what Pias's daughters wanted to do.

"Surely you know that is uncommon, even among our people."

"It says in the spell book that a Chuvani's blood is the most powerful," Emine said.

"We mean to steal your powers," Amara said and giggled.

"But I am not the Chuvani. I do not possess those powers."

"You are of lineage," said Emine.

"Yes, but the power—the magick was Vadoma's. I do not have it." She glanced at Sorina beside her. The woman looked confused, and guilt seeped into Pril's pores for deceiving her friend.

"Vadoma is dead. Your blood is blessed."

"Still you think drinking my blood is the key?"

The sisters nodded.

She sighed. "How were you going to obtain my blood after I was burned?"

Amara smiled.

"Oh, you were not to be burned until we bled you out."

"Bled me out?"

"Yes, sliced your wrists and allowed the blood to flow freely from you."

She shuddered.

Pias's daughters were twelve when Pril and her brothers had left the Renoldi clan. Four years had passed, and the playful sisters had grown into their father's image. Treason and supremacy reflected in their eyes and in their carefree statures.

"I am sorry but I cannot offer you my blood, nor am I willing to die for you," she said.

The sisters gazed at one another, and Amara smiled.

"As you wish," she said, tilting her head to the side.

A high-pitched shriek blew from Emine's mouth as she threw herself at Pril, knocking her backward and onto the ground. Long fingernails swiped at her face. Not quick enough to dodge the razor sharp talons, they sliced into her neck and chin. Her flesh howled, and she ignored the pain. No time to wipe the blood trickling down her neck, she brought her elbow up and rammed it into Emine's nose. The other woman yelped and brought her hands up to cover herself.

Pril took the opportunity and kicked Pias's daughter from her. She planted her palms into the earth, pushed up with her arms at the same time her legs kicked out and landed on her feet. Galius had taught her the move when thrown to the ground. Hands out, legs slightly parted she waited for Emine to come at her again. She heard Amara and Sorina, but didn't dare take her eyes from the icy sister.

Emine ran her forearm along her nose, smearing the blood across her mouth and cheeks. Her top lip curled, and she hissed, showing bloodstained teeth.

Pril waited. Every muscle in her body vibrated as she tried to anticipate the girl's next move. Emine stepped to the right and gave Pril a cutting glare. Pointed nails slashed at the air. She hissed again, dipped her head and charged straight for Pril.

She clenched her hands into tight fists, refusing to move. She waited until Emine was a foot from her and swung. She connected with the girl's chin but instead of being dazed she came back for more. Pril landed another blow to the girl's nose, and more blood poured from it.

Emine shrieked. Her chin tilted and eyes squinted, showing a wicked side to the homely-faced girl. She went for Pril, grabbed her hair and tossed her to the ground. Pril brought her hands up to protect her face as the young girl scratched up her arms and neck.

She needed to finish this, to find a way out from underneath the possessed girl. Her arms stung with each swipe of Emine's nails. Pril rolled, taking Pias's daughter with her. The girl struggled free and leapt into the air at the same time Pril kicked her left leg out, catching the side of her face, just below the jaw. A loud crack echoed in the darkness, and Pril opened her eyes to see Emine lying a few feet from her unconscious.

She scrambled to her feet and ran toward Sorina when an arrow flew past and rooted into Amara's chest. The young girl leaned backward. Her eyes grew wide and round, and her hands shook as she went for the arrow lodged in her breast. As she turned toward Pril, her green eyes watered, and her mouth worked. One tear slid down her pale cheek, and Pril felt remorse for the girl she'd known, but not the evil woman she'd become.

Amara reached out a trembling hand to her, and she went to take a step toward the girl when Kade touched her arm.

She stared back at him, and he shook his head.

"Let her die, Sister," Galius said as he walked through the trees and into the small clearing. It was his arrow that had struck the girl. Not a scratch on him, Galius stood tall and wide. His black pants scuffed with dirt and his white shirt marked with blood, he was a threat most took serious and steered clear of but not her. She loved him with her whole heart.

She ran to her brother and was relieved when his thick arms encircled her tiny frame. He was her protector always had been and always will be. She felt safe with him.

He shifted her back so he could gaze down at her. Her face had seen better days, and after Pias and Emine, she was sure to have a few scars.

"I have taught you well," Galius said and smiled.

"Indeed, Brother."

Kade helped Sorina stand. Her friend had welts around her neck from Amara.

"We must go," Galius said, "The Renoldis will gather and will want our blood."

"The horses are beyond the trees," whispered Sorina, and Pril figured her throat was sore from the strangling.

She went to the boy, picked him up and was surprised to see Kade when she turned around.

"I'll take him," he said, his lips turned upward into a half smile.

She nodded and handed the boy to him. The wanting returned inside her soul, and she yearned for Tsura. Her heart wept for her daughter, and she prayed Pias hadn't met the Monroes yet, and her baby still lived.

CHAPTER TWENTY

The sun peeked over the mountains, throwing bright rays across the land. Pril tipped her head and felt the warmth kiss her cheeks. She was exhausted. They rode through the night, stopping only once to water the horses and then carry on.

She leaned in, laid her head on Athos neck and inhaled. She hadn't expected Galius to have her prized horse waiting for them when they left the Renoldis. She glanced at Kade; her brother had brought his Goliath as well. She'd forgotten how kind he was, and how much she missed him since leaving her clan weeks before.

There had been no time for conversation, and she longed to have counsel with her brother. Was he healthy? How were his wounds? She watched him, hunched shoulders and taut back. He was not yet healed from the attack a few weeks before. She'd ask to have a look once they found somewhere safe to make camp.

Her own shoulders suffered from the sleepless nights and the encounter with Pias and his daughters. She'd smothered the cuts on her skin with beeswax to help heal them, but it didn't take the sting or ache from her bones.

Her uncle had her daughter and was taking her to the Monroes. Silas had the pendant, and she couldn't figure out how the eldest of the three brothers held the heirloom to her family. Had Vadoma given it to him? Had he stolen it? She didn't know. She worried he knew what the pendant meant and what it could do if used by the right person.

"We will rest in the forest for a few hours," Kade said beside her and shifted the sleeping boy in his arms.

"We will rest when I say," Galius spoke, and she didn't miss the challenge in her brother's voice.

"We are all tired, Brother. An hour or two within the forest walls would be welcome," she said.

Kade's bruised face smirked, and Galius scowled at him.

"I can see I am no longer in charge of your well-being," he said.

"I control myself, Brother."

"It stands to reason to take shelter there, does it not?" Kade said with his usual arrogance.

"Reason?" Galius spoke. "What reason had you captured by Pias and the Renoldis?"

Kade's jaw flexed, and she walked Athos in between them.

"There is no fault to be laid here, Brother."

"I cast blame upon the man who was to be your protector," he growled.

"Do you know your sister at all, dear Galius?" Kade asked.

"I know my sister better than anyone." He stopped his horse a few feet before they entered the forest and turned in his saddle to face Kade. "Do not think otherwise."

"Is that so?"

"It is."

Galius' arms tightened, and she watched as his nostrils flared.

"Do not speak as if I am not here," she said.

"Stay out of this, Gypsy."

"My sister has a name, and you chose to call her what she is instead? You have not been given that right."

"I don't give a damn about rights, is that not obvious to you?"

"How often has that landed you in trouble?"

"Not often enough," Kade said and flashed his teeth in a wide smile.

Sorina climbed down from her horse and walked into the forest.

"Where are you going?" Galius commanded.

"To find a suitable spot to rest," she said without turning.

"I have not commanded it."

She turned, and Pril was taken aback when she saw the flash of fire within her friend's blue eyes.

"I do not care."

She kicked Athos sides and followed Sorina.

"Gypsy?"

"Yes?"

"What do you think you are doing?"

"Have you no ears?" she asked.

"I do, but I have not said it's so."

She smiled and fixed her gaze on her brother and Kade.

"I take orders from no one. So you two may stay here as long as you see fit. However, Sorina and I have grown tired of your bickering and seek rest."

She clicked her tongue, and Athos followed Sorina into the forest, leaving Kade and Galius behind.

Pril leaned into the fire and yawned. She welcomed the heat to chase the tiredness from her bones. She glanced at Kade laying to her left, eyes closed and curled up tight into a blanket. He'd kept watch earlier while Pril and the others had slept. He'd been exhausted, eyelids half closed, dark circles shadowed his skin, and his sentences had become incoherent. He didn't argue when she'd told him to rest while she and the others kept watch. She figured he was asleep before his head hit his saddle.

A lock of blond hair lay clumsily across his forehead and cheek, stopping at the crease where his lips met. She thumbed the hem of her skirt to keep from tucking the errant hair back with the others and touching his bruised skin.

She was grateful for all of his help in searching for Tsura. She was sure he'd rather be on his vessel sailing far away from her. Instead he'd stuck by her side, through wolves, peculiar villagers and the Renoldis. He'd proven his loyalty, and other than her brother, he was the only man she'd ever trusted.

She hadn't known Pias would be involved with the Monroes, or in the search for her daughter. She sighed. She'd been naive to think Milosh and the Monroes were their only threat. Galius had warned her about the Renoldis. She'd ignored him and the danger they held. She'd been a fool, and the error could cost her Tsura's life.

Sorina sat across from her and rocked the boy in her arms. Her friend was growing fond of the child. It'd taken most of the day for the Witch's berry to wear off, and she wondered what kind of dose Pias had given him.

If she had the spell book she'd be able to create a tonic to counteract with the plant and flush it from his body, but lack of skills and knowledge forced her to wait for the berry to fade from him.

Galius had gone deep into the forest to hunt their dinner, and she was on watch until he returned. She placed her hand on top of the quiver and bow lying next to her. Three arrows were left. Galius had pulled the spears from their victims, the blood and flesh still stuck to the wood.

She stole another glance at Kade. She should release him of his obligations. With Galius here there was no need for his presence, and she was sure he'd be much happier back on his ship. Her belly tightened, and she tucked her bottom lip in between her teeth. Sadness wrapped around her like a warm blanket. She brought her knees to her chest and hugged them. She would miss Kade Walker, and that was unsettling.

Pril used Galius' knife to carve out an arrow. She'd been working for hours to sculpt the long piece of poplar and create a smooth exterior. She ran the blade along the wood, shaving off small bits until she was satisfied with the result. She didn't have the time, or the tools, to fashion the ends with metal and flint. So she shaped the wood into pointed spikes instead.

Galius turned the hare roasting over the fire. Her stomach rumbled as the meat sizzled. He had remained to himself after their confrontation earlier, and she worried about how she'd tell him Milosh was gone. Would he blame her for their brother's death? She dipped her head to hide the remorse swimming within her eyes. She didn't know if she could face his disappointment.

She glanced at Sorina. Her friend hadn't spoke more than a few words to her since escaping the Renoldis. Unease settled in her stomach. She leaned forward to relieve the pressure and the anxiety building within her.

"He is so small," Sorina said as she motioned toward the boy drawing in the dirt with Kade. "What is his name?"

"I do not know. He does not speak our tongue." She didn't think it was necessary to tell Sorina of her suspicions about the boy and his understanding of their language until she knew for sure.

"I see. What will you do with him once we find Tsura?"

"I have grown fond of him. I would hope he'd want to stay with us."

Galius stopped turning the spit to gape at her.

"He is without family, Brother. I see no reason why he cannot join our clan," she said.

"What is his background? Where did you find him?"

Galius' questions infuriated her. The boy was just a child, an innocent like Tsura, and yet his motives were still questioned.

"He was beaten bloody in one of the villages west of here. They locked him in a closet in their brothel," Kade answered.

Galius went back to turning the spit. She watched as his shoulders flexed, and his chest heaved. She wondered how Sorina convinced her brother to take her with him. He was not one who could easily be swayed.

"How did you come to be with Galius on this journey?"

"I followed." She shrugged. "He wasn't yet healed, but he was determined to find you. I refused him when he asked me to go."

"Thank you for not allowing him to go alone."

"I did not find him until two nights ago outside of the Renoldi camp."

"You are resilient, and I am indebted to you for your kindness."

She'd always known her friend had eyes for her brother and was delighted to see her take charge of the situation.

Silence settled over their meager camp, and she waited sensing Sorina had something else to say.

"You are of Vadoma the great enchantress."

She couldn't lie to her friend any longer. She'd been the only person who hadn't judged her or questioned Tsura's lineage.

"I am."

"And Tsura is her daughter."

"Yes."

Galius coughed, Sorina faced him, and Pril was shocked to see the glare he cast upon the woman.

Sorina held her lips shut and stared at the ground. All gypsies knew of the mighty Vadoma. She'd cast herself in such bad light that news of her evil doings spread like wildfire to each gypsy clan. When the Monroes set out to hunt and kill any gypsy girl after Vadoma's death they didn't factor in age, slaying any child under three.

"My sister was killed. My mother died saving her," she murmured, and Pril had to lean in to hear her. "I watched them. I saw it. I…I could do nothing." She wiped a tear from her cheek. "I still have nightmares."

"My dear friend, please know how very sorry I am for your loss."

Sorina watched her from across the fire. The blue in her eyes darkened.

"Apologies will not bring them back."

Pril hung her head. "No, they will not."

Kade stopped playing with the boy to listen.

"My sister, Sabella, has remained silent. She has not spoken a single word since the deaths of our family."

She wished there was something she could say or do to ease the pain she heard in Sorina's voice. She went to her and sat down beside her.

"If I could take your agony please know that I would." She touched her hand.

"All this time I've lived with the very child they hunted. The cursed one."

Pril stiffened.

Galius paused rotating the hare.

"Tsura is not cursed," she said.

Sorina pulled her hand from Pril's and stood.

"What would you call it then?"

"I would not call it cursed."

Sorina's eyes went flat all emotion gone within them.

"She is what they say. Cursed, spawn, evil."

"Sorina," Galius warned.

"My daughter is none of those things."

"She is not your daughter. She is Vadoma's spawn." The words spewed from Sorina's mouth like poison, and Pril felt the insult splash onto her soul.

"Tsura is just as much my daughter as if I'd bore her myself."

The woman she'd known, the friend she loved as a sister had betrayed her, and she understood why. She wanted to weep for the loss, beg Sorina to rethink her position, but knew she never would. How could she? If it were Pril she'd behave the same way.

Sorina had lost her family to the Monroes and their hate—to the damn blood curse Vadoma had placed. She was like so many who'd been destroyed by her sister's evil doings, and there wasn't a thing Pril could do to fix it. She couldn't change the past and make them see Tsura held no malice within her tiny body. She was a little girl who did not choose this life. She did not pick Vadoma as her mother, and she sure as hell didn't want people to die because of it.

"You should've let them kill her," Sorina hissed.

Pril's heart slammed into her rib cage, not prepared for Sorina's cold words. Fury flooded her senses, and her face heated.

"Those are cruel accusations," Kade said.

"Cruel is the truth I've faced. The death I've seen. It is the betrayal from the very people I loved," Sorina said.

"We did not betray you to hurt you, Sorina," Galius said as he removed the hare from the fire to lie on a nearby rock.

"No, you did it to save the devil's brood."

"That is enough!" Pril shouted.

"If I had a child with evil in her heart, one that caused so many deaths, I'd not think twice before ending her life."

"Then you are not who I thought you to be."

Sorina snapped her head up to glare at Pril.

"This from the very one who has done nothing but deceive others? How suitable."

"Why would any mother kill their own child, evil or not?" Kade asked.

Sorina's mouth curved into a devious smile.

"He does not know?"

Pril shook her head before meeting Galius' eyes.

"You have not told him who he searches for?" Sorina asked.

"What the hell is going on?" Kade snapped.

Pril sighed. She'd hoped to sit with Kade and tell him the truth of Tsura once they were far enough away from the Renoldis and out of danger, but Sorina had ruined her plans.

"Tsura is my sister, Vadoma's, daughter," she said.

"Vadoma, the one with the magical powers?" He snickered.

She nodded.

"He does not believe in such things," she said to Sorina and Galius.

"It is because he is of closed mind," Galius said. "For him to fathom something so surreal is too much."

"I understand it. I just don't believe it. Those are two very different things," Kade snapped.

"Tsura has Vadoma's powers. She is a Chuvani like her mother was," Pril interjected. "Vadoma laid a blood curse on the Monroes before they killed her. All of their daughters would die, and they believe by killing Tsura the curse will be broken."

"Will it?" Kade asked.

"Yes."

"Now do you see why she must die?" Sorina asked.

Kade frowned at the other woman. "No, I do not."

"You cannot get your words back," Pril said carefully to Sorina.

"I do not want them back."

"I cannot abide you speaking of my daughter in such a way." She stood.

"The truth may be difficult to speak, but you must understand."

"I cannot comprehend how someone could wish a child dead."

"She is cursed as Milosh said."

Pril's chest compressed as the loss of her brother hit her tenfold. The pain so raw, the wound still gaping seeped of anguish and misery. Her eyes watered, and the ache within her soul exposed the possibility of never seeing forgiveness for what she'd done. She hung her head, waiting for the pain to pass. She still needed to tell Galius of their loss, to repent of all her wrongdoings. She thought of Tsura, her baby girl, and anger bled into her veins to fuel her heart and ignite the fire within her soul.

She stepped toward Sorina ready to defend her daughter at all cost when Kade grabbed her arm.

"No, Gypsy. Not like this," he whispered into her ear.

Galius moved behind Sorina.

"I am sorry we have come to this. I can no longer stay within your company," she said, lips thin and unmoving.

Sorina lifted her shoulders. "Nor can I stay within yours."

"Brother, will you take Sorina back to our clan so that she may be with her sister?"

Galius was silent, his eyes locked with hers before he glanced at Kade and nodded.

"Fate has its way, and you, my Pril, will get yours," Sorina whispered.

"Get her away from me before I take my arrow and drive it into her tainted heart," Pril hissed before she walked away.

CHAPTER TWENTY-ONE

Pril walked into the woods. Disgust twisted her gut, and she folded her arms across her midsection. Sorina had acted out of fear and from the horrible loss she'd experienced. But no matter which way Pril weighed the situation she could not condone how the other woman spoke of her daughter.

Within the span of Tsura's short life, Pril had gone to battle with both her brothers, Magda and now Sorina. She loved them all. Regret showered her, drenching her in sorrow and dripped from her soul. She'd not been able to make them see—to help them understand that Tsura held no harm. She felt the loss of those she loved clear to her soul, and the agony almost too much for her to bear had ripped her in two.

How was she ever to feel whole again after the pain she'd caused? Where could she go that she'd be accepted—where her daughter felt loved for the child she was and not the gifts she had?

The Monroes wanted to kill her. Pias needed her as his pawn, and Milosh took her because of his own grief. She'd fed her daughter to the wrong people, handed her over without a fight, and she couldn't contain the tears as they slipped from her eyes.

She didn't believe in herself enough to count all of the spells she'd been taught. She didn't trust the magick within her to release the words and watch them do her bidding. She used the book day after day to try and create new spells to keep them safe, but she never read further. She never peeked beyond the pages to where she'd learn the craft. She'd been too afraid.

She didn't want to be like her sister. The power that came from the book, the knowledge inside of it frightened her to no end. What if she became as Vadoma? What if there was evil within her, too? She stayed away, only using the spells for necessity, for the children's safety. She wiped a tear, and even then she'd discovered she was a coward.

She heard Galius' steps as he came up behind her, and she used her shawl to dab at the tears upon her cheeks.

"The forest floor gives you away, Brother," she said, turning to face him.

He smiled, and she sighed. It'd been weeks since he'd shown any emotion. Most days he was in control of all situations, holding himself at arm's length away from everyone. He desired distance, he needed it to lead the clan, deal with his siblings and niece.

"How are you?" he asked.

There were so many things she needed to tell him, but first she had to confess the truth of Milosh. She had to tell Galius their brother was dead. She bowed her head. Her eyes misted. She hadn't come to terms with the loss and carried the regret upon her shoulders.

"Brother, we need to have counsel."

"Is that not what we are doing?"

She was quiet, the need to move her legs—to do something—overtook her, and she paced in front of him. Her hands were restless, and she folded them within her shawl several times before letting them hang at her sides. How was she going to tell him? She opened her mouth but nothing came out. She couldn't even whisper the words. Her chest constricted, and she could feel the tightness in her throat. She placed her hand over her neck and rubbed the skin.

"What is it?" he asked.

She halted. Her feet planted into the ground, and she hung her head.

"I am sorry, Galius."

He stepped toward her, and she retreated.

"Please do not come near me. I need to do this. I have to tell you without your comfort. I need to see the pain I've caused you and the despair within your eyes."

He straightened.

"Get on with it."

Her stomach contracted, and she bent. She forced herself to stare into Galius eyes and said, "Milosh is dead."

He didn't move, his eyes flickered but he masked the emotion she'd almost seen there.

"How?"

"He was murdered."

"How?" he asked again this time louder.

She swallowed and avoided his eyes.

"Hung from a tree."

She could hear him as he exhaled, forcing the air from his body in long puffs. She didn't know what to do. She peeked at him through her lashes, watching as he pumped his fists at his side and clenched his jaw several times.

"Brother, I am sorry."

He fixed his daunting gaze upon her, and she shuddered.

"Why do you apologize?"

"Had it not been for me, for my insistence on raising Tsura on my own, none of this would have happened."

He sighed.

"That is the past. You cannot keep living there."

"How can I not when the ones I love are being killed?"

"Milosh chose his own path, and though it saddens me to hear he is gone from us, I cannot abide what he did."

"Yes, but he was still our brother. I loved him no matter what he did."

"As did I."

"I never got to say I was sorry. I was too late. I shall never forgive myself for it."

"Milosh knew you loved him. He was driven by grief and nothing more."

She nodded but his words did little to comfort her.

"Do you know who killed him?"

"I feel it was Pias. When asked he denied it, but I know it was him."

He nodded.

"Rest easy, Sister. Milosh is with his sweet Alexandra now."

"I cannot help but feel regret for the things I have done. I feel responsible for the death of our niece, Milosh and Sorina's family. How can I ever come home knowing the fear still lives within our people?"

"They will accept you."

She smiled, pitying her brother for his ignorance to the matter.

"You cannot change the way our people think. When Sorina gets home she will tell them about Tsura and how we deceived the clan. We will no longer be welcome."

"The clan will listen to me. I can convince them Sorina is without mind."

"Brother, you need to cease and hear me. We will have nothing to go back to. I cannot take Tsura there knowing they will kill her."

Galius was silent, and she waited for him to speak.

"What of Tsura? Do you know where she is?"

She nodded.

"Pias has her, and he is taking her to the Monroes."

His head shot up.

"It seems Pias has been working with the Monroes for some time now. Silas has offered him the pendant in trade for Tsura."

"He has the talisman? But how?"

"I do not know. Vadoma could've given it to him before she died, in which case she deceived me."

"How so?"

"She told me the pendant belonged to me and if something ever happened to her to keep it safe. The night she died I searched for it within the cabin, but it was gone."

"Silas could've known it was there and took it."

She nodded.

"Does he know the power it holds?"

"No, I do not think so. But Pias does and…" She paused.

"What is it? What were you going to say?"

"He has the spell book, too. He stole it from my vardo the night they attacked us."

Galius ran his hand through his thick beard and growled.

"What will you have me do?" he asked.

She knew he struggled with his duty to take Sorina back. He wanted to be with her and Kade.

"You need to return Sorina to the clan."

He nodded.

"Shall I take the boy?"

"No. He remains with me."

"I will come back. I will not leave you to your own wits when it comes to Pias and the Monroes."

She placed her hand on his shoulder.

"I am not alone. For all his crassness and superiority, Kade Walker is good with a dagger and can throw his fists quite well."

"I will be two days behind you. Try to wait. We are stronger in numbers than alone."

He was right, but if she came to Pias's camp she would not wait to get her daughter.

"Yes, Brother, I will wait for you," she lied.

His shoulders dropped, and he opened his arms to her.

She went to him, feeling his strength and love.

"Go now, and know that I love you," she whispered.

He set her away from him and kissed her forehead. "As I you, Sister."

She watched as he walked away, knowing she may never see him again. Once she found her daughter, she'd take her to the other world far away from the dangers that lurked here.

Kade reached into the sack and pulled a handful of oats out for

Pril's horse.

"Here you go, boy," he said as the animal nuzzled his palm.

Pril had not returned from the forest after her disagreement with Sorina, and he was beginning to worry. He reached for the dagger fastened to his belt. He should go and search for her. What if something happened? He glanced at the boy drawing in the dirt. Galius hadn't taken him back to their clan when he left earlier with Sorina, and Kade guessed Pril had some say in the matter. She didn't want the boy to go with Sorina, and he couldn't blame her. He'd grown fond of the kid, and to send him with strangers would only cause him to escape. He didn't want to think of what could happen to him then.

With Galius gone he only had Pril to contend with, and he enjoyed riling her. He didn't care much for her brother or the way he commanded those around him. Kade controlled his own future, and no one would tell him otherwise.

Galius had asked him to wait for his return before taking Pril to Pias and the Monroes. He'd refused the other man. He wanted blood for what Silas had done to Sam, and no matter how much Galius begged, if he saw Silas or Jude Monroe he'd kill them without so much as a second thought.

He glanced toward the bushes where he'd last seen Pril. The woman perplexed him. He wasn't sure what to think when it came to her family and the mythical powers they held. Was what she told him true? Did the child possess magick? He'd witnessed Pril put the fires out when they were captured by the Renoldis but he still could not understand how it happened. Was his mind simply closed off to it as Galius suggested? Did he not have the capacity within his brain to comprehend such things?

Just thinking of it gave him a headache. He'd listened as Pias, Sorina and Pril's own brother Milosh spoke of the child. How they revealed their hate, greed and anguish. How death was the only way to rid them of the curse. The Monroes would kill Tsura. He was certain of it now. He knew that no matter what happened he'd never be able to hand her over to Silas and his brothers. He no longer needed the child to trade. There would be no barter. Silas was going to die, and Kade would kill him.

"I gathered some berries for the ride," Pril said as she walked from the bushes, her shawl tied to hold the blueberries she picked. He noticed the redness around her eyes and swollen lids. She'd been crying.

The boy bounced up from the ground and ran toward her, throwing his skinny arms around her waist.

"Oh my."

She smiled as she hugged him back.

"Sounds nice," he said and picked up the boy to place him on top of Athos.

"Thank you for saddling my horse and attaching my bow."

He nodded.

"Are you ready to leave?"

"After we've talked."

She froze while tying the shawl to the side of her saddle.

"About what?"

"Tsura."

"What of her?"

"Turn, and look at me, Gypsy."

He waited while she finished fastening the shawl and then faced him.

"Very well. What do you want to know?"

"I want you to tell me the story from the beginning."

"What story?"

"The one I've been hearing bits and pieces of for the last two weeks."

"It is a waste of time, and we cannot afford another minute."

He searched her over; the skirt and blouse she wore was tattered and dirty. Her thick red hair fell to her waist and reminded him of the auburn leaves on a cool fall day. Her pert nose tipped up, and full lips shaped into a frown enticed him. Her pale complexion offset the red in her hair, making her brown eyes vivid and alluring. She was beautiful. Had it not been for the sadness he'd seen in her eyes he'd have told her so.

"I am not leaving until you've told me what you know. I need to understand what we are up against."

She grimaced, and the urge to run his thumb across her lips overwhelmed him.

He turned from her and climbed onto Goliath.

"We will discuss it while we ride. Does that suit you?"

"Do I have a choice?"

"No."

She sighed, and he figured it had little to do with the predicament he'd placed her in but rather the events that had recently happened.

She mounted her horse, reins in hand, and eyed him.

"Where would you like me to begin?"

"Tell me about your sister, Vadoma."

"I have told you everything."

He clicked his tongue, and Goliath began a slow walk.

"No, you have not spoken about the curse. If I remember correctly you expressed it to be a myth."

"It is not."

"I figured so. Do go on."

"Vadoma placed the blood curse before she was hanged."

"She cursed the Monroes?"

"Yes."

"How did she come to know the Monroes?"

"She fell in love with Silas."

"But he was the one who hung her?"

"Yes."

"Explain."

"Silas had stopped courting Vadoma when she became with child. She'd grown cold and distant, striking out at anyone who defied her. I tried to talk with her, offer comfort, but she pushed me away."

"What happened to make the Monroes hang her?"

"Silas had come to fetch Vadoma one night after Tsura was born, begging her to come and help his father who was gravely ill. I knew why he'd come. I'd had a dream a few months before. I begged her not to go, but Vadoma ignored me and followed him into the forest."

Her face lost all color, and her eyes blurred, haunted by the past. He almost stopped her, but needed to hear the details.

"That evening, when the moon was high, Vadoma still had not returned. I went in search of her and heard the commotion in town."

"The whole town was in on her hanging?"

She nodded.

"The people of Jamestown had grown nervous around the Chuvani, and it didn't help that the Salem Witch hunts were still fresh within their minds. They didn't want to go back to that time and knew the magick Vadoma practiced was black. They'd come on several occasions to beg her to leave. They asked Pias, Galius and Milosh to speak with her, but she insisted on staying and scared them away with threats of spells and curses."

"She was that powerful?"

"If the magick is dark it can become very frightening, and so it isn't the measure of power one holds, but rather when it is done out of hate that scares so many."

"I see."

"Vadoma was an accomplished Chuvani. She knew the spells by memory."

"You said she could do other things."

"Yes."

"Such as?"

"Throw a beam—a force so strong it could knock an eight hundred pound ox through the air."

"That day I met you. Tsura did the same thing didn't she?"

He remembered being in Pril's wagon, seeing the child and then nothing more.

"Yes," she whispered.

"What else could Vadoma do?"

"Cause wind storms, burn things…her powers were plentiful."

"Can Tsura do all of those things?"

"She can and more."

"More than Vadoma?"

"I believe so, yes."

"Go on."

"When I was burned Tsura laid her hands upon me and healed my flesh."

"Bollocks."

"It is true."

He watched as she pulled her blouse down. He had to keep from examining her breasts and concentrate on her defined collarbone instead.

"I'll be. There are no scars. It is as if it never happened."

"Precisely."

He'd seen the burns on her skin and knew that even after she was healed they'd leave an awful scar. Her flesh was pink and unscathed. Unable to grasp the concept of a child with such powers, he changed the subject.

"Tell me when Vadoma laid the curse."

"I had crept into town and hid behind the livery. I watched as they bound Vadoma's hands and feet. Silas slipped the noose around her neck. I still remember feeling the rope as if it were around my own neck." She rubbed her throat. "Before he pulled the lever, Silas ordered Tsura hunted and killed. Vadoma went crazy. Her eyes glowed red, and she brought forth strong winds that bent the trees, tore off roofs and doors. The townspeople scattered, but Silas held tight to the scaffold. Vadoma cursed the Monroes, killing any daughter born to them right before he pulled the lever. She dropped from the platform, and her neck broke. Later they would burn her and bury the ashes within the forest."

"I'm sorry you had to see that, Gypsy."

She faced him. He saw the depth of her sorrow in the creases around her eyes and mouth. He wished he could take away her suffering.

"I used to believe my sister had her reasons for behaving the way she did, but as I've been on this journey I have realized none of them were acceptable. She was evil to the very core of her soul, and nothing I did would've made a difference."

"Tsura does not have the same evil within her?"

"I worry for her, but I do not believe so."

"But you're not sure."

"No, I am not."

What she said had made sense even if he couldn't wrap his head around the magick part. Tsura was a gifted little girl and by circumstance had become hunted by evil people such as the Monroes. He ran his hand through his hair. It was quite the predicament. Would the child ever be safe from harm?

The boy leaned against her, and he watched as she placed her arm protectively around his waist to secure him from falling. The horses trotted at an easy gait. He inhaled the freshness in the air, the smell of the grass, his horse and honeysuckle. The plant grew somewhere nearby, and as the sugary fragrance wafted toward him, he felt a craving for something sweet. He glanced at Pril. His groin tightened, and he shifted on top of his saddle.

"What direction are we heading in?" she asked.

"Northeast. Toward the water."

"I feared so."

Jamestown was where Pias's tracks were headed. Kade had every intention of killing Silas, and he knew the plantation owner would meet the Renoldi to trade the pendant for Tsura. He hoped Sam was still alive and healthy. He worried over his heart and how the Monroe's were treating him. Did he have enough water? Was Silas feeding him? The pain Sam must've felt when they sawed off his finger turned Kade's stomach and caused his forehead to perspire. His mouth watered, and he tasted bile upon his tongue. He shook his head and pushed the thought aside, unable to think of it any longer.

I will get to you. I promise.

He tightened his grip on the reins, pressed his heels into Goliath's sides, and the horse sped up. Goliath cantered across the open field. He didn't need to glance behind him to know Pril followed. Time was of the essence in more ways than one. He needed to reach Sam, find Tsura and distance himself from Pril and her gypsy heart.

CHAPTER TWENTY-TWO

The wide oak door creaked as Silas leaned into it. He stepped into the room. The small space was lit with two candles, one on the bedside table and another on a small shelf crooked and hanging from the wall. The air was damp and smelled of mildew. The wetness clung to his skin, and he felt dirty. He covered his nose with a handkerchief before going any further.

An old cot taken from the slaves' quarters, sat in the corner against a rock wall. The stones seeped from the dampness in the room. Samuel Walker lay beneath a thin blanket, his ragged breaths scarcely heard.

Silas came closer.

The sea captain's skin was pale. His cheeks were sunken in, and black circles shaded his closed eyes. Thin long gray hair fell onto his shoulders, unwashed and matted. Silas shivered when he saw the small bugs crawling across his scalp.

A sour scent came from the body, and he pressed the cloth further into his nose. He hadn't been back into the room after he'd cut the finger from the man's hand weeks before, and he could see no one else had either.

Jude and Hiram were the only ones who knew Samuel Walker was locked in the cellar below the stairs. It had been Jude's job to see to the well-being of the sea captain, and by the looks of it his brother had failed miserably.

He stepped closer. The bandaged hand was crusted with dried blood. The skin around where the cloth ended was a light shade of black. He lifted the arm, puss oozed through the cloth. The rancid stench wafted from the limb. He dropped the arm, stepped back and gagged.

"Damn it."

The man was his barter. He used him to get Kade Walker to search for the child. The bastard was near dead, dying of starvation and a ghastly infection. It mattered little to him that these were the man's last minutes, but he wanted the satisfaction of killing Sam Walker himself. He wanted to feel the proud sea merchant fight beneath the pillow he'd planned to hold over his sleeping face. Now he'd get nothing. The old bugger probably wouldn't even wake.

He turned to leave, disappointment dampening his mood, and he scowled.

"Silas..."

He heard the faint whisper of his name and twisted back around, shocked when he saw the old man staring up at him.

"You live?" he asked the cloth still at his nose.

"I...do."

"It is a shame."

For the little bit of life left in the old codger, he still had enough energy to narrow his sunken eyes at him.

"My son...will...kill you."

He smiled. Kade Walker would soon be dead. After he took care of the business with Hiram and Pias he'd hire a gun to kill the merchant runner.

"Your son will die before that happens."

The old man chuckled, the act stealing his breath, and he began to gasp.

"Your threats are a creek run dry, a dead man's last words. I am not frightened of you or your illegitimate son."

Sam wheezed his wrinkled lips strained as he tried to force the air into his lungs.

"Come...come...close."

The putrid smell seeped through the cloth across Silas' mouth and onto his tongue. He spat onto the floor to expel the revolting taste. He wiped his mouth and went to stand beside the bed.

The sea master's arm shot out of nowhere. A sharp piece of wood in his hand, he drove it into Silas' thigh.

Pain irrupted in his leg sending explosive signals up and down the limb. Silas screamed.

He had no time to block it or knock the weapon from the frail hand. His body shook with rage as his expression sagged into an evil grin. He jumped on top of Samuel Walker and threw his fists into the skeletal face. The bed creaked with each blow to the sea merchant's head. He pummeled him until his knuckles hurt, and he could not recognize the old man any longer. Blood seeped onto the pillow and turned Sam's white hair crimson. The bones in his face crushed and disfigured, his nose flat and pressed into his skull.

Silas removed himself from the corpse, wiped his hands on his pants and limped from the room. His heart raced from the exhilaration of what he'd done. He didn't feel the pain in his leg until he'd climbed the stairs to the main floor. He braced himself against the wall, sweat perspired on his brow, and his stomach lurched. The leg throbbed—the pain so intense it caused his head to spin and bile to rush up his throat.

A maid came out of the kitchen, a platter of food in her hand. She gasped, the dishes on top of the silver serving tray rattled.

"Find my brothers," he yelled, leaning into the wall.

She placed the platter on a small table in the hall before rushing to do as he'd asked.

He walked toward the study, dragging his leg behind him. The wound poured blood and pulsed with each step he took. He gnashed his teeth against the misery and stumbled, reaching out he steadied himself on a chair. His leg screamed for release from the constant agony, and he eyed the bottle of whiskey on the mantel.

Three more steps, and he fell onto the sofa, not caring about the blood on his pants or his hands. He glanced at the wood sticking from his leg and groaned. The damn thing needed to come out. His hand shook as he grasped it, feeling the rigid edges as he pulled. The wretched stick wouldn't move. He screamed his frustration and pain.

Jude and Hiram came running into the room.

"What the bloody hell happened?" Jude asked, panic on his pale face.

"I've been stabbed. What in hell does it look like?" Silas growled.

"I see that, but how?"

"Just get the damn thing out." He fell back against the sofa, too worn to do more.

"Where did all this blood come from?" Hiram asked his eyes big and round as he inspected Silas.

Silas ignored him. The snake was lucky it wasn't his blood.

"Brother, why are you covered in blood?" Hiram asked again.

He turned his eyes toward him, and let the hate show within the inky pits.

"I killed the bastard who stabbed me."

"A slave? Was it a slave?" Jude asked.

He shook his head.

"Then who?"

"Walker."

Hiram's face paled.

"You...you killed Walker? But *why*?"

Silas ignored him.

"Get this damn stick out of my blasted leg!"

"Hiram, go, and get clean linens. Tell Gertrude to boil some water," Jude commanded.

Hiram nodded.

"Wait," Silas called. "Whiskey, I need the whiskey."

Hiram went to the mantel, grabbed the whiskey from the shelf and brought the bottle to him.

He ripped the bottle from his brother's hands and pulled the cork free with his teeth.

"Get the damn cloths, Hiram," Jude growled.

Silas took a long drink from the bottle. The whiskey burned his throat and set fire to his gut. His leg ached, and he lifted the bottle again, downing another three swigs before the pain in his thigh began to numb.

"Why did you kill Walker?" Jude asked.

"We have no use for him. Pias has the girl. I was merely cleaning up loose ends."

"Yes, but Kade will not be pleased."

"Once we've taken care of the others, I will hire a gun to destroy Kade Walker."

"He won't die that easily."

"I am not concerned."

"You should be. Kade Walker adored Sam. Everyone from here to England knew it. He will seek revenge."

Jude's face blurred, and he blinked several times to clear his vision. The whiskey was working, thank the saints.

"If need be, I'll end the bastard's life myself."

Jude observed the room, concern stretched across his forehead.

"I fear you've made a grave mistake, Brother."

He couldn't believe what he was hearing. Jude questioned him on killing Walker. What did he think they were going to do with the bastard merchant when Kade brought them the girl? Let him go? Silas knew all along he'd kill Sam and enjoy doing it. He'd had his reasons for ending the weasel's life, and he wasn't sorry.

"You dare to question me about an old man, and yet you are willing to slay a little girl?"

"I...I was simply reminding you Kade Walker is not some vagrant we can just forget about. He is a skilled fighter and even better with his blade."

"Your weakness disgusts me. I thought you to be tough—cunning and lethal. You are no better than Hiram."

"It is far wiser for me to know what we are up against than to be fool enough to turn a blind eye."

Silas swatted the air. The room dipped, and he leaned to the side.

"Do not forget of the past, Brother," Jude whispered.

"I have not forgotten."

"I am not so sure."

Hiram returned with the cloths and water. He handed them to Jude.

"Brace yourself, this is going to hurt like bloody hell," Jude said as he wrapped the cloth around the protruding stick and pulled it from his leg.

Silas screamed and passed out.

CHAPTER TWENTY-THREE

Pril's backside ached, and her legs were cramped. She'd been on her horse since morning. The lull of Athos steps had her slipping into a trance where her eyes wanted to close, and a blissful rest waited. The sun receded toward the land, leaving the hills, plains and trees in shadows.

"When will we stop?" she asked, glancing at Kade who seemed to be almost half asleep in his saddle.

"There is a town up ahead."

He'd been quiet most of the day, offering one-word answers to her questions. She'd grown tired of trying to engage him and had decided to tell the boy a long story. She still wasn't sure if the child understood her or not, but he seemed enthralled with the tale she'd woven and watched as his eyes shone with amusement and uncertainty.

"He adores you," Kade said motioning with his chin toward the boy asleep in front of her.

"I feel the same way about him."

"I wonder how much of your story he understood."

"I'd like to think all of it."

He laughed, and she hadn't realized how much the sound would warm her heart. It'd been so long since she'd felt any joy, and the thought of having it without Tsura caused her eyes to mist. She missed her daughter and wished for a way to know if she was safe.

"We will find her soon," he said.

She glanced at him.

"How do you know?" she whispered desperate for reassurance.

"Because I will not give up until we do."

She'd responded to his kisses, his abruptness and his ignorance, but she'd not seen him like this, honest and true, and she didn't know what to say. His words had touched her in a way she'd never thought possible.

"Why do you study me so?"

"I've not seen this side of you."

He didn't reply.

"What is the strategy when we come across Pias?"

"I am hoping we get there before the Monroes."

She remembered what Galius had said—strength in numbers. If the Monroes were there before them, they'd be in trouble. It was better to deal with Pias, get Tsura back and flee to the other world before Silas and his brothers arrived.

"Yes, once we get Tsura you can go back to your vessel, and forget this ever happened."

"I won't forget, Gypsy."

"In good time you will. This day, and the ones before it, will all be a haze."

"How is it that Tsura hasn't used her powers on Pias?" he asked, changing the subject.

"He has drugged her. Used the Witch's berry he'd given the boy."

He nodded.

Had Pias not given the berry to Tsura. She could do anything out of fear or anger, and he knew it. The Renoldi was frightened of the little girl and with just cause.

"She is young and therefore cannot control what she does. It is my duty as her mother to teach her the ways."

"How are you going to do that if you cannot do the same things?"

She'd wondered this many times, and without the book she prayed she'd remember the spells, the herbs, oils and roots her mother had used, but more importantly she needed the words.

"I will need to have faith."

He regarded her, and she knew there would never be another man like him to enter her life. Resigned to a life alone, she'd grown to care for Kade Walker. It frightened and warmed her soul at the same time.

"How can you do that when you have no faith in yourself?"

"I beg your pardon?"

"Hold on, Gypsy, before you go off and tear me open. Hear me out."

"Very well." She fidgeted in the saddle.

"You can only count certain spells, correct?"

"Yes."

"Why is that?"

"I do not know."

"I believe it is because you do not trust in your own abilities. I can see how the death of your brother has affected you and Sorina's harsh words ripped you in two. You exist for Tsura. You wake each day for her and hence have forgotten to live for *you*."

"Nonsense."

"Truth."

"Absolute rubbish. I love my daughter more than life itself. Of course I'd put her above my own welfare, but for you to suggest I am not utilizing my abilities is absurd."

"You have not given yourself a chance."

"You are too foolish to understand."

"I understand more than you realize or give me recognition for."

"How dare you say I do not believe in myself?" She was shocked at his abruptness. He knew nothing about her, and yet what he'd said held truth.

"It is written on your face. In the way you walk, the set of your shoulders and the hesitance in your voice."

"I simply cannot do all of the spells. I have accepted it. Now leave it be."

"Ah, Gypsy, you are so naïve. Disappointment clouds me that you cannot see what I do."

"You know nothing of me."

"I believe I do."

"How can you be so crass?"

"All I propose is that you search within yourself. I bet you will be surprised at what you find."

"Bah! I have heard enough."

She couldn't let him know she felt the same way, had doubted herself from the very beginning. Vadoma was the gifted of the two sisters, and so she'd not even tried. When she had used the spells in the confines of the forest all alone…she'd failed.

"What of you?" she asked, tossing her hand in the air.

"What about me?"

"You're an unopened portal."

"There is nothing to know."

"Who is your mother?"

She knew the mention of his mother would light him up, and he deserved it for the things he'd said.

He clenched his jaw and frowned.

"Leave it alone, Gypsy."

"How convenient. You can spout off about me, and yet the mere mention of the woman who bore you sets you off."

"It is in the past."

"I've spoken of my past."

"You lied about your past, I just figured it out."

"No, I was not forthcoming. I did not lie."

"Your past is the reason we are both here right now."

This was true, but it did not stop her from wanting to know something personal about him. After all he knew so much about her.

"Did you know her name?"

He sighed.

"No."

"Where did your father meet her?"

"Sam did not know my mother in the way most men and women come together to make a child."

"I do not understand."

"Sam Walker raised me from the time I was an infant. He is not of my blood."

She didn't know what to say.

"I am sorry."

He eyed her.

"Do not apologize. Sam was the best thing that ever happened to me. Just because his blood is not within my veins does not mean he is not my father."

She nodded.

"If he hadn't taken me in, I'd be dead."

"You cannot be serious."

He nodded.

"My mother left me abandoned on the ship and never returned. If Sam hadn't been there to take pity on me, I'd have been thrown into the sea or sold as a slave."

Her heart broke thinking of how a mother could throw away her child.

"What was wrong with your mother that she'd give up her son?"

"I do not know."

"This Sam Walker must be a fine fellow."

"One of the finest."

"Where is he now?"

He clamped his lips and flexed his jaw.

"Kade, where is your father now?"

"The village is about half hour from here."

"Why will you not answer me?"

"I choose not to."

"But why?"

"We will need to find an inn that will feed us a bite to eat. The boy is probably as famished as I."

"What of your father?"

He blew out a long breath and faced her.

"I do not know."

Kade had spoken the truth to her. He didn't know if Sam was even alive, and the thought was almost his undoing. He tried to distract himself with thoughts of the child, Pril or the young lad but in the end his mind went back to Sam and how he fared. Would he be well when Kade saw him, his heart still slow, causing blackouts and dizziness? He was desperate for word, for any information to tell him Sam still lived. He rubbed his face, wiping the sweat from his brow.

Silas Monroe caused every muscle in his body to tense. Anger stirred his gut—his hands itched to strike out at the plantation owner and smash his bloody face in. He'd not rest until he knew that Sam was well, and Silas paid for what he did.

He glanced at Pril, stiff in her saddle, thankful she'd not pushed him further about where Sam was. He couldn't tell her the truth of why he'd been in the Peddler camp weeks before, blackmailed by the very man who'd hunted and killed her niece.

The boy leaned his back against her chest and snored. She was exhausted, yet resilient and always ready for battle. There were days he'd pushed her further than even he wanted to go. He was spent, and it took everything he had left in him to keep from closing his eyes. His muscles cried out for a soft bed and hot bath. It'd been weeks since he'd had either.

He led Goliath to a narrow gully of the Chicomine River and walked him across. He inhaled. The aroma of bannock filled his senses and caused his stomach to rumble. It'd been too long. He'd sacrificed everything to find the girl, leaving his vessel ported, his mates and the luxuries of his quarters. He missed them all, but he missed Sam more.

He should've never left him in the hospital alone, without a guard. He had enemies in almost every harbor, Felix Seller being one of them. The captain of the Seller Ship was his competition. For the last few years Kade had made his runs in good time. The other merchant hadn't been pleased that he was taking his work.

There were pirates and sea thieves he'd angered, not willing to give up his ship and what was on it without a fight. He hired the best seamen out there, fed and paid them well. In return, they remained at his side through it all.

He'd been blindsided by Silas. The wealthy bastard worshipped Kade, or so he made it seem, and he'd fallen into the trap. He blamed himself for Sam's capture—for his finger and his health. Had he not been so consumed with the loading of his ship, with the next delivery, Sam may still be with him and not locked up, being subjected to whatever means of torture Silas was inflicting.

He closed his eyes unable to think of his father any longer.

The small village hadn't grown in the four months since he'd been back. The town hosted an Inn nestled against the trees, and he led Goliath there. They passed homes with thatch roofs, the structures built with timber and scattered about the land in no particular order. Chickens ran loose across the dirt road, and he pulled his horse to the left so he didn't step on one.

A veil of darkness covered the land, the village asleep for the evening. A faint glow from the windows of the Inn lured him, and he let Goliath have control, taking them there. The Marrow Inn fell back against large oak trees and offered the privacy he desired.

He dismounted and stretched his tired legs.

"I will do the talking once inside," he said to Pril as he helped the boy down.

She nodded while sliding from Athos.

A fire burned in the large hearth against the far wall. A short counter made of pine stood between them and the man, fast asleep, resting his head on it.

Kade took his dagger from the sheath on his hip, and using the handle he hammered onto the wooden platform right next to the man's ear. The man jumped, knocking the book burrowed under his arm onto the ground. The Innkeeper wiped the spittle from his cheek and ran his hands through his thinning hair.

"A room is it?" he asked and glanced from Pril to the boy, then back to Kade.

"Yes, and warm water brought up for a bath please."

"Fine…fine." He wiped the sleep from his eyes.

"We've two horses out back that need tending."

"It'll cost extra for oats and a brushing."

"Very well."

He glanced behind them. "No bags?"

"No."

"Follow me." The short, portly innkeeper shuffled around the counter and down the hallway.

Kade went first, Pril and the boy behind him. The room was two doors down the hall from the front desk. He ushered Pril and the boy inside.

"We are famished. Is it possible to have something brought to the room?"

The man smiled, and Kade relaxed.

"Sure, sure. My wife, she made chowder soup."

"That will do. Thank you…uh—"

"Milo Mortis at your service."

"Much obliged, Milo."

Kade went into the room and closed the door.

Pril sat with the boy on the edge of the bed.

"I've asked for dinner to be brought," he said.

"Thank you."

The boy peered up at him with big round eyes. Kade reached out and mussed his hair.

"Famished are you?"

The child nodded, and he glanced at Pril.

"I've been suspicious for a while now," she said.

He knelt in front of the child and smiled.

"What is your name?" He'd asked him before but never got an answer.

The boy regarded him.

"Can you understand me?"

He placed his hand on Kade's cheek but said nothing.

A knock at the door took him from the child. He was delighted to see a plump woman with grey hair holding a tray with three bowls of chowder and a loaf of bread.

"Much obliged, Ma'am," he said and took the tray from her.

She smiled showing two deep dimples in her round cheeks.

"If you need anything, ring the bell," she said and pointed to a copper bell hung from the ceiling.

He nodded and closed the door.

"Red wolf," the boy whispered from behind him.

He placed the platter on the table and went to the lad.

"Red Wolf. It is nice to meet you." He put out his hand, and the boy lifted his brow.

"How come you haven't told us your name before now?" Pril asked.

He shrugged.

"We will not hurt you."

"I know this."

Pril smiled.

"Where do you come from?" Kade asked.

"I am Red Wolf son of Red Fox."

"Where is your father? We can take you to him."

The boy's eyes pooled, and when he blinked his lashes released two tears.

"Red Fox is gone from this world."

Pril placed her hand on his shoulder. "I am sorry, Red Wolf."

"What of your mother or other family?" Kade asked.

"It is but me."

The kid was alone much like himself, and Kade vowed to keep him safe at all cost. "How long have you been on your own?"

"I was slave to the white man for many seasons."

"You will be a slave no more, I can assure you of that," Kade said. He remembered the state the boy was in when he'd first seen him locked in the broom closet, and his gut clenched.

"You have no home then?" Pril asked.

"I am myself."

"You are welcome to stay with me for as long as you like," Pril said.

Red Wolf smiled. "Do you stay with Strong One?"

"You can call me, Kade."

He shook his head. "You are Strong One."

Kade shrugged.

Pril placed a bowl of chowder soup in front of the boy, and they dug into their evening meal. Red Wolf rambled on about his life before he was enslaved and his tribe of strong Cherokee people.

CHAPTER TWENTY-FOUR

Pril let Athos follow Goliath at an even pace into the forest. They'd left Red Wolf with Mrs. Mortis at the Inn. The elderly woman had a sweet smile and promised to take care of the lad, but Pril wasn't comforted. She'd not been happy with the arrangement, wanting to keep the child with her instead, but Kade refused to bring him and finalized things without her.

The trees shaded them from the afternoon sunlight as they went deeper into the woods, and she relaxed her squinted eyes. Tired from the night before, she'd not slept in anticipation of finally seeing her daughter today. She inhaled. How was her little one? Had Pias kept her drugged, sedated as not to cast a spell? Thoughts of all the wrong that could come to Tsura turned her stomach. If she was to have her wits today she needed to be prepared for anything, and that included death.

She recognized the branches drooping to the forest floor, the leaves similar to a veil, the crooked elm and the narrow creek to her left. She'd been here before. She shivered as memories invaded her mind. She closed her eyes, hearing the laughter of children and the scampering of feet about the leaf covered ground.

It had been here she'd grown. Where she watched as her mother took her last breath. It was the place Vadoma had reigned, frightening their clan and the people of Jamestown. It was from here she'd fled and taken her niece, promising to keep the child safe.

She didn't think she'd ever be back. She hadn't wanted to, and yet fate had led her here to the very place where it all began. Silas had done it on purpose, but why? What was the reasoning behind this destination for Pias to hand Tsura over? She tried to recall any recollection of the curse Vadoma had laid. Had her sister said anything of the place where Tsura had been born for it to be broken?

She searched her memory for the words—the blood curse, but neither showed it to be so.

"I have been here," she whispered.

Kade held up his hand, and she pulled on Athos reins. He swiveled in the saddle and glanced at her, his brow furrowed.

"I was raised within these trees. I ran upon this ground."

"You know where we are?"

"This was my home."

He scanned the area before his eyes came back to hers.

"Do you know where we might be going?" he asked.

She nodded.

"Vadoma's cabin."

"Cabin?"

"My sister was a Chuvani. She received the finest of things from her people. It is the same home my mother lived in. Beyond the tree of fire." She pointed past him to the red leafed tree within the forest.

"Magnificent."

"It is where my mother sleeps." She climbed down from Athos and walked him into the bushes.

"What are you doing?"

"We go on foot from here." She tied the reins around the trunk of a pine.

"Why?"

"It is sacred ground. A Chuvani rests here. No animals shall pass."

She waited while he dismounted and tied Goliath next to Athos. She shifted the quiver to rest it more comfortably on her back and gripped her bow tight.

He stood beside her, and together they walked toward the cabin ahead. She yearned to touch his hand and steal away the comfort that came with him. He'd been strong and unwavering throughout their journey. Without him, she'd have met death long before now, never seeing her Tsura again.

The cabin stood nestled in the comfort of tall maple, oak and pine trees. Overgrown bushes grew up the walls of the abode, and Pril couldn't help the unease as it crept into her soul.

"Not very inviting," Kade said from beside her.

"It has remained empty since my sister's death."

No one was here, and she couldn't hide the disappointment at not seeing her daughter. She caught her foot on something and fell forward. Kade grabbed hold of her arm, saving her from the hard ground.

"Thank you," she breathed.

The sound of a tree falling, and branches breaking, echoed around them. She turned just in time to see the log fall from the tree above, rope tied to either end of it.

"Run!" Kade yelled pushing her out of the way right before the log took out his feet and slammed his body face forward onto the ground.

She scrambled toward him, but was stopped when something cold touched the back of her head.

"Well, well if it isn't my dearest niece," Pias said. "I see you've brought your friend, hmmmm?"

On her hands and knees, she dug her fingers into the dirt. Kade didn't move, and she wasn't sure if he was injured or playing possum.

"Stand," Pias commanded.

She got to her feet, swept the hair from her eyes and glared at her captor.

"It seems you've escaped death." He tilted his head, and his eyes roamed her body. "Was it a spell? Is that what you did?"

"Where is my daughter?"

"You are without child, and yet you call your sister's your own?"

"I must see her."

"All in good time, my dear." He yanked her close, the gun pressed into her side.

"Damn it, Pias, tell me where she is."

"Tsk. Tsk. One in your circumstance shouldn't be so demanding."

She wrestled against his grip anxious for word on Tsura.

He gave her a shake before bringing her close. "Cease at once."

She could feel his breath against her cheek. She tried to pull away from him but her effort proved futile when he yanked her back toward his chest.

"Let me see Tsura," she shouted. Her insides cramped, her chest seized as she thought of a life without her daughter. Where had Pias placed her? Had he given her to the Monroes already? Was she too late? "You must tell me, does she live?"

His black eyes peered into hers, and she saw no trace of pity within them.

"Does she live?" she screamed.

The certainty she'd held onto all of this time and had kept her sane was now out of reach. She felt it falter and break. No longer able to control the anger, the fear, the dread, she lashed out, striking him with her free arm. "You bastard, I will kill you. I will kill you!"

Pias dropped his gun, grabbed hold of her hair and drove his fist into her mouth. Her skin split, and pain erupted from her lips to encompass the whole side of her face. The forest walls spun, she blinked to regain her composure and tried to focus on his face. Blood poured from the wound, and she tasted the metal upon her tongue.

He placed the end of the pistol to her head. "I will end you…"

She met his crazed eyes with a lethal stare of her own. If Tsura were dead what good would her life be now? She challenged him. Chin up, she pushed him to pull the trigger.

"Do your worst."

Kade's head pounded, and he blinked several times before his vision cleared. The fresh aroma of the soil mixed with the fragrant New England asters filled his senses and cleared his mind. He heard voices and lifted his head to see Pias holding Pril, his pistol to her head, blood on her chin and lips. Panic seized his chest, his ribs ached—his breathing was labored. Pril was hurt, and Pias was going to kill her.

"Pias," he called.

The Renoldi turned from Pril, the pistol still at her head, but his attention on Kade.

"Welcome, Mr. Walker. It is good to see you," he exclaimed. "Do stand, and if you try anything I will kill her."

"Take the pistol from her head first." He knew Pias spoke the truth, but needed to make sure Pril was okay first.

Pias sighed and removed the pistol from Pril's head and pointed it at Kade.

He held his arms out, keeping his hands visible.

"Your dagger if you please."

He pulled his knife from its sheath and tossed it onto the ground in front of them.

Pril struggled against Pias's hold. He skillfully wrapped his arm around her neck and jerked her against him.

"If you continue to fight me, you will expire, and so will your child."

The murderous look on his face frightened Kade. Without his dagger he was helpless against the wild man. Pril's life hung by a wire, and one wrong move by either of them could be fatal.

"Gypsy, do as he asks," he said, his eyes pleading with her to listen.

He stood still too afraid to move as he watched the play of emotions flicker across her red-brown gaze. She was scared. He wanted for some way to let her know he'd never leave her. He'd be by her side until Tsura was safe.

She relaxed, letting her shoulders fall.

He blew out a long sigh.

"Walk toward the cabin," Pias commanded.

"Where is Silas," she asked.

"I would imagine on his plantation."

"Is he not meeting with you for Tsura?"

Kade listened to the exchange, not missing the desperation in Pril's voice. He wished he could do something to help her, to set her mind at ease. He searched the area around the cabin for signs of Tsura. A blackened pit was dug into the ground, smoke cascaded into the sky from the small flame inside. A pot sat on a smooth rock beside the fire. Other cookware lay in front of the pit, but there were no signs of the girl…or the Monroes.

"Who are you meeting then?" Pril asked.

Pias glanced at Kade and smirked before taking the handle of his gun and smashing it over Pril's head. She crumbled to the ground.

Kade stepped forward, fists clenched, jaw flexed.

Pias swung the pistol toward him. His thin eyes became slits, and his high cheekbones lifted even more when he smiled.

"Do as I ask or I will kill her."

He growled and gnashed his back teeth together. He wanted to smash the Renoldi's face until there was nothing left.

"You will die this night."

Pias tipped his head back and laughed.

"You are amusing, my friend."

"I am not your friend."

"So sad. I had thought we'd become more than acquaintances."

The man was absurd. "I generally do not surround myself with lowlifes such as yourself."

"You hold yourself in high regard, do you? A merchant vagabond no less?"

"Higher than you."

The other man shrugged before he pointed the gun toward him. He walked Kade to the trunk of an oak. Pias pulled Kade's arms back to wrap them around the base of the tree and fasten them together. More rope was strewn around his middle, binding him to the trunk of the tree.

He glanced at Pril still unconscious on the ground, and he glared at Pias. Here he was again, helpless in the clutches of this bastard gypsy. He watched as the Renoldi tied Pril's ankles and wrists, leaving her on the ground. He took her quiver and bow and placed them against the log wall of the cabin.

"How did you escape my clan?" he asked, stopping at the pot to pull some meat from inside and place the fare into his mouth.

"Galius."

"Interesting."

"How so?"

Pias stared off, and when his gaze came back to Kade's he smiled.

"How long have you known the Peddlers?"

"Where is the child?"

"Safe."

"Where?"

"Within the cabin walls."

"Have you drugged her?"

"Why of course. You think me foolish enough to risk my life with a young Chuvani?"

"She is a little girl, what harm can she do?" Pril had told him of her powers, but he doubted her.

"You still do not believe?"

He shook his head.

"Such a shame. Such a shame indeed."

"I do not see how. I've not seen these powers or magick you speak of."

"Soon, soon, and you will want her too."

"If it is true, she is still a life. One that does not deserve to be hunted for her abilities and a damn curse."

Pias leaned against the tree beside him.

"You do not have powers?" He knew the Renoldi didn't. Pril had told him the magick was only bestowed upon women.

"My daughters can count the spells, but nothing like the Chuvani."

Pias's daughters were dead, but he wasn't going to tell him that. The crazed man would kill them for it.

"When do they arrive?" he asked. The Monroes hadn't shown yet. He was sure the trap Pias set had been for them. The Renoldi figured him and Pril for dead and was shocked to see them. He'd planned on killing the Monroes all along. "Will you kill them after they've handed you the pendant?"

Pias whipped his head around, his angled face framed by long black hair.

"I will."

"They are of three, and you are but one."

"I only seek one."

So it was Silas he was going to meet. The other brothers would remain home. It didn't make sense. Jude especially never left his eldest brother's side.

"Are you sure?"

"I am."

"The Monroes cannot be trusted."

"And neither can you, Mr. Walker. Tell me, does she know of your plan to steal the child?"

"Go to hell."

"Tsk, tsk. What will she say when she finds out you betrayed her?"

He pulled against the ropes, wanting to throttle the snake.

"You are afraid and rightly so." His eyes grew wide. "Oh, I see. I see indeed."

"You see nothing."

"You love her." Pias giggled and clapped his hands together. "Wonderful."

Kade growled.

"She will cast you to the wolves when she hears of your deceit. You will be but a poor man with a broken heart." He laughed a high-pitched breathy sound.

"She will know I had no choice."

"But you did. There is always a choice."

"I would not see my father killed."

"You chose his life for another's." He smiled. "A little girl's no less, but one with charm."

"I did not know Silas would kill the child."

"So sad…" Pias walked toward the cabin and disappeared inside.

"How could you?" Pril whispered as a tear danced down her blood-smeared cheek.

The agony within her words cut into him and wounded his soul beyond repair.

CHAPTER TWENTY-FIVE

Pril hung her head. She would not let him see the tears within her eyes. He betrayed her—duped her into his ruse, and she'd been the fool to think he was different. He wanted her daughter, hunted her like all the others and for the Monroes.

She held back the sob as it pressed into the back of her throat. Anguish sliced away at her soul, shredding any ounce of affection she'd had for him. How could she have been so blind? He'd tricked her, used her grief as leverage to get what he wanted…and he'd won.

"Pril."

"Leave me," she whispered as another tear dripped from her chin.

"Let me explain."

Her head shot up. "There is no need. You have deceived me."

She saw the remorse in his eyes and refused to acknowledge it.

"I had no other choice. You must understand."

"I understand nothing. She is a little girl." Her bottom lip trembled. "A baby."

"Silas has Sam. He is holding him captive unless I bring the child to him." He tried to stretch forward but the rope kept him still.

"You are a worm, Kade Walker."

"I wasn't aware Silas would kill the child. Do you think me so low that I'd watch a child be murdered?"

She sent him a chilling glare.

"I worried for my father." He paused. "I do not know if he lives even now."

She denied any sense of pity for him. He had conned her, pretended to care while plotting to take her child.

"Hush. I will not fall victim to your schemes any longer."

"I—"

"Enough."

Pias opened the door and walked out with Tsura in his arms. Pril gasped. Her baby was here. She was alive. Every muscle in her body screamed to be released from the bonds that kept her captive. Her arms ached to hold her little girl. She slid forward determined to make sure Tsura was well, to touch her—kiss her.

"Remain where you are," Pias said.

She stopped.

He laid Tsura on the ground and reached for the pistol tied to his waist.

"Can I see her?" she asked.

"Why of course…from where you sit."

"Please, please." She shimmied on her knees toward them. "Let me come closer."

The need to see Tsura, caress her face and hear her voice forced her to beg him. Was she well, had she fallen ill? What if Pias fed her an overdose of the Witch's berry? It was almost too much for her to bear. She gasped, and her flesh heated. She wanted to shriek, to pull at her hair, to lose control and spew vile obscenities at the scum who stole her daughter.

Pias went to where his horse stood grazing beside the cabin. He hadn't bothered to unsaddle the poor animal. A brown sack hung from the saddle. He reached inside and pulled out the spell book.

"It was to be the two of us, Pias. What is going on here?" A man Pril recognized as a Monroe, but was unsure which one, walked around the cabin. His navy blue coat hung past his hips to settle just above his knees and rest against the tweed breeches.

"Ah, Hiram, a pleasure to see you again." Pias smiled and walked toward him, the book held to his chest.

"We had an agreement."

"And we still do."

"Who are these people?" Hiram asked.

"I am Kade Walker, and this is Pril of the Peddlers. The child you seek is hers."

She watched as Hiram's face lost all color, matching the peruke upon his head.

"You've come for my daughter. To kill her," she hissed.

"Quiet," Pias commanded.

Pril planted her feet flat on the ground and stood. Her arms shot out in front of her to keep her balance. She wobbled back and forth, but did not fall. She'd destroy the bastard for all he'd done.

She hopped toward them.

"Cease," Pias shouted.

She angled her features into a scowl and hopped again.

"Stay put, Gypsy."

She ignored Kade and came closer to them

"Wait…you must hear me out," Hiram said.

She'd wait no longer. She wanted to hold her baby—to drive the end of her arrow into the hearts of both Pias and Hiram. The Monroe had conspired with Pias all of this time—she'd kill him first.

"I loved your sister."

The declaration stopped her, and she turned toward him.

"What did you say?" She was close enough she could hear Tsura's soft snores, and she released a breath.

"I loved her."

How could that be? Vadoma cared for Silas. He was Tsura's father.

"And she loved me."

"Enough!" she snapped. "My sister loved no one."

"I cherished her."

Hiram's eyes drooped, and she saw the sadness within them.

"If there was one she held affection for it was Silas."

"No, Silas was infatuated with her, but she cared for me."

"Lies."

"I speak the truth, please you must hear me."

"Silas courted her. I saw him come and seek her."

The corner of his mouth lifted.

"She used him to be with me."

"But why?"

"We wanted to run away together when she told me of the babe." His eyes glazed as he remembered. "I bought us passage upon a ship heading to the other world. We were to board the next day. Silas paid the captain to set sail without Vadoma. I couldn't get off. I was trapped at sea. When I finally was able to sail home, she refused to see me. She'd grown cold, resentful and dangerous. She no longer cared for me."

"You killed her. You and your brothers hung her."

"I did not know. When I found out what Silas had plotted I raced to save her…but I was too late. I could do nothing." He wiped the tear from his cheek. "I will never forgive myself for what happened that day."

She was stunned, shocked by what he'd said. She hadn't known, never suspected that Hiram Monroe was Tsura's father. All this time he'd been the one Vadoma had loved. Her sister had changed while love blossomed inside of her, and when he never returned she grew to be vile and spiteful. She became evil, inflicting the pain she'd felt onto those around her. The blood curse; it was why she'd placed it, her last spell to get back at Hiram for breaking her heart. Pril understood. The anger and resentment she'd felt toward her sister disappeared and was replaced with sorrow. Vadoma died of a broken heart.

"I have done some things I am not proud of..." He glanced at Tsura sleeping on the ground. "But I will not allow my brothers to kill my child."

She assessed him, trying to decide if what he'd said was true. Could she trust him? There was no valor or arrogance within his stance, and when she peered into his eyes she saw anguish and truth.

Pias clapped his hands together. "What a beautiful, tragic love story. I must say, Hiram, you tell it well. Bravo, my friend. Bravo."

"Go to hell," Hiram growled.

"Where is the talisman?"

"No! Do not give it to him," Pril begged.

Pias turned and aimed the pistol toward her.

"No!" Kade yelled.

A shot rang out, and she squeezed her eyes shut, waiting for the pain of the lead ball to pierce her skin. When nothing came, she slowly opened her eyes. Pias lay on the ground, eyes staring up at the sky as blood seeped from his chest.

Smoke billowed from Hiram's pistol which was still pointed at the Renoldi.

He went to Pril first, and she shielded herself with her arms.

"I will not hurt you," he said as he untied the bonds and set her free.

She ran to Tsura and picked her limp body up to cradle within her arms. A loud sob burst from her lips as she nestled her face within her raven curls. She was still drugged from the Witch's berry, but Pril didn't care. Tsura lived, and she'd found her.

Hiram's shadow loomed on the ground in front of her. She tucked Tsura into her side and stood. He wanted to see the child, to see his daughter's face for the first time, but she didn't trust him. He was a Monroe.

He reached across Tsura's sleeping form and laid the ruby pendant onto her chest. The stone flickered, growing brighter until it glowed.

"For you, little one."

The talisman she thought lost forever lay upon Tsura.

"Where did you get it?"

"The night Vadoma told me she was with child." He reached out and with the tip of his finger caressed Tsura's cheek. "She made me promise that if anything ever happened to her, this necklace would be given to you."

"To me?" Vadoma had promised her the pendant after she died, but Pril thought it only words. Now she knew her sister had spoken the truth.

Hiram nodded.

"She cared for you and knew the kind of love that was inside of your heart."

She often wondered if Vadoma knew she'd die that night four years past, if she placed the blood curse for more than the obvious reason. Now with the pendant being returned she believed it to be true.

"Thank you."

Hiram smiled.

"I cannot let you take her."

"Nor, do I want to. She is in good hands."

The weight of the past crashed down upon her. The regret, anger and fear slid from her shoulders, and relief overflowed from her lids to wash her face.

Hiram patted her back. "You'll do right with her."

"Brother, I am deeply hurt that you have betrayed me." Silas walked from the forest into the small clearing.

Pril grabbed the pendant, folding it within her palm and stepped back closer to the door of Vadoma's home. Three men walked with Silas, and she knew the white one to be his brother, Jude. Two Powhatan Indians stood on either side of the eldest Monroe. The tribe lived outside of Jamestown and was known for their lethal skills. Silas must've hired them. The urge to place Tsura somewhere safe overwhelmed her.

"I cannot allow you to continue your rampage any longer," Hiram said.

Silas' face turned hard and rigid.

"Is that so?"

"It is."

"And what of the times where you participated, Brother? We cannot forget that."

"Today it ends."

"Indeed it does."

Hiram raised the pistol in his hand and pointed it in Silas' direction.

"You are a weasel," Jude spat.

"It is true. I have done many things for which I am not proud," Hiram said.

Pril glanced down at Tsura's sleeping face. With the heel of her foot she pushed open the door and slipped inside.

She laid her on the ground. "Protect this little one. Keep thy evil and threats to none." She said the words, counting a spell to protect her daughter from the Monroes, and the evil that lay outside the cabin walls.

She took one last look at Tsura before she slipped the pendant over her head, hiding it beneath her blouse and exited the cabin, closing the door softly behind her. She spotted her bow and quiver to the left, and took a step toward them.

"I see you've done me a service yet, Brother," Silas said as he observed Kade still tied to the tree.

Kade struggled against the ropes. The veins in his neck protruded, his face crimson, his arms bunched.

"He will be freed," Hiram said.

"He will die." He leaned in close to Kade. "As your father did."

"You rotten bastard," Kade spat, pulling on the ropes with enough force to shake the tree.

Silas laughed.

"Did you think I'd let him live?"

Kade's lips thinned, his jaw flexed, and he growled low in his throat.

"You are more foolish than I thought."

"Brother, you cannot end his life. Have you forgotten what he is to you?" Hiram asked.

"He is nothing to me," Silas screamed.

"He is your blood."

CHAPTER TWENTY-SIX

Kade's head spun, and he blinked several times to regain his composure. Blood? He was blood to the Monroes? Impossible. It couldn't be. He'd been raised at sea by Sam, his mother a deserter.

"It is true," Hiram said.

He searched for Pril. He needed her strength—the abruptness and fire that was all her. He'd absorb her courage, her solidity, and confront the Monroes. But she refused to look at him, and he couldn't blame her. He was all the things she'd said and more. His gaze fell to Silas. His cravat was high around his neck, his waistcoat and breeches were of the finest fabric. The well-dressed aristocrat would die for what he'd done to Sam. He clenched his fists, anticipating the feel of his dagger as it sliced the man's throat.

"You are one of us," Hiram said. "You are a Monroe."

"Bullshit." He would not believe it.

"You are my twin."

Absolute nonsense. Hiram had fair hair and blue eyes, just like him, but so did half the country. They looked nothing alike.

"I was raised by Sam Walker. My mother left me on the ship, abandoned me."

"Our father wanted you dead," Hiram whispered. "He believed it was a bad omen to have two babies born together and forced our mother to be rid of you."

"She gave you to that bastard sea merchant instead of killing you like she was told to," Silas barked.

Hiram frowned. "She couldn't do it. She loved you and knew Samuel Walker would care for you as his own."

He'd always been drawn to Jamestown, to the Monroes. Could what they said be true? But why was it kept from him?

"Sam never told me."

"Mother made him promise not to speak of it to you. She thought of you even on her death bed."

"She was a lunatic, a narcissist who took to spirits daily," Silas sneered.

"Do not speak of the dead with little regard, Brother."

"I will speak what I want." Silas cocked the pistol and aimed it at Kade. "I've grown tired of this day. Where is the child?"

He could feel the ropes loosening around his arms and pushed away from the tree. He was thankful Pias hadn't tied his ankles. He pressed the bottom of his foot into the trunk, stretching the ropes.

"She will remain with Pril," Hiram spoke, his pistol still pointed at Silas.

"No one will stand in my way of killing the girl."

"She needs to die for ours to live," Jude said.

"There has been enough bloodshed. I will not condone this."

"I care not what you say. My daughters have all perished because of that spawn, that witch." Silas pointed toward Pril.

"I am not a witch, nor was my sister or her daughter."

"Spells, potions and that blasted curse say you are!"

Pril sighed. "I cannot undo what my sister has done in the past, but I can end the blood curse."

Silas smirked, and the wrinkles around his mouth stretched upward. "You will break the curse?"

She nodded.

He laughed.

"A mere gypsy with no gifts other than the hole between your legs?"

Kade heaved against the rope around his chest. He winced as the twine dug into his skin cutting the flesh.

"Be still, Strong One."

He paused. The whispered voice belonged to Red Wolf. He was supposed to be back at the Inn. "How did you find us?"

"It was easy. Your horse has light step."

He tried not to smile at the kid's response and remained unmoving while the boy worked the bonds.

"The child must die." Silas motioned with his free hand to the Indians beside him.

The two men pulled their tomahawks from their bare backs and ran toward Hiram and Pril. Kade's chest constricted, his ribs pressed into his stomach. He launched forward, rustling the leaves. He needed Red Wolf to hurry, or Pril would die.

Pril went for her bow and quiver. No one would get through the door of the cabin. Bow and arrow ready, she aimed at the beefy Indian, screaming as he ran toward her. She steadied her bow, took a deep breath and released the arrow. She watched as it soared through the air and stuck into the Powhatan's neck. The man fell to the ground, convulsing as blood spurted from the wound.

She spun, arrow ready, and watched horrified as the other Indian drove his tomahawk into Hiram's chest. She set her sights on the Powhatan and loosed the arrow. The stick lodged into the tall lengthy man's back. He pulled his tomahawk from Hiram's chest and turned deadly eyes toward her.

She reached inside her quiver but it was empty. The Indian came toward her. She froze; her body would not move. Silas and Jude went for the cabin. *Tsura!* She dove to the ground, pulled the arrow from the Powhatan she'd just killed, rolled onto her knees and drew her bow. The man was two feet from her, his bloodied weapon raised high. She squeezed her eyes shut and fired. The ground beside her shook when the Indian fell, the arrow lodged in his chest.

She grabbed the spell book and clutched it to her. Her arms ached from the tight hold, but she'd not lose it again. She raced to beat Silas to the cabin door when Jude yanked her backward by the hair. The pinch in her scalp caused her to cry out as he held her tight.

"That was amusing," he said and tried to pull the book from her.

She refused to give it to him, keeping the book tucked under her right arm.

He jerked on her hair again, and she was sure he'd pulled the tresses from the scalp. Her hold on the book loosened, and he wrenched it from her grasp.

"What is this?" he asked.

She didn't answer him.

"It appears to be the devil's work." He tossed the heavy book into the fire.

"No!" She reached out her arms and thrashed the air as the flames devoured the book and every written word inside of it.

She struggled against him, but he held her still. When Silas came out of the cabin with Tsura in his arms, she ceased. She prayed the protection spell she'd spoken earlier worked, and her daughter would be safe.

Silas laid Tsura onto the ground and grinned at Pril.

"You bastard. I will kill you," she screamed.

"Quiet her," Silas yelled to Jude.

Before she could defend herself, Jude struck her with his closed fist.

Pain exploded on the right side of her face. She shook her head, pushed through the dizziness and the nausea to glare at him.

"A tough one are you?"

She spat in his face.

He backhanded her, snapping her head to the side. Blood dripped from the cut on her cheek, and she left it there.

Silas pulled a dagger from his belt and knelt beside Tsura. The end of the blade pointed toward her heart. He was going to kill her.

"No!"

He lifted his arms high into the air above the girl, ready to drive the knife into her chest.

"Blast not what ye have done but what ye prepare. Cast thy weapon far into the air." The pendant grew warm against her heart as she spoke the words.

Silas' hand shook as he tried to hold onto the knife, but Pril's spell was too strong, and the dagger flew from his hand and into the air to land at Kade's feet.

"You bitch," Silas shouted, and he dove for the blade the same time Kade became free from the ropes.

Kade jumped onto the Monroe, and she watched helpless as the two wrestled on the ground. She wriggled against Jude. She had to get to Tsura. She needed to protect her. Jude held her tight against him. He was stronger and could easily restrain her, but she wasn't giving up. She tossed her head back into his chin. The force vibrated down her neck and into her back. She stomped her heel onto the top of his foot, but his hold on her grew tighter.

Silas pounded his fists into Kade's sides, and she could hear his breath as it whooshed from his lungs with each blow. She cringed, helpless to do anything other than watch.

Kade grabbed Silas' peruke and threw it into the bushes. He smashed his fist into the other man's nose. Blood shot from the open wound, but Silas did not stop his relentless beating of Kade's ribs.

Tsura sat up and wiped her eyes.

Pril struggled against Jude, driving her elbow into his side as she surveyed the danger all around her daughter. Her stomach dropped. She prayed the Witch's berry still had Tsura dazed, and she'd not understand what was going on around her.

A low, threatening rumble came from Kade. She turned from Tsura just as he plunged the blade into Silas' side again and again until he fell on top of him, unmoving.

Jude threw her to the ground and went for Tsura.

She scrambled for a weapon but there was nothing within her reach. He was almost to her, and she didn't have time to stop him. Fear slammed into her stomach, and she reached out, grasping at the air around her.

She heard the whistle of an arrow right before it embedded itself into Jude's back. Three more followed one after the other, but he kept going determined to kill her daughter.

"Tsura run!" she called to her.

Her daughter turned toward her. Confusion folded her forehead, and her pudgy hand brushed the ringlets that had fallen into her eyes.

Jude reached out to grab her.

Kade shoved Silas from him and threw the dagger. The blade struck Jude in the chest. He fell to his knees, his hand still out, he stretched for Tsura. A slow exhale exited his lips before he fell to the ground dead.

Pril released a sob and ran toward her daughter. She scooped her up and smothered her with kisses.

"My darling, thank God you're safe."

"Mama, I knew you'd come."

"I did, my sweet." She kissed the top of her head. Her eyes overflowed with tears as she rocked Tsura in her arms.

Red wolf walked from the bushes and into the clearing. He held a bow she did not recognize at his side. He resembled a warrior, much older than his twelve years. He stood away from them, and she sensed his confusion. She opened her arms, and he ran into them.

He smelled of pine and dirt, and she squeezed him to her.

"You saved her life."

"As you saved mine," he said.

"Where did you get the bow and arrows?"

The boy smiled. "I borrowed them from Mr. Mortis."

She nodded.

"What is her name?" he asked, staring at Tsura.

Before Pril could answer, Tsura sat upright and said, "I am Tsura."

"I am Red Wolf."

Tsura placed the palm of her hand to the boy's cheek, and his eyes grew big.

She smiled. Her daughter had shown Red Wolf a hint of magick.

"Gypsy, I need you," Kade called as he leaned over Hiram.

She didn't trust him, and as much as it hurt her, after today she would have no more to do with Kade Walker. She lifted Tsura off of her and went to Hiram. The Monroe was still alive, his breathing shallow, his skin a light shade of grey. She unbuttoned his long coat and folded it away from the wound. Blood surrounded the gash in his chest and stuck to his white shirt. There was nothing they could do. The tomahawk had gone too deep, and he'd lost too much blood.

Hiram reached for Tsura, and she placed her hand within his. Pril had never told her who her father was, but as she watched Tsura lean closer to him, she saw that the girl knew.

"I've not known you at all, but I always loved you," he wheezed.

The girl ran her hand over Hiram's eyes to close them, he inhaled short quick puffs of air, and she knelt beside him. She placed both hands one on top of the other covering the wound and closed her eyes. Her arms shook, her cheeks heated, the softness on her face contorted as she rocked back and forth. Sweat dripped from her forehead, and she pitched forward.

She opened her eyes, glassy and bloodshot, turned to the side and vomited onto the grass. Pril went to her.

Hiram sat up, the wound no longer visible, his flesh closed and healed.

"Bloody hell," Kade whispered.

She smiled into the top of Tsura's head.

"You did it, little one."

"As I did for you, mama." Tsura placed her hand onto Pril's chest, and she remembered the burns her daughter had healed.

"Yes."

"The child has her mother's gifts," Hiram said, staring in wonder at his healed flesh.

"She does." Pril reached for the pendant around her neck and handed it to Tsura. "Come closer," she said to Hiram.

He knelt in front of them. Without Pril telling her, Tsura took her father's hand.

"Do you know the words?" she asked her daughter.

Tsura nodded.

"Cast ye from thy blood curse. Revoke thy spell, remove thy verse."

Hiram glanced at Pril.

"It is done," she said.

He put his arms out, and Pril's hold on her daughter tightened.

"Mama, it is okay."

Her daughter was growing into a strong Chuvani. Her sense for right and wrong was unlike Vadoma's, and the worry Pril had felt all this time, eased from her soul.

She released her and watched through tear filled eyes as Tsura hugged her father.

Hiram wiped a tear from his own eye and kissed the girl's cheek. "My love will be with you until the end of time."

"I know."

He stood and observed the bodies of his brothers. "You are the only blood I have left," he said to Kade. "You will always be welcome home."

Kade nodded but did not respond, and she wasn't sure if he'd accepted that he was a Monroe yet or not. Such things took time, and he would need plenty.

"I bid you farewell." He took one last look at the cabin. She knew he was remembering Vadoma and the love they shared.

She stood with Tsura and Red Wolf as Hiram disappeared into the forest.

Kade stepped toward them, and she pushed Tsura behind her. He'd broken her confidence therefore she'd not allow him near her daughter.

He stopped, and sadness reflected in his eyes. "I mean no harm."

"Is it because Silas is dead along with his brother?"

"No, I decided long ago that I would not take the child to them."

"Bah!" Anger consumed her. She'd begun to care for Kade Walker, and he'd shown her his true side. He'd manipulated her, and she'd been so caught up in finding her daughter that she'd believed every word he'd said as truth.

"You must know I'd never harm a child. I am not that kind of man."

"You are many things to which I cannot speak of right now." She glanced down at the children on either side of her.

"My father's life was at risk? For all the good I tried to do, Silas still killed the only person I ever cared for."

She'd seen how the news of Sam's death affected him, and a part of her wanted to comfort him, but she could not see past what he'd done. She straightened.

"Look around you at the bloodshed, at the lives lost for your child. Can you not see the sacrifices made?"

"I see a traitor and nothing more."

His shoulders fell, and he shook his head.

"Take your leave." A small piece of her did not want to see him go, but her stubbornness refused to forgive him.

He glanced at Tsura and then Red Wolf.

"Where do you wish to stay, boy?" he asked.

Red Wolf peered up at Pril, his bottom lip trembled, and his brown eyes misted.

"I wish to go with Strong One."

Pril's heart broke. She was sure he'd want to stay with her. He had become a part of her, and she loved him. She could see he battled with his decision and wanted him to know it was okay.

"I have grown to love you, Red Wolf, but you must go where your heart speaks. Strong One will care for you and keep you safe. I shall miss you."

He released a sob before he jumped into her arms and squeezed her tight.

"Go now, and carry me in your heart, for you will be in mine always." She kissed his cheek one last time before he went to stand with Kade.

"Sister, are you well?" Galius asked, concern stretched across his face as he surveyed the bodies strewn about the ground.

She spun surprised to see him.

"Brother...you are here. You have come."

"I did." He frowned. "You were to wait for me."

She averted her gaze from his unable to see the disappointment within the dark realms of his eyes.

"I could not. You must understand. She is my life."

He smiled.

"As she is mine." He glanced at Kade. "Thank you for protecting my sister and niece."

"It was an honor." His eyes met hers. She saw the torment within them and glanced away.

"I see you've done well, and all but one Monroe is dead."

"Hiram will remain alive. He is Tsura's father."

Galius' eyes widened.

"It is true. Vadoma had us fooled into believing Silas to be Tsura's father."

"How can that be? We watched her go off with him."

"Yes, but Vadoma did not want us, or anyone to know of her love for Hiram."

"Why?"

"She wanted to run away with him. They were to sail to the other world when his brothers shanghaied him. Silas wanted Vadoma for himself."

"I remember he'd come to call on her several times."

"And she refused."

"And he got angry."

"Hiram did not return until after she'd had Tsura, and by then it was too late."

"She'd surpassed the evil we'd seen in her and became far worse than any of us had ever expected."

She nodded.

Galius' eyes clouded, and she knew he thought of how he'd spoken of his sister all these years. He blamed Vadoma for the blood curse—the reason they'd been hunted, and so many had died. She placed her hand on his shoulder.

"Time will heal your wounds, Brother."

CHAPTER TWENTY-SEVEN

Kade waited. He did not want to leave Pril. Not like this. Not with hard feelings. Not with his insides in turmoil, and his chest aching so fiercely he was sure he'd die.

She kept her distance from him, and when he tried to explain she closed him out, refusing to hear him.

There was nothing left to do but say goodbye. Now that Galius was here, she was in safe hands. He could leave knowing all would be well with her and the child. He took the boys hand in his.

"Goodbye, Gypsy."

She lifted her head. He memorized every feature on her face—her short nose, pointed chin, high cheekbones, rose-colored lips and fire-red hair. He embedded her image into his mind.

"Goodbye."

She was strong, and he knew she'd forget him before he was out of her sight. The thought struck him, almost taking him to the ground as he walked away. He'd be forever changed because of her—a man who cared only for himself, and his problems had grown to care for a little girl he'd never met and her mother. He'd seen into Pril's life and grew compassion for the things she'd dealt with.

He sighed. It was far better this way. He glanced down at Red Wolf. He had the boy. He thought of Sam. He'd never see him again. He swallowed past the guilt in his throat. He wouldn't hear Sam's rustic laugh, see the twinkle in his eye or ask him for advice. He was gone. The thought stopped him, and his life with Sam replayed in his mind.

Red Wolf tugged on his arm.

"Strong One?"

He focused on the boy's face. Faint lines creased the sides of his eyes.

"Yes?"

"Your thoughts make you sad."

"They do."

"Why?"

He didn't see any sense in hiding how he felt about Sam Walker.

"My father has died."

"The man with the slanted face killed him." It wasn't a question, and he was taken aback at the boy's keen sense of the things that had gone on around him.

"Yes."

"We have both faced this death."

The boy had seen hardships far worse than Kade. He'd watched his father die, and was kept a slave for many years.

"I will not leave you."

Red Wolf's words nestled into his heart, and his chest ached with affection for the lad. The days they'd spent together the child had not spoken. Afraid and unsure, he'd remained mute. Last night he'd rambled on about all sorts of things, and Kade listened, enjoying the way his voice grew with excitement.

Goliath stood where Kade had left him hours before, and he ran his hand along the smooth coat.

"Hello, boy."

Goliath whinnied and stomped his feet.

"Your horse has great affection for you," Red Wolf said.

"Think so?"

He nodded.

Kade lifted Red Wolf up onto Goliath's back and climbed up after him. He clicked his tongue, and the horse set out at an even gait. The tops of the trees swayed, rustling the leaves together as a light breeze blew against them. He inhaled, smelling the sea. The salt lingered in the air, and he could taste it upon his tongue. He was almost home—to his ship, his mates and his cabin. He yearned to run his hand along the wooden rail, feel the uneven boards as he walked across them. He thought of Pril and the urge to look back. To see what he'd left behind. He tensed. He would not seek her face among the trees.

"Strong One?"

"Yeah, lad?"

"You love, Gypsy?"

"Love does not exist." He still believed this to be true. Love was a fairy tale he wanted nothing to do with. He desired real emotions, not flippant spurts of joy followed with a pain so deep you wondered if healing would ever come. He needed none of it.

"Then why do your eyes tell me so?"
"No more questions."
"Does your heart beat for her?"
"Quiet."
"She has become a part of you."

He didn't answer. There was no reason to. The lad wouldn't listen, and he was tired of talking. He wanted to forget the last few weeks, board his ship and set sail to the farthest place from here.

Pril picked up Tsura and faced Galius.
"Where do we go now?"

He assessed their surroundings before he answered her. "I see no reason to go anywhere. Hiram does not want the child, therefore she is safe here."

She eyed him. Why would they stay here? In the very place their sister died?

"I'd rather not. We should set sail to the other world and start fresh."

"What purpose do we have to move? She is well. Nothing else matters." He lifted Silas' body and carried it into the trees. She watched as he picked up each corpse and one by one took them into the forest.

He grabbed the shovel leaning against the south wall of the cabin and went back into the woods to bury the men.

She did not want to stay here. Her stomach clenched, unsettled, and she glanced about the area trying to distinguish why she felt so anxious. Galius was here, and all would be well, but the knowledge did nothing to ease her mind. She picked up Tsura, and the child laid her head on Pril's shoulder.

"Why did the man go, mama?"
"He was no longer needed."
"But you need him."

She peeked at Tsura. The girl had shown she was far beyond her years, but how did she know what was in Pril's heart?

"I have all I need here, darling. You and Uncle Galius."

Tsura shook her head, and the black curls whipped Pril's face.

Her last words to Kade permeated her mind and replayed over and over. She'd been harsh, cutting even, but was unwilling to set him free from her anger. How was she to ignore what he did? She could not look the other way and pretend it never happened? She had begun to care for him in a way she never thought possible. She trusted him, had sacrificed her life to save him. When she thought of all they'd been through hope arose within her chest, but as quickly as it came, she squashed it with the reality of the deceit he had shown her.

She would miss Kade Walker, his arrogant comments and rude behavior, but that was all she'd allow herself to do. There was no room left inside of her heart for anything else. She could not abide what he'd done. Ill circumstances or not, he wasn't the person she thought him to be.

Tsura wiggled free from Pril's arms and sat on the ground.

She watched as her daughter drew the shape of a pyramid in the dirt.

"What are you doing?"

The child looked at her, her green eyes glazed. She was seeing something Pril could not.

"What do you see, Tsura?"

She drew four more pyramids, all in different sizes. Her small hand shook as she continued to use her finger and shape another picture. When Pril saw it she gasped.

It was Kade's dagger, the symbol of the lion on the blade.

Tsura dropped her head and exhaled.

"The man who bears the pyramid has killed many."

"Does he live?"

She nodded.

"What of the dagger? Tell me what you know of the knife."

Her small forehead crinkled. "I do not know. I saw the knife but I cannot tell if it brings good or evil."

She scanned the area. The cabin was covered in overgrown branches and shrubs. The grounds eluded to a warm invitation but the longer she stayed a strange sensation took hold. She felt the tug on her soul, the push from behind telling her to leave this place and never return.

Galius came from the woods, shovel in hand, dirt smeared on his wide shoulders and arms. She stepped toward Tsura's drawings and messed them with her boot. Until she understood what Tsura's vision meant she'd not be showing anyone, not even her own brother.

Galius searched among the ground kicking up twigs and rocks. The skin on his forehead wrinkled, and even though his lips were covered with his beard, she knew he frowned.

"What is it you seek, Brother?"

"The talisman. You said the Monroes had it—Silas coveted it."

"Yes."

"I've searched all of the bodies, and none showed signs of the pendant. Nor can I find the spell book. I've gone through the cabin but it is not there."

"Jude Monroe threw the spell book into the fire. It is gone."

"And the pendant?"

"I have it here."

His step was too quick, and she retreated, her senses alert.

"Why do you want it?"

He gazed behind her at Tsura before meeting her eyes and shrugged. "It is the only way to break the blood curse."

"It has been broken."

Galius' stance shifted, and he smiled.

She released the clenched muscles in her back. She'd been leery of everyone and with just cause. Tsura's drawing hadn't helped, but now she felt terrible for the mere moments where she'd suspected Galius.

"Tsura has lifted the curse. All is well now, Brother."

"I know Hiram is not of concern, but I thought it best to remove the curse all together."

"You need not explain." She went to Tsura and picked her up.

"I still cannot fathom Vadoma and Hiram."

"We were not searching for it. Our eyes watched someone else. Vadoma planned it that way."

"Yes, I see it now." He frowned.

"What is it?"

"I cannot help my anger still even after all this time."

She knew he spoke of the blood curse and why their sister had laid such a burden upon them. She no longer held the blame within her heart. She'd let it pass through her when Hiram spoke of Vadoma, and how much she loved him. Pril understood why she'd cursed the Monroes, and she could forgive her sister for it.

"The anger will seep from you like nectar from the flower. It will take time."

She placed her arm around him, and he wrapped her in his embrace.

"Together we shall remain strong," she whispered. Her stomach growled, and she giggled.

"I will hunt our dinner." Without waiting for her reply, he grabbed his quiver and walked into the forest.

Pril eased onto the ground, keeping Tsura in her arms.

"Mama, your face is hurt."

"It is." She'd forgotten about the cuts and bruises upon her skin until now. The flesh on the right side of her face was the most tender, and when she blinked the bruise stung.

"Want me to make it better?"

"No, my sweet. I will be fine." She didn't want to see Tsura get sick like she did when healing Hiram.

How had she received such a gift, to heal with her hands, without words from a spell book? It was amazing and dangerous all at the same time. She thought of Kade, and her gaze went to the trees where he'd left. She'd not lay eyes on him again.

He'd placed himself in danger on many occasions during their brief time together, and for that she was grateful, but she still couldn't understand why he hadn't told her the truth. There had been several opportunities to speak it, yet he held the information inside—afraid.

She knew fear all too well. She'd lived with constant guilt, shame and agony, but with all of it came a strong need to love. She yearned for freedom, to give herself entirely without fear and reservations pushing her away. Love was a difficult thing, one that came with many daggers to the back. Love had shown her deception, betrayal, hatred, anger, lust, agony, warmth, exuberance and a contentment she'd never thought possible. Love had given her Tsura. No matter what Vadoma did, Pril would be forever grateful to her sister for the gift she'd bestowed upon her.

CHAPTER TWENTY-EIGHT

Pril leaned against the trunk of a tall pine. Tsura's head lay on her lap while she napped, and Pril relished in the tranquility of how much her life had changed in the past two days. They'd remained at Vadoma's cabin, Galius was insistent on staying through until the cooler seasons passed. She disagreed and wanted to start fresh some place else. She needed to venture to the other world where Tsura would be safe.

Galius was adamant in his argument that no more hunted the girl. He was sure all of the evildoers had been killed, and with the blood curse removed the threat was now gone, but she knew better. Magda would not forget. She'd seek vengeance on them for what the curse had done to her husband and child. Sorina posed a different threat, one that Pril feared could have grave consequences. The woman she once called a friend was gifted in the way of the earth. She could create almost anything, and Pril had wondered if she could count the spells, too.

Unease drenched her soul, leaving the hairs on her arms tall. She heard the sinister cries of those seeking justice, and she could not deny the truth any longer. They must leave this place.

Galius placed another log onto the fire and flipped the catfish sizzling on a rock next to the flames. She wasn't fond of the bottom feeders, but she hadn't eaten since morning, and she was famished.

"The fish is almost done, Sister," Galius said. Amusement lifted his voice, and his eyes twinkled.

"Do not tease me so." She frowned. "I am practically wasting away as I wait for you to finish cooking our fare."

He laughed, picked up a rock, placed the cooked fish on top of it and handed it to her. She used her fingers to pick the skin from the catfish and placed the meat into her mouth.

"Brother, I cannot help but worry that Sorina and Magda will hunt

Tsura. They will rally the Peddlers and come for us."

He took a bite of his fish and shook his head.

"You must see the danger which they hold."

"I see nothing. They are but women, with no magick or skill with a weapon."

"They do have a weapon. Revenge."

"They are weak. I am not threatened."

"Why are you so insistent to stay here? I do not desire to sleep within the cabin where my sister lived before her death. Nor do I care to sleep outside on the grounds." She stared at him, her eyes pleading. "I wish to leave here and never come back."

"You speak like a child. Your wants and needs? I ask you to cease your whining, and leave me in peace."

She was stunned at his reply. Galius had never spoken to her in such a manner, and she rubbed her neck to ease the ache there. She glanced down at Tsura, snoring softly, and blinked through the tears. She would not cry. Her fish forgotten, she pushed the rock to the side and sat in silence.

Galius finished his food and tossed the bones into the fire. The flames grew as they licked the fish bones, and she watched them until they resumed their normal height. She waited for his apology, but it never came. He stood and went inside the cabin.

She prayed that soon their life would go back to the way it was before they'd left Jamestown. The worry and tension drained from her muscles, and all would be well once more.

An intense pain twisted in her stomach, and she leaned forward, squishing Tsura between her chest and lap. Galius exited the cabin and came toward her. Without a word he took the girl from Pril's lap and laid her close to the cabin, placing a blanket over her.

"Brother, I do not feel well."

He gazed down at her as another spasm sliced through her insides, and she screamed from the intensity of the pain. Her lungs burned as she tried to inhale. What was wrong with her?

She reached her hand toward him, but he turned from her and walked away. Her vision blurred, and she blinked to focus. He leaned over the fire to add another log, the sun bright on his back. His white linen shirt worn and faded showed the skin underneath. Three red scars glowed—three creating a pyramid that lay in the middle of his back.

NO. It cannot be.

She blinked unable to accept what she saw—what Tsura told her. The pendant heated, burning the flesh on her chest, and she swatted it away. What did it mean? Was the talisman telling her Galius was the one? She looked at him again. Three scars from the arrows she'd pulled from his back shouted at her to be seen. *"The man who bears the pyramid has killed many."* Tsura's words echoed in her mind, and she could not see past what was in front of her.

"How could you?"

"Devil's porridge," he said from across the fire.

She recognized the name immediately, a small bush that grew around Jamestown and was known for its vicious effects. He'd poisoned her. Galius, the brother she'd admired, counted on and loved unconditionally had fed her poison. If he'd given her enough of the porridge she would die from it.

Her stomach convulsed, and she leaned to the left vomiting onto the grass. She wiped the sweat perspiring on her brow and left her arm to drape over her forehead. She gagged. Her stomach heaved, but she refused to give in. She needed to know the answers.

"Why?" she cried.

Galius came toward her and knelt down so she could see him.

"Because of her."

Pril's hands and legs convulsed, and she purged again this time all over herself. She tried to move her head to search for Tsura, to see her, but her limbs would not cooperate.

"What do you want with her?" The words were slow as she began to lose all ability to move her lips.

"Her magick."

"You have no need for it."

"Ah, but I do, Sister. With the pendant I can use Tsura to aide me in all that I want and need. I will never be without again."

"But she is…a child."

"I mean not to kill her as I did Alexandra, but she will be a slave to me."

Pril gasped. He killed their niece? Her heart wept for the girl, and how she must've trusted her uncle to bring her home, not knowing he'd end her life.

He sat down beside her.

"I needed Milosh to lose his sense, and he did. He took Tsura which allowed me to end his life also."

She vomited again, the remnants of her fish ending up in her hair and on the side of her face. How could this be? Galius was her rock, the one who kept the family together, and all of this time he'd been plotting to take her daughter. He'd killed his own brother and niece!

"Soon, Sister, you too will expire."

She spat onto his leg.

"You will die for what you've done…" She tried to place a spell, but she could not take a breath, and she just wheezed.

"You cannot do it. The effects of the plant have taken over your body. You are defenseless against me."

She shivered, her teeth chattered, her throat swelled. She retched down the front of her blouse. Unable to fight back, her body useless, her mind fogging, she searched for her daughter. She spotted her sleeping frame, and before it was too late, before she inhaled her last breath, she whispered, "I love you."

One tear slid from the corner of her eye as her body stilled.

CHAPTER TWENTY-NINE

Kade clenched every muscle in his body. He'd been riding for the better part of the day. His mood was sour, his backside ached, and when he found the boy he'd be lucky if Kade didn't throttle him. Red Wolf had ran off just as he pulled the anchor to set sail this morning.

They'd been in Jamestown two days, and after a much-needed meal and clean clothes, he and Red Wolf went about rounding up his crew. The seventeen men hadn't gone far, most in the brothels on the wharf, the others in whorehouses further inland or still on the ship. He instructed the men to scrub and clean the entire boat, while he ordered others to load the vessel with goods to take across the sea. He pushed them hard, forced them to work into the wee hours all with one path in mind…get as far away from the memories as possible.

Now he was stuck backtracking across familiar land while the kid played a game he was not fond of. He knew without a doubt the boy had gone to see Pril and, damn it, he was not happy about it.

He entered the forest around the gypsy cabin where he'd left Pril and her daughter two days before. He pulled Goliath to a stop and climbed down to survey the ground. Red Wolf's prints had disappeared. The lad had made it quite clear where he was going, often pushing his heels into the dirt so Kade wouldn't miss them, but now they were gone. He searched the trees around him.

The birds were quiet, and the only sound was the occasional rustle of leaves. His gut tightened, and he reached for his dagger. Instinct told him something was off. He left Goliath and took light steps toward the cabin that stood past the trees.

An owl hooted from above. He paused mid-step and looked up. Red Wolf sat high up in an oak tree. The boy placed his finger to his lips before he silently jumped from branch to branch, cascading down the tree until he was at the bottom.

Kade waited until the boy stood in front of him before he said, "What in hell—"

"Shush, Strong One. He will hear you."

He peered around the lad but saw only bushes.

"Who?"

"The man who looks as an ox."

"Galius?" He shrugged. "He is Pril's brother."

The boy shook his head.

"No, he is evil."

"Nonsense." He grabbed Red Wolf's arm and tugged him toward Goliath. "We are leaving."

"This Galius, he…he…"

Kade turned toward him and was met with round eyes filled with terror. Red Wolf moved his lips to tell him something, but no sound came from them. Whatever he was trying to say tore the child a part. Kade knelt in front of him, took both his arms within his hands and faced him.

"Nothing can hurt you. Speak what you need to."

Tears formed to soak the black lashes surrounding the lad's eyes, and Kade watched defenseless as they fell down his cheeks. He pulled him into his embrace and listened while Red Wolf released two heart-wrenching sobs that shook Kade to the core.

"I cannot say it, Strong One. I do not wish it to be true." The boy broke down. His body trembled as more tears fell from his eyes.

"You must tell it for me to help you, Red Wolf."

The boy pulled himself from Kade's embrace and wiped his eyes with the back of his hand. He inhaled a deep breath, and when he looked at him, Kade knew it would be something awful.

"The gypsy lady, she…she is dead."

"Pril? You must be mistaken." He didn't believe the boy. It was impossible. Galius would protect her. He wouldn't let anything happen to his sister or her child.

"Yes, it is Pril."

He shook the lad.

"No. No, it cannot be." He moved past Red Wolf and went deeper into the trees. He'd see for himself. The cabin stood in the clearing beyond the tall elm and pine trees. He refused to believe she was gone. Surely the lad was wrong. Pril was safe. She was smiling and content beyond the trees. She had to be.

Red Wolf grabbed his arm.

"You cannot go, or he will kill you, too."

"Galius is not a threat."

"Please," Red Wolf begged, and the truth of what the lad was saying sunk in.

He inhaled the air around him and held it within his lungs until they burned. He needed to clear his head. The lad was right, if danger lurked near the cabin, it was best if they came up with a plan. But first he needed to make sure Pril was alive.

He nodded and placed his finger to his lips to quiet the child. He crept toward the clearing and crouched down to hide behind a thick of Alder Buckthorn. He spotted Galius first. The large man seemed well-rested. His hair was wet and combed, and he'd donned clean clothes. There were no smudges under his eyes from lack of sleep. Kade could see no sign of a killer within the man.

He spotted Tsura sleeping beside the cabin, a brown blanket covering her.

Galius disappeared behind the cabin and within minutes emerged carrying a shovel across his right shoulder. He walked into the trees across from where Kade, and the boy sat watching.

The area had been cleaned, and he figured Galius had buried the other men and tidied the camp. He spotted Pril. She lay next to the fire. Her long red hair stretched out behind her. He couldn't see her face and stepped into the clearing when Red Wolf pulled him back.

He glared at him, but when the boy pointed behind him, he turned to see Galius coming through the bushes. The gypsy went to his sister and gave her a kick with the front of his shoe.

Kade winced.

Pril did not move.

Dread stole the color from his cheeks causing his vision to go in and out of focus. His jaw worked, and sweat formed on his brow. She could not be gone. He willed Pril to thrust a leg out, move an arm—flex a bloody finger, anything to indicate she lived.

She was still.

He waited. His lungs stilled as his mind scolded her to wake, to show him she lived, but she did not move. He shook his head, unwilling to believe it.

He needed to rescue her. He had to act and fast.

"Red Wolf, aim your arrow for the man's chest."

The boy nodded as he readied his bow. He pulled the arrow back with strong arms and steady hands while he waited for Kade to give him the signal.

Galius leaned over Pril and slapped her face. The sound echoed throughout the forest, and Kade felt the punishment to his core.

She did not flinch.

Kade's fists opened and closed at his side. When Galius stood, he nodded to Red Wolf to release the arrow. The dart flew through the air and penetrated the skin beneath Galius' collarbone.

"Again," he said to Red Wolf.

The boy released another arrow to puncture Galius' stomach. The gypsy fell onto his knees, and Kade ran from the bushes, dagger held high. He slammed into the bigger man knocking him backward. The arrows snapped, and the jagged ends poked into his skin. He did not care. He would kill Galius. Kade swiped his blade across the man's chest.

Galius snarled and replied with a strong punch to the side of Kade's head. The earth spun, and he drove the knife into his opponent's side. The brute was not giving up. His large meaty fists pummeled Kade's ribs without respite. Each blow robbed him of his breath and any strength he needed to win this fight.

Blood seeped from Galius' shirt and onto Kade's. He pulled the knife from the gypsy's side and aimed it for his heart. Galius was too quick and drove his fist into Kade's chin. His teeth snapped together with such force that one broke, and he spat it out onto the ground.

He was running out of steam and needed to end the fight. He thought of Pril and what she'd been through these last weeks to now be betrayed by her brother. He slammed the blade into Galius' chest. The knife penetrated his heart, killing him in seconds.

Kade rolled from Galius and lay with his back to the ground. He panted, his cheek swelled, and his muscles ached. Ragged and sore he stared up at the sky. Blood ran from his nose down the side of his face and into the dirt beneath him. He had no energy to wipe it. He heard Red Wolf's steps as he ran from the forest toward him.

"You live?" he asked.

Kade wiped his face and sat up. "I do."

Red Wolf went to Pril and fell onto his knees beside her. He laid his head to her chest and wept.

His eyes watered, and his throat ached. The bruises Galius had given him were nothing compared to the hurt and desolation that now cried within his heart. He went to them. The need to hold Pril in his arms consumed him, and he shuddered. He pulled her lifeless body onto his lap. Her crimson hair, long and flowing, framed the pale face marred with cuts and bruises from the battles she'd won.

"Ah, Gypsy."

Vomit permeated her hair and clothes, a sign she'd been poisoned.

Emotions stirred in his gut. Agony, sorrow and the hunger—the need of wanting her with him spilled from his soul, and he hung his head. He pitched forward as the pain of losing Pril spliced across his back. He should've never left her. He should've taken her to the other world. Everything within him ached, and he clutched her to him. The misery and regret sat heavy upon his soul as he acknowledged his love for her. He was to blame. He was the reason she lie dead in his arms. Had he not deserted her she'd still be alive.

He moaned.

She was gone. He couldn't continue to console himself with visions of her happy and content without him. She lived no more. The need to scream overtook his whole body, and he trembled from the grief.

Why had he been so stubborn? What had he gained from his arrogance—from his pride? He was a wretch, a vagabond and a derelict. He deserved nothing, and yet he yearned for her—thirsted for her. His heart beat for Pril, his soul belonged to her. He sucked in a sob, and his tears fell onto her ashen face. Without her, he had nothing.

He placed his lips to hers and wept

CHAPTER THIRTY

Kade covered Pril's body with a blanket he'd found inside the cabin. He'd moved Galius into the forest to be eaten by the wolves and bears. He examined the shrouded area for somewhere he could bury Pril. He didn't want to place her in the middle of the clearing, or even off to the side. She deserved to be laid to rest somewhere peaceful and calm.

He spotted the red leaves. The tree of fire Pril had spoken of when they first arrived here. Her mother was buried there, and it only seemed fitting she be placed there, too.

He stood and picked up the shovel when a small hand touched his arm. He knew it wasn't Red Wolf. He'd sent the boy into the forest to find some branches he could fashion into a cross.

He turned to see Tsura. When he'd checked on her an hour ago she was sound asleep, and he wondered how she didn't wake through everything that had happened. When he took a closer look, he realized she'd been drugged and figured Galius had used the Witch's berry Pril had told him about.

"You came back," she whispered.

Kade crouched down to her height. The weight of what he had to tell her pushed him lower still until he sat on the ground in front of her.

"There is something I need to tell you," he said and opened his arms for the child to sit on his lap.

Without hesitating, Tsura went to him.

The words were difficult to speak, the pain fresh and raw within him, but the child needed to know her mother had died.

"I am sorry but…" He swallowed. "But your mother has perished."

Tsura's head whipped around, and her black curls smacked his cheeks.

"No."

Kade nodded and pointed to Pril's covered body lying on the ground.

The girl went to her mother. She pulled back the blanket. He closed his eyes and waited for the wail—the sobbing—the shriek to bring her back, but the child was silent. He opened his eyes and was met with Tsura's smile.

"She sleeps," the child said.

"Yes, a deep sleep," he said, trying to make it easier for the girl to understand.

She waved him close.

He went to her.

She pointed to the red pendant around Pril's neck, and he could've sworn it glowed, but when he looked again it remained the same.

"See, she sleeps."

"I do not understand."

Tsura placed the pendant in the palm of her hand. "It saved her."

He shook his head unable to fathom what the child said.

"She was poisoned."

"The talisman protected her."

"But how?"

"My mother has the gift, as I do, but she cannot see it. The pendant can feel it, and together they saved her life."

Hope sprung in his chest, and he reached for Pril, placing his hand over her heart.

Tsura laid her hand upon his and closed her eyes.

"Feel mine heart strong and true, rid thy self of toxin undo. Awaken now to see mine soul, and embrace mine love to make thy whole."

Kade's palm heated as Tsura said the words, and he didn't move a muscle, too afraid he'd break the spell. His eyes widened when he saw Pril's lashes flutter. He could not contain the excitement. He could wait no more. He pulled her up and into his arms.

"Kade?" Pril said.

He squeezed her to him. When her arms wrapped around him, he let the tears fall.

"You came back, Gypsy," he whispered into her hair.

"As did you."

He held her from him, and when she smiled, he sighed.

"I shall never leave you again. I will take you wherever you want to go."

"Do you mean that?"

"Of course."

"I wish to be with you."

He eased her lips toward his and pressed them together in a soul-drenching kiss. He poured himself into her, drinking from her the love he'd thought never to find. For the first time in his life, Kade Walker was home.

EPILOGUE

One year later...

The cabin lay nestled within the forest, secluded at the bottom of a valley and surrounded by the Appalachian Mountains. Flowers bloomed in the windowsill. A garden of herbs and vegetables were planted out front.

Inside the log walls they huddled over a low fire.

"What do you see?" Magda asked.

"I need more herbs…and the blood from our mare," Sorina said.

Emine took the jar from the counter and walked outside. No mirrors hung within the home, and she refused to look at her reflection in the glass she held. Her face was lopsided; the jaw busted a year before never healed right. She was disfigured—a *monster*—and hate stewed inside of her for the woman who had made her that way.

She plucked a few sprigs of thyme from the garden and moved toward the mare. She placed her fingernail against the horse's neck and slid the nail along the skin. The flesh opened, and blood dribbled from the cut. She held the jar under the wound and watched with narrowed eyes as it filled.

She ran her finger along the cut. "Heal thy wound upon mine touch."

"Emine, hurry," Magda called from the doorway.

She rushed inside and handed Sorina the jar.

The other woman dumped the contents into the cauldron and stirred them with a wooden spoon.

"Gather around," Sorina said.

The women stepped closer as smoke billowed from the pot.

"Find thy child." She stirred some more. "Tell us where she hides."

"I see nothing. You must be saying the wrong words," Magda said.

"She is right," Emine took the wooden spoon from Sorina. "Cauldron do thy duty, mix thy goods to bind, show the marked girl when she's near…find, find, find."

A blue haze wafted from the pot above their heads. When they peered into the cauldron, a young woman with black ringlets and green eyes stepped off of a ship onto the docks.

"She will come back to us a young lady," Magda said.

"We will wait until she returns." Emine smiled.

"And ready ourselves to kill her," Sorina hissed.

~ * ~

If you enjoyed this book, please consider writing a short review and posting it on Amazon, Goodreads and/or Barnes and Noble. Reviews are very helpful to other readers and are greatly appreciated by authors, especially me. When you post a review, drop me an email and let me know, and I may feature part of it on my blog/site. Thank you. ~ Kat

katflannery@shaw.ca

Dear Reader,

After I finished *LAKOTA HONOR*, Book 1 in the Branded Trilogy I knew I needed to give my readers an explanation as to where the gift of healing had come from. It became clear to me early on that this story would have more of the paranormal feel to it than the book before it. I decided to place the book two hundred years before and in doing so needed to do a lot of research, which is why I write historical.

During the process of writing *BLOOD CURSE*, I fell in love with Pril and Kade as I do with all of my characters. However, these two have stolen a piece of my heart. I cried with them, laughed with them, and grew angry with them. I cherished them each for the strong willed, caring and loyal individuals I'd created…and I will miss them.

BLOOD CURSE was my labor of love and I am pleased to give it to you. I hope you enjoy Pril and Kade's journey, and within a few pages adore them as I did.

Love,

Kat

About The Author

Kat Flannery's love of history shows in her novels. She is an avid reader of historical, suspense, paranormal, and romance. A member of many writing groups, Kat enjoys promoting other authors on her blog. She's been published in numerous periodicals.

Her debut novel CHASING CLOVERS has been on Amazon's Bestsellers list many times and was #62 over all their titles. LAKOTA HONOR and HAZARDOUS UNIONS are Kat's other two books and both have made bestsellers lists. BLOOD CURSE is Kat's fourth book and she is currently hard at work on her next.

When not researching for her next book, Kat can be found running her three sons to hockey and lacrosse. She has her Certificate in Freelance and Business Writing.

www.katflannerybooks.com
https://twitter.com/katflannery1
http://www.facebook.com/pages/Kat-Flannery/131065966999142

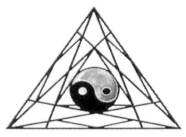

IMAJIN BOOKS
Quality fiction beyond your wildest dreams

For your next eBook or paperback purchase, please visit:

www.imajinbooks.com

www.twitter.com/imajinbooks

www.facebook.com/imajinbooks

Made in the USA
Charleston, SC
19 September 2014